THE
WEEK BEFORE
THE WEDDING

Center Point
Large Print

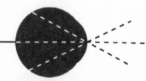

**This Large Print Book carries the
Seal of Approval of N.A.V.H.**

THE WEEK BEFORE THE WEDDING

BETH KENDRICK

CENTER POINT LARGE PRINT
THORNDIKE, MAINE

This Center Point Large Print edition
is published in the year 2013 by arrangement with
NAL Signet, a member of Penguin Group (USA) Inc.

The text of this Large Print edition is unabridged.
In other aspects, this book may vary from
the original edition.
Printed in the United States of America
on permanent paper.
Set in 16-point Times New Roman type.

ISBN: 978-1-61173-830-8

Library of Congress Cataloging-in-Publication Data

Kendrick, Beth.
 The week before the wedding / Beth Kendrick. – Center Point Large
Print edition.
  pages ; cm.
  ISBN 978-1-61173-830-8 (library binding : alk. paper)
  1. Weddings—Fiction. 2. Large type books. I. Title.
 PS3611.E535W44 2013b
 813′.6—dc23
                                                    2013009793

For Danielle Perez,
friend, champion, and editorial rock star

ACKNOWLEDGMENTS

A weepy, wine-soaked "I love you, man" to:

Kresley Cole, who dragged me over the finish line, the starting line, and every damn line in between.

My amazing agent, Amy Moore-Benson, without whom I would be living in a van down by the river.

Marty Etchart, who introduced me to the "Wrap it up!" rule of writing and some really good pinot noir.

Film producer Tai Burkholder, who routinely demonstrates how to get to yes. Remind me never to negotiate with you!

Chandra Years, Barbara Ankrum, Kathie Galotti, and Erica Ashcroft, who provide invaluable personal support and professional guidance.

The many friends and family members who offered encouragement, chocolate, and free child care while I played fast and loose with my deadline. I am so fortunate to have you in my life, and I count my blessings every day.

CHAPTER 1

"I'm Emily, and I'll be your cautionary tale tonight."

Emily McKellips struck a pose, her hands stretched over her head and her hips swiveling in tight low-rise jeans that barely covered her ass. The two-room dormitory suite was packed in flagrant violation of the campus fire code, with everyone dancing and laughing and crowding around the keg in the corner. The bass on the stereo was cranked so high she could feel the downbeat vibrating through her body, and her lungs filled up with the familiar Friday night smells of smoke, sweat, and stale beer.

"Finally!" Summer rushed over, thrust a red plastic cup into Emily's hand, and tugged her toward the suite's second room. "We've been waiting for you. You *have* to see this."

"See what?" Emily twisted her unruly auburn hair up into a bun. "I've seen everything there is to see around here."

Summer, Catherine, and Jess were clustered by the bunk beds, giggling and nudging one another. Emily elbowed her way into the trio of blondes

7

and grimaced as she took her first sip of cheap, lukewarm beer.

She tried to follow the direction of their gazes, but the room was too dark and the overhead strobe light too disorienting. "Give me a hint. What are we looking at?"

Jess pointed her index finger. *"Him."*

Emily squinted into the shadowy fray. "Who?"

"The hot transfer student," Summer said.

"He's in my film studies class. I didn't hear a word the prof said today." Catherine grinned. "I don't think I even kept my tongue in my mouth."

"This is about a guy?" Emily coughed as a marijuana-scented cloud of smoke billowed their way. "No, thank you."

"His name's Ryan," Jess said. "And if you hadn't lost your mind and switched majors last spring, you'd probably have met him already. See? This is what happens when you take boring accounting classes full of boring people. You miss out on all the hotties."

"Yeah, but just imagine how much *more* boring the accounting classes would be without me," Emily pointed out. "I'm doing a public service, really."

"Whatever. I will never understand how you can sit around crunching numbers and studying graphs with all those future corporate sellouts. I thought you were allergic to conformity and responsibility."

"Conformity, yes. Earning potential, no."

"Doesn't the thought of wearing a suit and working in a cubicle give you hives? I can't picture you wearing panty hose."

"Never," Emily vowed. "Death before panty hose. Which reminds me—I just ordered a new leather miniskirt today. It'll be perfect for when I finally track down the lead singer of Wake Up Will and get arrested trashing a hotel room with him and show up on a bunch of celebrity blogs."

"Didn't you already do that last summer?" Catherine asked.

"That wasn't Wake Up Will," Emily said. "It was the Ice Weasels. And we only got arrested because Summer kept flashing people from the balcony."

"We were in New Orleans." Summer shrugged. "That's how you say hi in New Orleans. I was just immersing myself in the local culture." She got a little glint in her eye. "God, I love hotels. The maid service, the little bottles of shampoo . . . I have no idea what I'm doing after graduation, but my future job's going to involve staying in lots of hotels. Mark my words."

"And my future job's going to involve leather miniskirts and the singer from Wake Up Will."

Jess laughed. "And you need an accounting degree for that *why?*"

"If you'd grown up with her mother, you'd understand," Summer said. "Now focus. We're staking out the new guy, remember?"

"Not interested," Emily said. "I've benched myself from dating until graduation. What was I thinking when I enrolled in this tiny little school in the middle of Minnesota, of all places? Ten thousand lakes and no decent guys."

"How can you say that?" Catherine cried.

"You don't even give them a chance!" Jess said. "You just meet and delete!"

"They delete themselves by puking in my car or kissing like they're giving my tonsils a deep-tissue massage or using the phrase 'ipso facto' while asking me out." Emily shuddered at the memories. "I'd love to find someone I could really connect with, but I give up. Six hundred men on this campus, and I've screened every last one of them."

Summer gave her a look. "Don't bench yourself just yet."

"Too late—I'm out for the rest of the season."

"You haven't even met him."

"Fine." Emily drained the rest of her beer. "Five hundred ninety-nine screened, one to go."

"You only need one," Jess said. "Maybe this guy is it."

Catherine nodded. "He doesn't look like the type to puke in your car."

"Ooh." Summer batted her eyelashes. "Sounds like soul mate material."

Emily almost gagged. "There's no such thing as

a soul mate. And if there were, he definitely wouldn't be a film studies major."

Summer grabbed Emily's chin and swiveled her head until she was staring at the back of some guy's head. A guy with broad shoulders, a flannel shirt, and thick black hair. "Look. There he is."

"Well, ah do declare." Emily made a big show of fanning her cheeks with her hand. "That's one fine-lookin' cranium he's got there."

Then he turned around.

He turned around and looked right at her, and Emily froze on the spot, her lips parting and her eyes widening.

"*Psst*. Put your tongue back in your mouth," Catherine murmured. "Don't be like me."

But Emily wasn't listening. She couldn't feel anything except the deep, steady pulse of the bass thrumming through her body.

He stared at her.

She stared at him.

And then the lights came on.

"Security!" boomed an authoritative male voice. "Break it up!"

The overhead fluorescent lights blazed down, temporarily blinding Emily, but she barely blinked. She didn't want to look away.

She didn't want to sever the connection.

All around her, kids scrambled to extinguish their cigarettes and stampede out the door before they got busted for underage drinking.

"Come on," Jess yelled, yanking on Emily's hand.

"I'll be there in a minute." Emily held her position and waited.

Sure enough, he came for her.

She lowered her face to hide her smile as he approached. *Men. So predictable.*

He stood directly in front of her, waiting for her to look up at him. "We should go." Then he offered his hand, as if he had no doubt whatsoever that she would take it.

And she did, allowing him to lead her out the door, down the hall, and into the cool, clear night. When they got outside, she took a deep breath. The fresh evening air was mixed with his scent: soap and shaving cream and a hint of spicy cologne.

Cologne usually did nothing for Emily; she found it cheesy and synthetic and a little desperate. But something about this particular scent on this particular guy made her want to locate his pulse points and lick them.

His grip on her hand tightened as they started across the grassy quad.

"Where are we going?" she asked, though she already knew the answer: his dorm room, his off-campus apartment, or his car.

He surprised her again by saying, "Want to see a secret?"

"Depends. Is it the kind of secret where I end up dismembered under your floorboards?"

Because he was still ahead of her, leading her

farther and farther into the dark, she couldn't make out his next words, but one of them sounded like "tunnels."

"What?" she asked. "Did you say 'tunnels'?"

"Yeah. There's an underground tunnel system below campus."

"No, there isn't."

"Yes, there is."

She laughed and squeezed his hand. "Look, I know you're new here, but the underground tunnel story's just an urban legend. Like jackalopes. Or snipe shooting."

"You're sure?"

"Positive. I know everything about everything at this school. Why don't we just go back to your room?"

He turned suddenly and tugged her up a flight of stone steps to a dormitory. She assumed he'd seen reason and was going to lead her up to his room, but once they were inside, he took her down three flights of stairs to the basement, where the bluish glow of the vending machine lit up the deserted laundry room.

"Here." He turned a corner and pointed to a battered metal door, which had been marked with a triangular sign depicting a bolt of lightning: DANGER! KEEP OUT!

Exasperated, Emily snatched back her hand and folded her arms. "That's not a secret tunnel —that's a bunch of circuit breakers."

Why were the cute ones always crazy?

The guy sifted through the flotsam in his jeans pockets—lighter, lint-covered mints, ticket stubs, and coins—until he fished out a brass key, which he inserted into the door lock.

"Where did you get that?" Emily demanded.

A puff of warm, stale air wafted out as he pulled the door open, revealing a narrow corridor with no discernable destination.

"The tunnels," she marveled, sticking her head into the blackness. "They're real. How the hell did you find this?"

"I like to know things no one else does." His hazel eyes met hers and his smile was slow and subversive. "When they built these dorms in the seventies, they dug tunnels between some of the buildings so students could go to class without freezing their asses off in winter. But there were problems with asbestos, so they sealed off the whole system."

Emily took a step over the threshold, into the dark. "So we're not supposed to go in."

"Automatic expulsion if you get caught."

A little thrill ran up and down her spine. *Rules? Made to be broken. Lines? Drawn to be erased.* "Well then, we better not get caught."

She walked farther into the darkness, trailing her hand against the gritty stucco wall, and he joined her, closing the door behind them.

For a moment, she experienced total sensory

deprivation: no sound, no sight, nothing except the cool solidity of the wall. Then, slowly, she registered the rush of her own heartbeat in her ears and the steady, shallow rasp of his breathing. She could smell the cologne as he came nearer, and her own breath caught in her throat.

There was a faint metallic click; then a flickering light cast a warm golden halo around them as he held up his cigarette lighter.

"I'm Ryan, by the way. Ryan Lassiter." He watched her face. "But you already knew that."

He waited a beat for her to introduce herself, and when she didn't, he straightened up and illuminated the path stretching out in front of them.

Emily rubbed her nose as the stale, humid air settled back into stillness. "You'd think it would be freezing in here, but it's warm."

He nodded in agreement, then pulled off his flannel shirt to reveal a well-worn white T-shirt. Through the dim, flickering light, Emily could make out the logo of her favorite band.

She rounded on him, pressing her palms against his chest as he ran into her. "Where'd you get that shirt?"

He glanced down at the block of text, which read WAKE UP WILL. "I saw them at a club in Minneapolis two years ago. Right before they broke up."

"Lucky." Emily traced the W with her index

finger, both envious and desperate for more details. "I'd kill to see them play live. Hell, I'd kill for that T-shirt."

The tunnel went dark again as he released the lighter. Through the blackness, Emily heard the soft rustle of cloth and felt the heat of his skin inches from hers.

Then, his voice, low and warm in her ear: "Put your hands up."

She didn't hesitate, not even for a moment. She didn't know what he was going to do to her, and she didn't care. She knew only that whatever it was, she wanted it.

She felt his hands on her shoulders, then sucked in her breath as the damp air hit her stomach. He pulled her shirt over her head, then skimmed his hands along her sides as he pulled the soft, worn cotton of his shirt down over her.

She turned her head and sniffed the shirt's collar. It smelled like him, warm and spicy.

"You just gave me the shirt off your back?"

"What can I say? I'm that kind of guy."

She reached out blindly until her palm connected with his chest again. He'd just held her hand for five minutes, but this skin-on-skin contact felt completely different. "What kind of guy is that?"

She could hear the smile in his voice. "A literalist."

"I like it."

His lips brushed against her cheek as he asked, "What's your name?"

"Emily."

"Nice to meet you, Emily."

She responded by kissing him in a manner that would warrant immediate expulsion, tunnels or no tunnels. And the thin, flimsy layer of cotton between them only served to intensify the slow, steady slide of his body against hers.

Both of them were laughing and panting by the time they came up for air.

"Emily?" Ryan said.

She traced his lips with the tip of her tongue. "Mmm?"

"You're kind of unbelievably hot in my shirt."

"I'm that kind of girl." She wrapped both arms around him and whispered in his ear, as sultry and sinful as any soap opera vixen, "A temptress in a T-shirt."

They collapsed, still laughing, his body cushioning her from the floor.

And just like that, in the middle of the tunnel, in the middle of the night, they fell in love.

SATURDAY

CHAPTER 2

Ten years later

The world's most perfect man had one hand on the steering wheel and the other on Emily's thigh.

She settled back into the Audi sedan's spotless leather upholstery and smiled at her fiancé. "I'm so glad you could make the drive up with me."

"Right on time, too." Grant took his gaze off the road just long enough to glance at the Swiss watch on his wrist and amend that to, "Okay, *almost* on time. I told you I'd be out of surgery before rush hour."

"You did, indeed."

"And I made it. Even with a ruptured artery." He gave her a look of mock innocence. "I don't know how you could ever doubt my word. I'm the picture of punctuality."

"Uh-huh." She placed her hand over his on her leg. "I've heard all this before, buddy. You just want to get me into bed."

"I want to get you down the *aisle,*" he corrected. "But yes, bed sounds pretty good right now." He gave her fingers a gentle squeeze. "We can do a little catching up before all the guests get here tomorrow. My mom should be at the airport around ten, and what time did your mom say she'd arrive?"

"Who knows?" Emily stifled a sigh, trying not to ruin the soft pink glow just before sunset with thoughts of impending family drama. "She operates on Georgia Standard Time. And she's on the prowl for a new 'beau', so you'd better lock up your male relatives."

Grant laughed. "I seriously doubt Georgia would want anything to do with my great uncle Harry."

"If he's got a healthy stock portfolio, she'll take him." Emily had long ago given up trying to reform—or even understand—her mercenary, man-eating mother. "Don't underestimate her— that's how she sucks you in."

Grant's smile was warm and indulgent. "Don't be too hard on her, angel. She's not as smart or responsible as you are, but she raised a great daughter."

Emily bit her tongue and changed the subject. Men, regardless of age or marital status, were incapable of seeing Georgia as she really was. Which was why Georgia, still an incorrigible and indiscriminate flirt in her fifties, preferred male company to female. "Women are so catty and two-faced," she would remark while filing her nails or trying on earrings sent by a besotted suitor. "You just can't depend on them. But men! So charming and agreeable!"

Georgia manipulated men for security and profit, and Emily had rebelled in her adolescence by selecting boyfriends who could provide her with thrills, drama, and explosive physical chemistry, all of which she categorized as "fun." She treated love like a double dare, a tightrope without a net. But while Georgia continued to search for men to keep her safe, Emily learned to rely on herself. She'd spent the last ten years accumulating an MBA, a closet full of under-stated dark suits, and a conservative, well-balanced investment account. And despite the vow she'd made to her college friends a decade ago, she'd worn panty hose just that morning.

Emily didn't take double dares anymore. She preferred the sure thing.

"You're quiet tonight," Grant said. "Everything okay?"

"Absolutely," she assured him. "Just going over my to-do list in my head."

"How many items are on that list of yours?"

She tilted her head, considering. "Seventeen . . . no, eighteen thousand."

"Make you a deal: You forget the list exists for the next few hours, and tomorrow I'll take care of at least ten thousand items."

"Done." She reached over and touched a button on the dashboard console. The soft, soothing strains of a violin concerto poured out of the speakers as the car dipped and rose along the road leading them up through the Green Mountains.

"We're here," Grant announced as they passed a painted wooden sign welcoming them to the town of Valentine, Vermont.

Emily gazed out the window at the abundance of green branches and vibrant summer blooms. "This is gorgeous." Her voice was hushed. "I didn't know towns like this existed outside of Nick at Nite reruns."

As they turned off the highway onto a charming little Main Street lined with shops, Emily saw children digging in a sandbox at a grassy park and couples walking hand in hand to a little shop advertising homemade fudge and maple syrup candy. Families carrying beach towels and coolers strolled back from the lakeshore. A pickup truck, complete with hound dog sticking its head out the window, rumbled by on the opposite side of the road. It was like a promotional postcard come to life.

And the air! Emily lowered the car window to breathe in the crisp, fresh mountain breeze. If this air couldn't clear her mind and cleanse her soul, there was no hope for her.

Planning a wedding in Vermont while relocating from Minnesota to Massachusetts for Grant's new job had been a logistical nightmare, but Emily felt sure that all the hard work would be worth it.

"You were right about this place," she said. "It's the American dream come to life, right down to the white picket fences."

"And the eighteen thousand items on your to-do list." Grant squeezed her hand again. "Not everyone could plan a wedding in two and a half months. When I first told my family we were setting the date for the Fourth of July, they didn't think we could get everything done, but you pulled it off."

"Not yet," she cautioned. "We've still got a week to go."

"Yeah, but the hard stuff's done, right? We just have to figure out a few last-minute details." He regarded her with pride and admiration. "You're amazing."

She laughed, relieved and grateful that none of her last-minute details could rupture an artery and bleed out on the operating table. Organizing an out-of-town, black-tie wedding for a hundred and fifty guests in eleven weeks, all the while coordinating a cross-country move, interviewing for a new position in a financial firm, and house hunting for a classic Cape Cod in a good school district had required the strategy, discipline, and cunning of a top secret black-ops military mission. But Emily had always been decisive, and her years of experience in the business world had taught her how to prioritize and keep her eyes on her goals without ever glancing back. "Fix it or forget it" had been the mantra of one of her B-school professors. And fix it she had.

In a perfect world, she would have had a year to sample caterers, deliberate over first dance songs, and pore over bridal magazines for bouquet and centerpiece ideas. But on the night Grant proposed, he mentioned that he wanted to hold the wedding at a rustic family resort called the Lodge in Valentine, Vermont—the site of his parents' and grandparents' weddings. The Lodge was special to his family, and Emily desperately wanted to become part of that history and tradition.

When they'd called the resort to ask about available dates, they'd discovered that the Lodge had recently been featured on a national talk show as an "ideal destination wedding locale," and every weekend for the next sixteen months had been booked.

This hadn't deterred Grant. Like most surgeons, he wasn't known for his ability to take no for an answer. He'd asked for the resort's manager, made small talk for a minute or two, reminisced about his family's summers at the inn, and then said, "You know my mother has her heart set on me getting married at the Lodge. There must be something we can do."

He'd listened and nodded, then hung up the phone in triumph. "Great news," he reported to Emily. "There was a fiftieth anniversary bash scheduled for the Fourth of July, and the husband just died."

"Score!" After they high-fived in triumph, Emily said, "We're going to hell."

"Why? It's not like we killed him," Grant said. "Anyway, the manager says we can have our wedding that weekend if we book it today."

"Fourth of July?" Emily did a quick calendar check in her head. "But that's only two months away."

"It can't be that hard to plan a wedding, right?" Grant shrugged. "It's just food, flowers, and invitations."

"Aw." She'd patted him on the head. "You're so pretty."

"What? It's not just food, flowers, and invitations?"

She tried to explain. "It's more like planning a full-scale invasion of Russia. With ground troops. In winter."

He considered this for a moment. "Then forget it. You've got enough on your plate, and I'll be too swamped with starting the new job to help much. If you can't do it, we'll find someplace else and my mother will just have to deal with it."

"No, no, no." Emily held out her palm. "Hold on. I didn't say I couldn't do it."

"You said Russia with ground troops in winter."

"Yeah, and Saint Petersburg is going down." She drummed her fingers on the kitchen counter as she mulled over her next move. "Family traditions are very important." Or so she'd heard.

"Not more important than your sanity."

Emily pressed the phone into his hand. "Call them back and tell them we'll take the Fourth of July."

"Are you sure?"

"Very sure. I'll make it happen."

And she had.

As she looked around the idyllic village, she felt a little pang for the kind of upbringing she'd wanted but hadn't had. "It must have been great to grow up here."

"Yeah, Mom and Dad booked a cabin at the Lodge for the whole month of August every year. There were no TVs, no video games. My sister and I used to drive them crazy, complaining about how bored we were."

"But somehow you survived."

"Hey, when you're eight years old, all you need for hours of entertainment is a really big stick. And then, when I was ten, they sent me to the summer camp on the island in the middle of the lake."

"Was this camp called 'Alcatraz,' by any chance?"

"I loved it. When I was in college, I came back to be a counselor."

"I didn't know you were a camp counselor," she said. "But you know, I can totally see it. I bet you were super cute in your hiking boots and your khaki shorts."

"I was in charge of water sports. Sailing, canoeing, water-skiing."

She smoothed the crisp fabric of her white linen skirt. "That didn't happen. You're just flipping through an L.L.Bean catalog and making stuff up now."

"I won't even tell you about all the archery and the capture-the-flag tournaments." He grinned. "Didn't you ever go to summer camp?"

"Right. Do you really think my mother would send me into the woods with a bow and arrow? We honed our survival skills at Nordstrom's semiannual sale. That woman will shed blood to get the last pair of Ferragamos in her size." Emily laughed at the memories. "She never understood the appeal of the great outdoors."

"The summer camp's still going, as far as I know," Grant said. "Maybe we'll send our kids someday."

He turned the car off the main road and onto a gravel path that wound through towering pine trees until the forest opened up to a vast lawn featuring putting-green-quality grass, white Adirondack chairs, a charming gazebo, and an actual croquet set.

Emily's eyes widened as she stared at the hotel. "This was worth every second of wedding planning insanity."

The Lodge looked like something out of a Hollywood film set—luxury accommodations downplayed by a rugged and rustic exterior. The main building was long and low, with porch railings and window casings inspired by Frank Lloyd Wright and a roof that the property's Web site claimed was shingled with antique slate sourced from a nearby quarry. All of the guest suites were outfitted with high-thread-count linens and cavernous spa tubs, and many had fireplaces and screened patios. Every night, the housekeeping staff distributed truffles from a local chocolatier. Beyond the porch, Emily could see the sparkling shoreline of Valentine Lake, dotted by a tall lifeguard's chair, a string of white buoys, and a long wooden dock.

"We're never leaving," Emily informed him. "I'm serious. We're taking up residence."

Grant laughed as he unbuckled his seat belt, then got out of the car and came around to open her door before he unloaded two suitcases and a garment bag from the Audi's trunk. The breeze blowing in from the lake was thick with humidity and mosquitoes.

"Ooh, I'll get that." Emily grabbed the garment bag and carried it with her hand above her head so that the bag didn't fold or touch the ground. "That's the dress."

Grant watched her, his brow furrowed with confusion. "It's made of cloth, right? Not plutonium?"

"It's sixty-year-old lace and tulle. I'm afraid to even look at it the wrong way."

He led her up the stairs to the lobby. "Let's stash that in a closet somewhere and see if we can squeeze in some quality time before anyone else figures out we're here."

Emily gave him a flirty little hair flip. "And by quality time, you mean . . . ?"

"It's almost the Fourth, right? We can get the fireworks started early."

She dabbed at her forehead with her free hand. "How convenient. I'm already hot and sweaty."

He picked up the pace and approached the front desk with brisk efficiency. "Grant Cardin, checking in. We need a room and a door with a lock on it, stat."

But the clerk, apparently a longtime employee of the hotel, recognized Grant and settled in for a newsy little chat. Soon a throng of staff members was clustered around them, offering handshakes and hugs of congratulations:

"You've gotten even handsomer than the last time I saw you."

"Heard you're a big-shot surgeon now. You always were a smart kid."

"This must be your beautiful bride."

"We've reserved your mother's favorite room for her. Is she bringing her famous macaroons?"

Clearly, Grant was Valentine, Vermont's version of a rock star—and Emily had dated enough musicians back in the day to know this was her cue to stand back and let him have the spotlight. Ever mindful of the delicate wedding gown, she ducked out of the crowd and waited under the huge wrought-iron chandelier for the groupies to disperse.

A few minutes later, Grant extricated himself and urged her down the hall toward the guest rooms. "Now where were we? I believe you were hot and sweaty?"

When they reached their suite, he dropped the bags and smacked his palm to his forehead. "I left my laptop in the backseat of the car."

She unlocked the door and ushered him inside. "Be right back."

"Don't worry. I'll get it."

"Honey, you've done more than enough." She slipped her hand into his pants pocket and fished out the car keys. "Go inside and prepare to be seduced. Oh, but first, please hang the dress up. And make sure you don't look at it, touch it, or breathe on it."

"No looking, no touching, no breathing. Got it."

Emily managed to retrieve the computer from the car in three minutes flat. Running the gauntlet in the lobby proved a bit more time-consuming. For fifteen minutes, she answered questions about the wedding cake and appetizers, harpists and hairstyles. She listened to hotel employees gush about the Cardin family in general and Grant in particular, and by the time she got back to the room, her thoughts had veered from hot and sweaty sex to bouquets and boutonnieres.

When she opened the door to their guest suite, she found Grant sprawled across the bed, snoring with one arm flung over his eyes. The closet door was open—before he'd passed out, he'd stowed the garment bag safely away.

Poor guy. He'd been working for forty-eight hours straight before he started the four-hour drive. In slumber, his face had gone slack and unguarded. After years of grueling all-day surgeries, he'd become expert at hiding his fatigue, but despite his constant show of stamina and strength, he was only human, and as she gazed down at him, she felt both protective and vulnerable.

He was her future husband; her partner, for better or for worse; the kind of man she'd always wanted but hadn't dared to hope for.

She hated to wake him, so she tiptoed across the carpet to the French doors leading to the patio, and looked out at the darkening sky.

A series of early fireworks exploded over the lake. She watched the dazzling display of lights and colors through the spotless glass, then reached out to touch the smooth, hard surface with one finger.

SUNDAY

# CHAPTER 3

The mothers arrived the next morning.

At first, Beverly had insisted that she'd take a shuttle van from the airport to the resort. "I don't want you kids to go to any trouble," she'd said on the phone. "Heaven knows you've got enough to deal with already." She and Stephen, Grant's father, used to drive up to Valentine Lake in their wood-paneled station wagon, but after Stephen died two years ago, Beverly had balked at making the drive alone.

Grant had overruled his mother's insistence, and after a ten-minute volley of increasingly heartfelt entreaties that the other not go to any trouble, Grant played his trump card ("It's what Dad would want") and arranged to meet her at the baggage claim at the Burlington airport. Emily accompanied him, a bit nervous. She'd met Bev only once before, at the Cardins' holiday celebration, and was anxious to earn her mother-in-law's approval.

Emily hadn't realized what a huge potential stumbling block in-laws were until she announced her engagement to her girlfriends. The initial reaction was always the same: First, the friend would ooh and aah over the ring, but then she would pull Emily aside to ask, in the manner of a drug fiend trying to score black-market heroin, "So? How's the mother-in-law situation?" Emily laughed it off the first few times, then started to really freak out. But she couldn't have asked for a nicer group of people to marry into. To hear Grant tell it, his family was devoid of rivalry or feuds. Emily had been skeptical until she sat down to Christmas dinner with all of the aunts and cousins and grandparents. No one bickered. No one screamed or drank too much or argued about politics.

Instead, everyone inquired with genuine interest about one another's lives and helped to set the table with Bev's holly-themed china plates. After the meal, everyone gathered around the baby grand and sang along while Grant's sister Melanie played Christmas carols. Bev and her sisters, Rose and Darlene, exchanged thoughtful gifts like hand-knit sweaters and framed family photos. At the end of the evening, Emily and Grant were sent home with a round of hugs and kisses, a cooler full of leftovers, and a pair of rose-scented candles that Aunt Darlene had crafted with love in her own kitchen.

"Oh my God," Emily had said as they backed out of the driveway and started home. "Norman

Rockwell is alive and well and hiding out at your mother's house."

Then she had called her own mother on her cell phone, and Georgia had answered from a beachside resort in Hawaii where she'd gone with her beau of the moment: "I can't talk now; we're about to go snorkeling. But Merry Christmas, baby girl. I'll have a cranberry cocktail in your honor tonight. Cheers!"

Bev was one of the last passengers off the plane, but she didn't seem impatient or annoyed. With her sensible shoes, tasteful pearl earrings, and matronly gray pageboy, she maintained an air of perpetual serenity. She greeted Grant and Emily with long, tight hugs, then unzipped the large, floral-printed tote bag over her shoulder.

"I made your favorite." She handed Grant a ziplock bag full of cookies. "Coconut macaroons." Then she handed a small cardboard box to Emily. "And I wasn't sure if you liked coconut, dear, so I whipped up a batch of double-fudge brownies, too."

"I adore coconut," Emily assured her. "Brownies, too. But I'm on a strict diet until the wedding. Have to fit into the dress."

"Of course you'll fit into the dress," Bev said. "I can't wait to meet your family. Has your mother arrived yet, dear?"

"I have no idea. All I know is that she'll be here sometime today. I begged her to send me her flight schedule, but she kept saying she hadn't finalized her plans yet."

At this, a slight ripple appeared in Bev's calm complacency. The Cardins all prided themselves on their organization and punctuality, and it was beyond comprehension that someone would be unable or unwilling to pull together an itinerary for her own daughter's wedding.

Emily looked to Grant for guidance on how to defuse this potential source of in-law tension, and he put his arm around his mother's shoulder and steered her toward the baggage claim. "Georgia will be here soon enough, Mom. You'll love her. She's the life of every party."

Bev, whose idea of partying began with a game of bridge and ended with half a glass of white wine and a ten p.m. bedtime, looked even more dismayed.

"She'll want to hear all about your knitting," Emily said, ignoring Grant's raised eyebrows. "She loves crafts."

Bev brightened at the mention of knitting. "I had to put my yarn tote into my checked luggage. The nice young men at the security station said I couldn't bring my knitting needles on the plane."

Grant's mouth was too full of macaroon to reply, so Emily made sympathetic noises while they waited for Bev's bags to appear on the revolving carousel.

"I had some trouble deciding what to wear to the wedding," Bev confessed, as she pointed out one giant suitcase and then another. "So I just brought a little bit of everything."

Emily grinned. Maybe there was a chance Georgia and Bev would get along, after all.

Back at the hotel, as the desk clerk handed Bev her room key and Grant helped the bellhop load a flotilla of tan leather luggage onto a wheeled cart, Emily heard a familiar voice singing with Broadway-level gusto and volume:

"Now I've . . . had . . . the time of my liiiiiiife. . . ."

A round of applause broke out at the far end of the lobby.

"Goodness." Bev looked taken aback. "What in the world is that?"

Emily plastered a smile on her face and braced herself. "That would be my mother."

Right on cue, Georgia rounded the corner with a theatrical twirl, both hands swishing her skirt in time to her a cappella performance. She'd been the belle of the ball in her youth and had refused to concede to middle age without a kicking, screaming brawl. In accordance with her personal motto—"All glamour, all the time"—she wore a tight leopard-print top with a long black peasant skirt and glittering jewelry bedecking her ears, throat, fingers, and wrists. As always, her thick red hair was impeccably coiffed. She looked like a cross between a carnival fortune-teller and a Saks-y socialite.

41

Reveling in the attention, Georgia sashayed across the lobby with a group of hotel guests and employees trailing behind her, as though she were the pied piper in inhumanely high-heeled gold sandals.

"*There* you are! The young lovers!" She kissed Grant's and Emily's cheeks, leaving smears of pink lipstick on each. "*Bonjour, bonjour.* I have arrived!"

"So I see." Emily stepped to one side to introduce Bev. "Mom, this is—"

"I simply adore this hotel." Georgia flung out her arms. Her gold bangle bracelets clattered. "It's so *Dirty Dancing*!" She finally deigned to acknowledge Bev with a tight little half smile. "Don't you agree?"

Bev started to speak, but her lips seemed incapable of articulating the word "dirty." After a moment, she cleared her throat and replied, "I'm afraid I don't know what that is."

Emily jumped in to explain. "It's a movie. Set in the Catskills in the 1960s."

Georgia threw back her head and laughed. "I'm expecting Patrick Swayze to show up at any moment."

Bev reached back and clutched Grant's arm for support. But she stood her ground and seemed more determined than ever to make a good first impression. "Care for a coconut macaroon?"

"Thank you. How kind." Georgia took a tiny

nibble of the cookie Bev offered, then folded the rest into a tissue. "Long flight, Mrs. Cardin?"

"Please, call me Bev."

Georgia motioned Bev in for a bit of girl talk. "Frankly, honey, you look positively bedraggled. Care to borrow my lipstick? I've got a lovely shade of plum that will do your complexion a world of good."

"Mother," Emily hissed.

"What? I speak the truth."

Bev patted the corner of her mouth with her index finger and tried to keep smiling. "You know, I think I'll just go to my room and freshen up."

"Nothing more refreshing than a cocktail." Georgia clapped her hands. The bellboy abandoned Bev's tower of luggage and snapped to attention. "Two Bloody Marys, please."

"Oh, I don't drink," Bev said.

Georgia craned forward as though she couldn't have possibly heard this correctly. "At all?"

"Well, I might have a glass of wine with dinner," Bev said. "On special occasions. Certainly not hard liquor in the morning."

"Fascinating." Georgia glanced at Grant as though this cast his entire family under a dark cloud of suspicion.

Bev tried to duck back behind Grant, but found herself blocked by Georgia at every turn. Finally, she gave up trying to escape and faced Georgia head-on. "Emily mentioned that you enjoy knitting?"

Before Emily could die a slow death of shame and humiliation, a hotel employee with the body of a personal trainer and the face of a boy band singer emerged from the back office.

Georgia pointed one long, glossy fingernail at him. "And here he is—Patrick Swayze!"

The young man looked behind him, obviously confused. When Georgia continued to coo over him, he said, "I'm, uh, Brad. Brad the concierge."

"Even better!" She coaxed him out from behind the counter and looped her arm through his. "I just checked in and I'm positively parched. Show a girl the way to the bar, won't you?"

Brad glanced at his manager, who nodded. "I'd be happy to, ma'am."

"Darling, men with muscles like yours"—she gave his biceps a little squeeze—"call me Georgia. And I'm sure you're too much of a gentleman to let a lady drink alone." She turned her tractor-beam smile on Grant. "Care to join us?"

Grant took half a step toward her, then noticed his mother's expression and hung his head. "I'd better help my mom get settled." He pushed the luggage cart across the lobby. "Let's catch up in a bit. We can all have lunch together."

"Anything you say, Doctor." Georgia shifted her focus to her daughter. "Emily." It was not a request. "Care to join me."

As Bev and Grant headed toward the elevator, Emily could hear Bev's voice, urgent and despairing: "Who on earth does that woman think she is?"

"I'm a woman who knows how to use fashion, hair dye, and makeup to my advantage." Georgia tossed her auburn mane and waved her hand dismissively. "Though I certainly can't say the same for that mousy little creature." She whirled around, pinning Brad the concierge with a sly, demanding smile. "How old do you think I am?"

Brad's complexion went from pink to red to sickly white. "Well . . . uh . . ."

"Don't be shy," Georgia purred. "I'll give you a hint: I had my daughter when I was practically a child myself."

Brad adjusted the collar of his maroon polyester uniform jacket.

"Just say she looks like my sister," Emily told him. "My *younger* sister. It's the only answer she'll accept."

"Darling, don't be a wet blanket." Georgia whapped Emily with her woven straw handbag. "Like that dowdy old lady Bev." She wrinkled her perfectly powdered little nose in disgust. "*Bev.* What a name. So provincial and old-fashioned."

"Be nice to her," Emily warned. "Grant's whole family's going to be here this week, and I want *both* of us to make a good impression."

At this, Georgia came to a halt and dug her

stiletto heels into the carpet. "Don't you talk to me about making a good impression. Little Miss Lemon Lips ought to worry about making a good impression on *me*. *I* am the mother of the bride. *I* am the hostess of this wedding."

In actual fact, Emily and Grant had paid most of the expenses, but Emily knew that her mother was in no mood to be bothered with such trifling facts. She was on a roll.

"Traditionally, the wedding is supposed to take place in the bride's hometown," Georgia pointed out. "But did I make a peep of protest when the Cardins insisted on making all the guests trek up here to the back of beyond? No, I did not. And when that woman—"

"Beverly," Emily supplied.

"When *that woman* bullied you into wearing her threadbare old pile of rags from the fifties—"

"It's actually a lovely vintage gown. Wait till you see it. And nobody bullied me; I wanted to wear it."

"—did I kick up a fuss? Indeed, I did not. You're my only child, and I'm supposed to be planning your wedding. Especially since I wasn't even *invited* to your first wedding."

"Mother." Emily held up her index finger and got serious. "We do not speak of the first wedding. Ever."

Georgia ignored her. "Then that June Cleaver wannabe insists on doing everything her way, even though she already had her chance when her own daughter got married. But have I complained?"

"Um . . ."

"No!"

"Well, I'm glad to hear you're not bitter about the whole thing. But listen, Mom, I'm not kidding. I don't want you bringing up my first—"

"You know I make a point of being gracious under difficult circumstances, but *really*. Women like Bev give the fairer sex a bad name."

"Uh-huh."

"I don't think I care for your tone, young lady."

"Sorry about the tone," Emily said. "It's just . . . sometimes I think you have unrealistic expectations of other women."

Georgia threw back her shoulders and resumed walking toward the bar. "I have no idea what you're talking about."

"Be honest, Mom. It's not like you've ever had a lot of female friends."

"I have plenty of female friends. Like Summer. I absolutely adore Summer."

"Summer doesn't count; she's your step-daughter."

"Former stepdaughter," Georgia corrected. "And the fact that I still adore her, despite her nightmare of a father, and the fact that she dares to be younger and prettier than I am, just goes to show how forgiving and easygoing I am."

Emily picked up her cue, and said, between a laugh and a sigh, "No one's prettier than you are."

47

"No one," Brad threw in.

Georgia beamed. "Flattery will get you everywhere." She batted her eyelashes at Brad, but Emily steered the conversation toward the point she really wanted to underscore:

"And speaking of Summer. I know how you two get, and I'm warning you: Do not terrorize the wedding guests."

Georgia's smile went from flirtatious to diabolical. "Just stay out of our way and no one will get hurt."

"Mom, I'm begging you, just for this week, can't you please try—"

"Oh, Emmy, stop being such an old lady. Try to have some fun." Georgia gave a dainty little finger wave to two older gentlemen seated at the bar.

"Georgia!" They fell all over themselves pulling out a chair for her and beckoning her over. "You look great! What'll you have?"

"Two Bloody Marys for me and my gorgeous daughter." Georgia laughed. "But don't get any ideas, fellas—she's taken!"

"Just water for me," Emily said. "I'm off alcohol, carbs, and sugar until the wedding."

Brad slipped away, mumbling excuses about work, but Emily noticed the concierge glancing back at her mother as he returned to the lobby.

"Come on, let's mingle." Georgia grabbed Emily's elbow and pushed her toward the men.

"Wait. Who are those guys?"

"Bankers from New York. I met them on my way in, over by the tennis courts. Aren't they dashing?"

"How do you do it?" Emily wondered aloud for the thousandth time. "You're like a Svengali or something."

Georgia winked. "Oh, you know how it is, sweetie. I just do a little dance and sing a little song, and people eat it up."

This statement would have sounded immodest if it weren't so true. Maybe it was the red hair or the lilting laugh or her silly self-indulgence, but males of all ages had always been willing to stop whatever they were doing to help Georgia get whatever she wanted.

Which was not to say that her life had been easy. Georgia tended to go to extremes—the highest highs, the lowest lows, opulence or poverty. In her eyes, moderation was akin to cowardice, and moral obligation was like slavery of the soul.

Growing up with Georgia for a mother had been a thoroughly exhilarating—and exhausting—experience.

Even now, every time Emily buckled herself into the passenger seat of Grant's car, she couldn't help reflecting on the contrast between her smooth and structured adult life and her turbulent childhood. Grant had bought the Audi after he finished his surgical residency, to celebrate signing on as a transplant surgeon at a university hospital in Boston. With his customary practicality, he'd chosen an understated sedan over a flashy Porsche or Mercedes convertible. Georgia, on the other hand, had always preferred to make a statement with her vehicles. She'd let all of her daughter's friends pile in—seat belts be damned! The automobile model and manufacturer had changed over the years, from a tiny red Mustang to a cushy Cadillac to a cavernous Range Rover, but certain factors remained constant: The floorboards were always littered with sunglasses, tubes of lipstick, and valet parking stubs. The music was always loud, and all passengers were required to sing along. (Emily knew the lyrics to every song on Madonna's *True Blue* album by the time she was four.) And when Georgia got pulled over for speeding or running a stop sign, Emily and her friends were to remain silent while Georgia simpered and pouted until the officer let her off with a warning.

The red Mustang and Range Rover eras marked periods of prosperity, when Georgia was newly married or freshly divorced. But when she was single, things were different. There were tiny, thin-walled apartments instead of spacious suburban homes; waiting at bus stops in sleet storms instead of tooling around in shiny new cars; phone calls from collection agencies at all hours of the day and night.

"You need to get a job," eight-year-old Emily had instructed her mother one day when she opened a letter from the electric company threatening to disconnect their power. "A real job."

"I'm going to do better than that for you, baby," Georgia replied. "I'm going to get a new husband."

Even as a third grader, Emily knew that this was not how responsible adults behaved. She would stare grimly at her mother, only to have Georgia stare right back and say, "What am I supposed to do? I can't type. I can't teach. This is my skill set. This is all I know."

And Emily had never been able to argue with that. Her mother had been raised in material splendor, the beautiful, spoiled youngest daughter of well-to-do parents who doted on her, fulfilled her every wish, and sent her off to find a suitable husband at a posh all-girls' college. Georgia had been a nineteen-year-old sophomore when she met Cal, the carpenter who came to fix a splintered shutter at Georgia's sorority house.

Two months later, Georgia was pregnant, Cal proposed, and Georgia's parents threatened her with disinheritance if she married "that wastrel."

Georgia went ahead with the marriage because she was madly in love. Cal was no wastrel. He was funny and hardworking, and he doted on Georgia. Emily didn't have many detailed memories of her father, but she knew that their little family had been a team. He had anchored them with a quiet sense of confidence and security.

Like Grant anchored her now.

Cal's death sent Georgia into an emotional and financial free fall. Though she had somehow managed to scrape by paycheck-to-paycheck with him, she started spending impulsively without him. She declared that while being poor was worth it for the right man, the right man was gone forever, and there was no point in being both heartbroken *and* penniless.

"I'll never stop loving your father," she explained to Emily. "But I'll never stop loving you, either, and he wanted the best for you. He wanted the best for both of us."

When Emily was still in elementary school, her mother married Peter, a type-A entrepreneur who'd started his own telecommunications business. When Emily was in middle school, Georgia divorced Peter and traded up for Jules, a temperamental poet who came from a very wealthy family. Jules had a daughter, Summer, who was Emily's age, and although Emily and Summer bonded instantly, Jules and Georgia barely made it to their first anniversary before splitting in a vicious two-year court battle. After that divorce, there was a lengthy and terrifying bout of deprivation, during which Emily started finding ways to earn her own money: babysitting, dog walking, busing tables at the pizza parlor down the street, which was owned by a family friend.

She was fourteen. She could help fend off the collection calls and the threatening notices from the utility companies.

She could not, however, understand why her mother refused to take the same course of action.

"Get a job!" Emily yelled at Georgia when she came home from school to find an eviction letter on the apartment door. "I don't want to hear about your 'skill set' or whatever! Go work in a fancy bar or something, where you'll make good tips."

Georgia, for once, had listened to reason. "You know, Emmy, you may be onto something." She'd selected a chic black sheath dress and applied for a hostess position at the country club where she and Jules used to play golf and lounge by the pool.

It didn't bother Georgia that her former friends were sneering at her lowly new status as a server. She was too busy catching the eyes of all the movers and shakers who came in for a scotch and soda after a long day at the office.

Exactly five days after she'd started hostessing, Georgia greeted Dr. Walt Bachmeier, a retired ear, nose, and throat specialist. The wedding took place six months later. And Emily, awash in adolescent angst, refused to act as maid of honor, or even to attend the ceremony.

"I'm not going to this farce," she informed her mother with an air of moral superiority only attainable in high school. "You don't even know this guy. You're just marrying him for money."

Georgia put down her mascara wand and crossed her arms over her silk dressing gown. "That's simply not true. Walt is a delightful man."

"He's ancient, Mom."

"He's *established,*" Georgia corrected. "Age is just a number; you'll find that out for yourself when you get a bit older. The important thing is, he still likes to dance and go out and see the world. He loves me; he loves you. That's all that matters."

"All that matters is his bank account," Emily countered. "You don't love him."

She drew back a bit, half expecting Georgia to slap her for such temerity, but her mother surprised her by looking thoughtful and really considering her reply.

"You're wrong, honey. I absolutely adore him. I don't love him the way I loved your father, true . . . but we have a more mature kind of bond. We're companions, not soul mates. He's smart, he's funny, and he has the most beautiful manners." Georgia had adjusted the fresh flowers in her hair. "Besides, you're starting college in a few years. That tuition's not going to pay itself."

Emily, enraged to be reminded that she stood to benefit as well as her mother, retorted with, "Oh, now it's my fault you have to get married to a senior citizen who wears plaid pants?"

Georgia laughed. "It's golf wear, honey. Lighten

up. I think you might really like Walt if you give him a chance."

Even as she scowled and stomped her feet, Emily had to admit her mother was right. Walt wasn't rigid and controlling like Peter or moody and demanding like Jules. He had kind blue eyes, he actually listened to Emily when she talked, and he loved Georgia way more than she deserved.

Her mother had magic, and she used it to charm other people into taking care of her. And when Emily headed off to college with a tuition check signed by her stepfather, she vowed that she would learn to take care of herself. She would become an accountant or an actuary, instead of a poet or a beauty queen. She told herself that she didn't need magic, and she wouldn't succumb to anyone else's spell, either.

But she had been wrong. Falling in love with Ryan had been easy—it took all of ten minutes —and the magic had dazzled her. Blinded her.

Even now, ten years later, she still caught herself wondering. . . .

"Smile, honey, you're getting married!"

Emily snapped back into the present to find her mother pressing a glass of vodka and tomato juice into her hand. She started to protest, then realized that resistance was futile and appealed directly to the bartender. "May I have ice water, please?"

Georgia's magnetism drew a crowd, and soon Emily was surrounded by strangers, most of them male, all of them congratulating her and wishing her well and asking her where she was going for her honeymoon.

Emily sipped her ice water and tried to quell the flutters of panic in her chest. *Deep breaths.* She was not and never had been a panicker.

I can handle this. For the next week, she was going to be the belle of the ball, the center of attention, and she could do it. She could do anything for seven days.

A low, teasing voice murmured into her ear. "You look like you need someone to take you away from all this."

She whirled around to find Grant standing at her side. "What are you doing here?"

"I walked my mother to her room and promised her I'd pick up my sister and my aunts at the airport tonight. That gives us"—he consulted his watch—"five hours. Want to get out of here?"

"Yes." She slid off the leather barstool and grabbed her purse strap. "I'm all yours."

"Hey!" Georgia snagged the other strap of Emily's bag. "Exactly where do you think you're running off to, missy?"

Emily pointed at Grant and let him do the talking. "I need to steal the bride-to-be for a little while." He gave Georgia his most charming Dr. Suave smile. "Urgent wedding business."

"You can't leave," Georgia protested. "We're celebrating. Join us! Pull up a chair."

Grant shook his head, then dug out his wallet and ordered a round for the house.

"I'll have her back before dark." Grant took Emily's hand in his and led her outside to the resort's parking lot.

"Where are we going?" Emily asked as he opened the Audi's passenger side door for her.

"It's a surprise." He walked around the car and settled into the driver's seat. "I thought you could use a little treat."

"But I'm not allowed to indulge in anything," she said as they drove down the bumpy dirt road toward town. "No booze, no sugar, no butter . . ."

"You can still enjoy yourself," he assured her.

"Unless it's ice water and lettuce, I can't enjoy it until next Sunday." She pulled one knee up to her chest. "You better brace yourself, buddy, because the honeymoon is going to be nonstop indulgence. I'm talking strawberry milk shakes for breakfast. Not smoothies—*milk shakes.*"

"I look forward to it." He patted her foot.

"Bora-Bora." Just saying the words sent a little shiver of anticipation up her spine. "I can't wait."

"It's going to be great. No cell phones, no e-mail, no emergencies at the hospital. Just you and me and a bungalow for two."

"Bungalow." She grinned. "I think I like saying that even better than 'Bora-Bora.' "

"Ten days," he said. "I can't remember the last time I took ten days off work."

"That's because you've never taken ten days off work. You've never taken five." Emily paused. "Have you ever even taken a whole weekend?"

"I took off three days when my sister got married."

"Which was how many years ago?"

"Uh." He coughed. "Six."

Emily laughed. "But you don't have a problem. You can stop working *anytime you want.*"

"The point is, I'm overdue for a real vacation. We should pack extra sunscreen, because my flesh might literally crumble to ash in the sunlight after all these years in the hospital."

"I know it's tough for you to get away for so long." Emily leaned over and kissed his cheek. "So I'll try to make it worth your while."

The words were saucy, but her tone was sweet. After years of playing the temptress and leaving men before they could leave her, she had allowed herself to be soft and vulnerable with Grant.

Well, she was trying, anyway. The whole vulnerability thing was still a work in progress. She trusted him completely; she'd trust him with her life. But she didn't always trust *herself* to be the kind of woman he deserved. She wanted to be perfect for him, and as much as she regretted her past mistakes, she could never undo them.

She would always be the counterfeit with the checkered past in the idyllic Norman Rockwell tableau.

Grant returned her kiss when he braked for the only stoplight in town, then continued along a narrow asphalt road until he pulled over in front of a low-slung lakeside building with a swirly-lettered sign in front: VALENTINE SPA.

"I hear that even ice water tastes delicious while you're getting a massage."

"I love you." Emily threw her arms around him. "Will you marry me?"

"Six days," he said into her hair. "Ready or not."

CHAPTER 4

"So what'll it be?" Bonnie, the Valentine Spa manicurist, offered up three shades of polish. "Pink, pink, or pink?"

Emily examined the choices, then selected the palest of the bunch. "What the hell? I'll go with pink."

"So you're getting married?" Bonnie uncapped the little bottle and got to work. "When's the big day?"

"Next Saturday. It's kind of a wedding-slash-reunion for my fiancé's family."

"That was your fiancé who dropped you off? He sure is nice. Cute, too."

"He's the best." Grant had delivered Emily to the spa's front desk with instructions to give her a paraffin mani-pedi before he returned to join her for a couples' massage. "I'm really lucky."

"That's the right attitude to start off a marriage." The manicurist nodded with approval, then began a mini-massage of Emily's left hand. "Relax, hon. Try to release all the tension from your arms and shoulders."

"Sorry." Emily made a conscious effort to calm down. "There's a lot going on. All the last-minute details."

Bonnie turned on some soft, *plinky-plunky* harp music and worked her way from Emily's thumb toward her pinky. She paused when she reached the left ring finger. "Ryan, huh? Is that your fiancé's name?"

Emily snatched her hand away and tucked it under her thigh. "No. He's Grant. My fiancé's name is Grant."

"Gosh, I'm sorry." The other woman looked stricken. "I didn't mean to—I just saw the tattoo on your finger and I thought . . ."

"Of course." Emily forced herself to put her hand back on the counter. "That's a reasonable assumption. But I didn't realize it was so, um, obvious still."

She'd paid a lot of money to get Ryan's name off her body—it ended up being more expensive than she'd expected. More painful, too.

Signing up for tattoo removal turned out to be a much bigger commitment than signing a marriage certificate. After pricing out the treatments at laser clinics in her area, Emily had to wait until she'd received her first corporate bonus to afford the expense.

Then she had to talk to the medical staff and set up a series of appointments.

"It's a small tattoo, and relatively recent," the

bubbly blond nurse had told her. "You're lucky —you'll probably need only two or three treatments. And black ink is the easiest to remove. If you'd written 'Ryan' in red or purple, that'd be a much bigger production."

"Will it hurt?" Emily asked.

The nurse shrugged. "Everyone's different. Some people have a really high pain threshold; other people cry. A lot of our patients say it feels like a rubber band being snapped over and over on their skin."

"I'm not going to cry," Emily said firmly.

And she hadn't. But it had been excruciating, like pushpins being shoved into the tender flesh of her finger. She forced herself to keep her expression neutral and her breath steady during the treatments.

But the nurse had picked up on her pain and given her shoulder a squeeze. "If you want, we can give you some numbing cream."

"No, I'm okay," Emily insisted. "I'm good."

And she was good—most of the time. She was maturing into a new woman. The kind of woman who would never dream of doing something so headstrong and impetuous as getting a tattoo. Or eloping with some hot guy she barely knew.

"Do you do this a lot?" she'd asked the doctor as he applied an antibacterial ointment and gauze bandages. "Erase wedding rings from people who thought they'd be together forever?"

The doctor handed her a pamphlet on proper post-treatment skin care. "Every day."

Emily finally allowed herself to wince after she walked out to the medical plaza parking lot. She could tell, from the swelling and moisture she felt beneath the bandage, that her finger had already started to blister.

After the third session, the doctor pronounced her finished.

"But I can still see it," Emily had protested, staring down at the faint white outline of Ryan's name on her skin.

"That's hypopigmentation—just a lightening of the skin. It's pretty common. Hopefully, it'll fade over time."

"Hopefully?"

"Everyone's body is different." The nurse gave her a consolatory pat. "Your mileage may vary."

The scars never faded. She could still see Ryan's name, etched in stark relief, whenever she typed or sliced vegetables or scrubbed the bathtub.

Grant had never commented on the scar. As much as she wanted to convince herself that he'd never noticed it, she knew better. He saw it, but he understood she wouldn't want to discuss it, so he never pressed her. Neither one forced the other to acknowledge the faded tattoo or the reason it existed.

"I picked out a wide wedding band," Emily told

the manicurist. "It'll cover the scar completely."

"It'll be like the whole thing never happened," Bonnie agreed. "And I mean, honestly, I can barely make it out. I could kind of see an 'R' and a 'Y' and I just took a guess."

"Uh-huh."

Bonnie looked up with a little twinkle in her eyes. "Did he get a tattoo ring, too?"

"Ryan? Yeah."

"Does he still have his?"

"I haven't seen him since the day we broke up," Emily said. "But I'm sure he's gotten rid of it. And I'm sure he didn't bother with a fancy laser clinic, either. Knowing him, he probably carved a chunk of his finger out with a pocket knife."

Bonnie looked like she was trying to decide if it was okay to laugh at this.

"He was twenty-two at the time," Emily elaborated. "And a horror movie junkie."

Bonnie shook her head. "The men we date when we're twenty-two."

"Exactly."

"So what'd he end up doing with his life?" Bonnie asked. "Besides hacking up his ring finger?"

"I don't know." Emily said this with equal parts defiance and pride. "And I don't care."

"You never Googled him? Looked him up on Facebook or anything?"

"Nope."

"Wow. You must have a lot of self-control."

"Not really," Emily said. "I just prefer to look ahead instead of behind."

"Well, with a second husband like yours, I can't say I blame you." Bonnie smeared some warm wax over the scar bearing Ryan's name and glanced up. "What was his name again?"

"Grant."

"You two seem really happy together."

"We are."

"And a big band of bling beats a tattoo any day of the week." Bonnie redoubled her efforts with the paraffin wax. "So let's get your hands all ready to show it off."

"Your skin feels so soft," Grant said two hours later as he and Emily lay side by side on towel-draped massage tables.

"I got the works: wax, pumice stone, moisturizer, eight different kinds of cuticle oil." Her eyes were half-closed in the darkened room, and she didn't try to stifle her yawn. "Sorry if I fall asleep. I already had my hands and feet rubbed down, and I'm pretty sure they're pumping sedatives through the vents in here."

The massage room was muted and hushed, with low light and a faint sound track of mellow flute music. The scent of mint and lavender wafted through the air.

"Smell that?" Grant said. "That's the smell of Zen."

They rested next to each other, shoulder to shoulder, in a comfortable cocoon of intimacy. When the masseuses entered and began to knead the tension out of their shoulders, they lapsed into companionable silence. Emily knew, as she drifted in and out of wakefulness, that this even-keeled contentment had been worth waiting for.

And she'd had to wait a long time. Their courtship had started off slowly. No spontaneous combustion or love at first sight.

Of course, she'd been too terrified to fall in love on the day she first met him. The August afternoon had been stifling, with record temperatures and humidity levels in Minneapolis. Emily had just stepped out of her office building and rounded a corner downtown when a FedEx deliveryman collapsed on the sidewalk right in front of her. The short, stocky man had swayed on his feet, then dropped an armload of Tyvek envelopes as he crumpled to the concrete without a single word. Emily stared at him for a moment, frozen and mute with shock, until a bright puddle of blood started pooling beneath his head.

"Help!" she'd cried, glancing left and right. The sidewalk was deserted in the midafternoon swelter. "Help!"

She'd just come out of a business meeting, so she took off her black Armani blazer, folded it, and slipped it under the man's head, both to cushion his skull and stanch the bleeding. She had no idea what to do next, but she knew she had to do *something*.

"Oh God, oh God," she said, then addressed the FedEx guy directly: "Don't die. Okay? Hang on."

She pulled her cell phone out of her briefcase to call 911, but her hands were shaking and she dropped the phone.

As she picked it up, Emily heard footsteps behind her. Then a calm male voice said, "I'm a doctor. Tell me what happened."

She didn't look up at first. She remained in a kneeling position on the sidewalk, the hot concrete ripping her stockings, and kept her focus on the flushed, unconscious man. "I'm not sure what happened. He just keeled over."

"Sir. Sir, are you okay?" The newcomer crouched next to Emily and shook the FedEx guy's arm. When there was no response, the doctor leaned forward, put his cheek above the guy's mouth, and then placed his fingers on the guy's neck. "He's breathing and he has a good pulse. He probably just collapsed from the heat, but we need to call an ambulance."

"Right. I'm on it." Emily reached for her dropped phone, but he beat her to it. When he gave it back to her, their hands touched and she finally turned to look at his face.

And stopped hyperventilating long enough to

notice that he was pretty cute. Very cute. Actually, between the chiseled jaw and the thick, sandy hair and the broad shoulders, he kind of looked like a Ken doll. A living, breathing Ken doll with an MD and a humanitarian streak.

Emily kept her gaze on his open, handsome face while she dialed 911. "Hi. I'm Emily."

"Grant Cardin." He offered his hand and she took it. His grasp was warm and sure, with just the right amount of pressure.

A Ken doll with an MD, a humanitarian streak, and good hands.

Too bad her makeup was running down her face in sweaty streaks. *Note to self: Next time you stop to administer first aid to a random stranger, wear waterproof mascara. And maybe some stronger deodorant.*

After Emily relayed the pertinent details to the 911 operator, Grant resumed his brisk examination of the patient. "Hopefully he'll be all right after they get some fluids in him, but that's a nasty gash on his head. I'd like to get him out of the sun, but I don't want to move him with that head wound."

So the two of them stood over the fallen man, creating a human awning from the brutal midday sun.

"It's a good thing you showed up," Emily said. "I didn't know what to do."

"I was in the hotel elevator." He tilted his head

toward the conference center across the street, which featured domed glass elevators on each side. "I saw him fall. I saw you stop to help him." He paused, waiting until she looked up at him through her melting clumps of mascara. "Not everyone would do that."

A few minutes later, after the ambulance arrived and the paramedics loaded the fallen FedEx guy onto a gurney, Grant picked up Emily's blood-drenched jacket and tucked it under his arm. "I'll get this cleaned and return it to you." Before she could argue that he'd done more than enough, he'd asked for her card and continued on his way.

Emily had spent the rest of the day watching her phone, wondering if the doctor with the dimples would call.

He didn't call. Instead, two days later, he hand-delivered the dry-cleaned jacket to her office and asked her to dinner. At the end of their first date, he kissed her on the cheek. At the end of their second date, he barely brushed his lips against hers. At the end of their third date, he'd given her another perfunctory peck, and Emily had called in her best friend and former stepsister, Summer, for a consult.

They'd scheduled an emergency strategy summit at the dressing room of the poshest department store in the city.

"He keeps asking me out," Emily explained as she pulled a simple but brilliantly cut black cocktail dress over her head. "And he keeps checking out my rack when he thinks I'm not looking, but the man will not make a move."

"Objection." Summer stopped paging through a fashion magazine long enough to give Emily a critical once-over. "You said he kissed you. Twice."

"Yeah, but they weren't steamy, passionate kisses. They were like . . ." She wrinkled her brow, searching for the right term. "Smooches. He smooched me. Like you'd smooch your cat or your cute little cousin."

Summer turned a magazine page. "That's what you get when you date a Ken doll. You get Ken-and-Barbie kisses."

"But I sense he's holding back. I know he has potential."

"Potential is an urban legend. Dump him."

"No!" Emily adjusted the bodice of the dress, examining her cleavage in the mirror. "He's awesome. Smart and funny, and I can tell he's got quite the body going on under those tailored shirts. And, PS, did I mention he's a surgeon?"

"I don't care if he's emperor of the universe. The man *smooches*." Summer shuddered. "Next."

Emily twisted her hair back to see how the neckline would look with an updo. "But I really like him."

"Why?"

Emily gave the matter some thought before

70

replying. "He's kind. He's a great guy, with great values, and he makes me feel . . ."

"Like a femme fatale?"

"No. Like a—"

"Shameless hussy?"

"No. Like a lady."

Summer grabbed the wastebasket and pretended to retch. "And that's a good thing?"

"Yes. I see potential in him, and I think he sees potential in me." Emily felt a girlish little smile starting as she related the next part. "And when we go out, I feel taken care of. Not in a financial way, although he does insist on paying for everything. It's the little things. He pulls out my chair; he makes sure my water glass is always full; he puts his hand on the small of my back when we're walking through a crowd."

"The hand-on-the-lower-back thing is hot," Summer conceded. "Gets me every time."

"That's what I'm saying. He's a gentleman. It makes me all fluttery inside."

"Despite the Ken kisses?"

"I never should have said the 'K' word to you." Emily rolled her eyes. "So what if he didn't throw me up against the wall and ravish me at the end of our second date? Did you ever stop to think that maybe he's just biding his time and being considerate?"

"Little does he know who he's dealing with."

They both laughed.

Summer tossed the magazine aside and said, "I vote you just rip his clothes off and be done with it. Since when do you wait for a guy to make the first move?"

"Ugh." Emily speared her fingers into her hair. "Since I became a lady and started dating gentlemen."

Summer lifted one eyebrow. "I have to tell you, I strongly disapprove of this trend."

"Stop editorializing and help me pick a dress, will you?" Emily turned in front of the mirror and peered over her shoulder at her reflection. "Which one says 'unzip me with your teeth,' the black one or the red one?"

"From my very limited understanding of ladies, I don't think they wear red dresses. They leave that to the shameless hussies like me."

"Hmm, good point." Emily returned the red dress to its hanger. "I'll go with the black. I'll wear it with no panties and hope he can pick up on the 'I'm-not-wearing-any-underwear' vibe."

"This is stupid. Just unzip *him* with *your* teeth and go for it," Summer advised.

"Ahem. That's not who I am anymore."

"Oh, please. You got an MBA, not a personality transplant. Stop pretending you're Audrey Hepburn. You're Mae West and we both know it."

Emily gasped. "Shut your mouth. I am Grace Kelly."

"Yeah. Keep telling yourself that." Their gazes

met in the mirror and they both grinned. Summer had known Emily since middle school, and she knew all the dirt: the skipped curfews, the forbidden older boyfriends, the acting out and the double dares and the tender wounds that still made her flinch, even after all these years. The two of them had run wild together through their teens and early twenties, each trying to outdo the other with her outrageous behavior.

And now Emily was about to get married to a restrained, respectable surgeon, and Summer was going to wear a mint green bridesmaid's dress with crinoline.

Emily didn't realize she was laughing until Grant nudged her ankle with his foot.

"What's funny?" he demanded.

"Summer in her bridesmaid's dress," she murmured. The masseuse had worked her way down Emily's spine and had moved on to her legs. Delicious, dreamy torpor seeped through her.

"She'll pay you back someday," Grant predicted. "She'll make you wear black leather to her wedding."

"With fishnets," Emily added.

"You look exhausted." He leaned forward to kiss the tip of her nose. "You should take a nap when we get back to the hotel."

And she did—after making Grant swear that he'd wake her before he left to meet his aunts and his sister at the airport.

"All these people have come all this way." She yawned as he tucked her in beneath the huge, fluffy white comforter. "I want to have dinner with everybody."

"You've been running nonstop for two and a half months." Grant walked into the bathroom and filled a glass with water. "Get some rest. You let me sleep yesterday; today it's your turn."

"I just need a power nap. Wake me up in thirty minutes."

"I'll wake you up in thirty minutes." He put the water glass on the bedside table.

"Promise?"

"Promise."

Hours later, Emily startled awake in pitch-darkness, her heart thudding. A drop of sweat trickled down her temple and into her hair. She flung out her arm and rolled over to find Grant sleeping next to her. He didn't stir and his breathing remained slow and even.

She raised her head from the pillow, her ears straining to detect the slightest disturbance, but there was nothing. The room remained dark and cool and peaceful. The digital alarm clock on the nightstand read 2:56 a.m.

Swinging her bare feet onto the floor, she sat up, then pushed her hair out of her face and fumbled for the water glass next to the clock. She took a few sips of the lukewarm liquid and concenvtrated on slowing her pounding pulse.

The stress is getting to you, she told herself. *Just six more nights and you won't be waking up in a cold sweat.*

But the more she willed herself to settle down, the more her body rebelled. Her nerve endings practically crackled with sensitivity, and she was hyperaware of the swish of her soft cotton nightgown against her legs and the clammy varnished floorboards beneath her bare feet.

As she pulled back the drapes and cracked open the French doors, she heard the low, growly rumble of an engine and the crunch of tires on gravel in the parking lot. A door slammed. A dog barked. A man laughed.

And there was something in that sound, in the depth and timbre of that laughter, that jolted her heart out of its galloping thud and into a skittering staccato. Something stirred deep in her soul, and for a moment, she couldn't draw air into her lungs.

She still couldn't see anything, but she heard the jingle of dog tags and the receding echo of footfalls. And then . . . silence.

The sweet, fresh night breeze gusted across her cheeks, and she found her focus, one breath at a time. Her fear and panic ebbed as she gazed up at the huge white moon suspended over the treetops.

She closed the window, crept back to bed, and stretched out next to Grant. But she couldn't fall back to sleep. She couldn't bear to be still any more. She tossed and turned for hours, until the first gray light of dawn crept in through the curtain folds and the rest of the world woke up.

MONDAY

CHAPTER 5

If the flower girls didn't trash Emily's wedding gown, the mother of the groom and the mother of the bride were going to spill blood on it. While the seamstress attended to last-minute alterations, Emily crossed her fingers and hoped Bev and Georgia might start bonding after a few cups of chamomile.

"You look like an angel straight from heaven," Beverly gushed as she gazed at Emily.

Georgia shot Bev a withering glance over the edge of her gold-rimmed teacup. "It's very *Mad Men* chic, I'll grant you that, but truthfully, Emmy, you could do better. You look a little . . . *missish.*"

Bev stopped sniffling and dabbing. "She looks demure and elegant."

"She looks like she's taking her first Communion."

"Stop bickering, both of you, or I will turn this car around." Emily cringed as one of Grant's nieces careened by, brandishing a harmonica in one hand and an open bottle of nail polish in the other.

"Ava!" Grant's sister Melanie chased after the giggling little blonde. "Put that down! You're going to—" The rest of her sentence was lost in a blast of harmonica music.

Georgia made a face and put her hands over her ears.

"Sorry about that." Melanie confiscated the nail polish from one daughter and a tube of glittery lip gloss from the other. "Aunt Rose bought them both makeup kits at the airport gift shop. And then Aunt Darlene gave them a harmonica and a pennywhistle."

Georgia grimaced. "Do your aunts secretly hate us all?"

"Mother." Emily shot her an admonishing look. "Rose and Darlene are amazing." A wistful note crept into her voice. "The whole family is so thoughtful. They're always giving each other gifts, and you can tell they really put a lot of time and thought into it."

Georgia regarded Bev with a mixture of pity and disdain. "Honey, where I come from, letting a preschooler loose with a harmonica is considered an act of war."

"My sisters mean well." Beverly maintained her placid smile. "They forget what it's like to have small children underfoot."

"I'd hand them over to Matt," Melanie said, referring to her husband, "but he's in bed with a massive allergy attack."

Bev tut-tutted. "Again?"

"Every time we come up here." Melanie didn't try to hide her exasperation. "You know how the ragweed pollen knocks him out. And he forgot to get his prescriptions refilled before we left."

"Poor Matt. Well, if he needs medicine, just talk to Grant." Bev beamed. "Grant will take care of everything."

"Hold still," the seamstress ordered.

Emily obeyed, standing motionless while the seamstress crab-walked around her feet, pinning and stitching. The dress technically fit, in that the fabric encompassed her body, but the margin of error was mere millimeters. She prayed the gown wouldn't rip at the seams as she walked down the aisle.

Don't sneeze, don't sneeze, don't sneeze. . . .

Although she adored the vintage style and the exquisite details—the dainty pearl buttons, the lace appliqué hand sewn across the sheer illusion bodice, the airy tulle netting that floated around her calves in a full tea-length skirt—she couldn't enjoy wearing it because she was too busy being terrified she'd inadvertently ruin it.

"I feel like I have one foot on a live grenade," she said.

"Relax," Bev urged. "Smile."

"And change your lipstick," Georgia added. "That peachy shade is washing you out."

"Alexis!" Melanie let out a little shriek in the

adjoining bathroom. "Is that thing *alive?* Put it back outside, this instant!"

When Grant and Emily had first called his mother to announce their engagement, Bev had offered up the traditional Cardin family gown, which she and her mother had both worn at their weddings.

"It's good luck," she'd assured Emily. "And it's gorgeous. My mother bought it in 1950 from Priscilla of Boston and we've taken very good care of it over the years."

Emily had accepted at once, relieved that she could skip the hassle of shopping and rush-ordering a new gown from a bridal salon.

She'd been so relieved that she'd neglected to ask about the dimensions of the dress. A major oversight, as it turned out. Who would have guessed that modest, matronly Bev had once had a waistline like Scarlett O'Hara?

The tailor had let out the seams on the bodice as much as she could, but in order to fasten the back buttons, Emily had to cinch herself into a boned corset so tight, she could practically feel her blood circulation trickling to a halt.

"Oof." She exhaled and sucked in her stomach even more as the seamstress examined the panels of silk. "Hear that? It's my liver screaming for mercy. Didn't people eat in the fifties?"

"They wore girdles," the seamstress explained. "And women didn't work out the way you girls do today. Their shoulders and chests were much narrower."

"Are we almost done here?" Georgia glanced at her delicate gold wristwatch. "I've got a date."

"You do?" Bev was shocked. (Emily was not.) "With whom?"

"Tennis with Ted at two and cocktails with John at four thirty," Georgia replied.

"Who are Ted and John?"

"Some lovely gentlemen I met in the bar this morning."

Bev looked as though she, too, were cinched into a constrictive corset. "So you're . . . you're socializing with strange men?"

"Just as long as you're not socializing with Cardin men," Emily said.

Georgia toyed with her emerald cocktail ring like a scheming movie villainess. "I make no promises."

"These stitches should hold," the seamstress mumbled, a pair of straight pins clamped between her lips. "As long as you don't dance too much or hug too many people."

Don't breathe, don't eat, don't move until after the wedding reception on Saturday night. "No problem."

"Hey! Watch yourselves, girls," the seamstress snapped at Ava and Alexis, who were now racing around the room brandishing sticky rainbow-striped lollipops.

Melanie appeared to be on the verge of tears. "Where did you two get those?"

"Auntie Rose." Alexis took a bite from her sister's lollipop, setting off a chubby-cheeked, blond-ringletted riot.

Georgia fished through her purse and extracted her wallet. "Time for a game, girls. It's called 'Who Can Sit Down and Be the Quietest.' Winner gets twenty dollars."

Ava and Alexis raced for the sofa.

"Finished." The seamstress stepped away, dusting off her hands with satisfaction. "Well? What do you think?"

Emily gazed into the mirror and raised her hands to smooth back her long dark hair, then lowered her arms as she felt the tulle straining across her shoulder blades. "I look like Jackie Kennedy."

"If only my mother could be here right now." Beverly twisted her handkerchief. "She would love you as much as I do."

Georgia glanced up from the compact mirror she was gazing into. "I know you're obsessed with tradition, darling, but I'd suggest something a little more modern and slinky for your next wedding."

Bev's smile vanished. "What do you mean, her next wedding?"

Georgia waved her hand airily. "Oh, you know, just in case things don't work out down the line."

"Mother," Emily hissed.

"Don't be so sensitive. I'm only teasing." Georgia glanced at her ring finger, then amended, "Or maybe I'm not. Men can be flighty, you know. They have midlife crises and lapses in judgment and sordid affairs with their secretaries."

Bev was staring at Georgia with a mixture of shock and horror. "We're not talking about *men;* we're talking about *my son.* Grant will never have a sordid affair. I raised him better than that."

"Don't mind her." Emily reached over and squeezed her future mother-in-law's hand. "This is my one and only wedding gown, and I love it." She leapt to one side as the seated, silent flower girls started dueling with their lollipop sticks.

"I love that your family has so many traditions," Emily told Bev. "Thank you for sharing them with me."

"It's your family now, too," Bev said. "After the wedding, we'll have it dry-cleaned and treated, and someday your daughter can wear it for her wedding."

At this, Georgia sat up a little straighter. "Our family has traditions, too, you know. Plenty of traditions. And you know you could have worn any of my gowns for this wedding. The Vera Wang, the Monique Lhuillier—oh, and the Amy Michelson was simply exquisite."

Melanie and Bev exchanged a look, and then Melanie asked, "You've been married three times?"

"Four," Georgia corrected. "It's an art form."

There was a knock from the hallway, and as the door swung inward, Grant said, "Hey, Mom, have you seen—"

All the females in the room started screaming.

"Don't come in!" Bev cried.

"You can't see her in her dress!" Georgia flung herself across the sofa to shield her daughter from view.

"It's bad luck!" Emily ducked out the sliding glass door and onto the balcony.

In her excitement, she'd left her silver satin sandals in the bedroom, and the rough-hewn wooden planks on the balcony floor pricked her toes. But when she inspected the gown for damage, all the material looked intact: no stains, no tears, no splotches of sweat.

I belong in this dress, she assured herself. *I can pull this off.*

And for a moment, shaded by the pine trees and inhaling (in shallow, non-girdle-busting breaths) the fresh mountain air, she believed it. She listened to the birds calling and the faint sounds of splashing from the lakeside, and reminded herself what really mattered. The dress, a hotel full of wedding guests, all the flowers and French champagne—none of those things really mattered. What mattered was that she knew who she was and what she wanted. What mattered was being a good partner to the man she'd chosen to share her life with.

A shrill, two-toned catcall knifed through her moment of Zen.

"Nice dress, babe."

Emily inhaled sharply, caught a bug in her throat, and dissolved into a coughing fit. Her fingers curled around the wooden railing as she leaned forward to see who had whistled at her, then flung herself backward just as fast.

She felt the tulle start to give way along her bicep, but she didn't even glance at the damage. She was too busy fending off a full-blown panic attack.

It wasn't. It couldn't be. *You're having a girdle-induced hallucination.*

But then the deep, amused male voice spoke again, this time directly under the balcony. "Are you wearing pearls? It's official: Hell just froze over and the devil is serving gelato."

Emily edged back toward the railing and peered down at the ground, where a shaggy tan dog was wagging its tail next to a tall, dark, and devastatingly handsome man.

He looked so different, she didn't even recognize him at first glance. But when she closed her eyes, she knew.

And when she opened them again, he was still standing there, staring up without a trace of surprise.

"Ryan?"

CHAPTER 6

"What are you doing here?" Emily demanded.

"You seem less than thrilled to see me." Her ex gave her a thorough once-over, his gaze lingering on her lace-encased bosom.

She felt dizzy and breathless from sprinting down the stairs, through the hotel lobby, and across the gravel parking lot in her bare feet. She might have blown by Grant in her desperate race to get to Ryan before anyone else could. Her groom might have seen her in her wedding gown.

But she didn't care about that right now. All she cared about was Ryan.

Oh, and breathing.

She knew that the slightest sign of weakness would be detected and used against her. She had to remain calm. Cool. Untouchable.

He took in her panicked hyperventilating and offered her a steadying hand. "Can I get you anything? Maybe some smelling salts?"

"No," she wheezed, swatting away his outstretched fingers. "I'm fine."

"Obviously."

"I'm fine."

"Okay, then let's start over. Hi, Emily, it's nice to see you again."

She stalked toward him, her hands clenched into fists by her side, and backed him around the corner so that no one from the Lodge's parking lot or front lawn could see them. "You're not here. You cannot be here."

He didn't argue with her. Instead, he settled back and watched her with disconcerting intensity. She had forgotten how completely he could focus, shutting out everything else in the world. And right now, he was focused on her.

Ninety-nine percent of her was horrified and irate. But the other one percent . . . well, she'd deal with that later.

He watched her watching him and gave her a slow, sexy smile. "I missed you, too."

Cursing her own lack of self-control, she glanced down at his left hand. He wore a blackened silver skull ring on his third finger.

She glanced back up at his face and asked, "Did you get remarried?"

"Does that look like a wedding band to you?"

"No, but, I mean, you're not exactly a traditionalist."

He took off the ring to reveal her name, still tattooed on his finger. "It tends to kill my game when women see 'Emily' already branded into my flesh, so I try to cover it up." He paused, his gaze roaming all over the sweet, frothy gown—the gown that Georgia had accurately described as "missish." He was not looking at her as though she were Grace Kelly or Jackie Kennedy.

He was staring at her as if he wanted to unzip her gown with his teeth.

She started to cross her arms, then stopped when she realized she was straining the shoulder seams. "Keep looking at me like that and you're going to lose an eye."

"I can't help it. You're a temptress in a tutu."

Emily stopped glaring at him just long enough to look over her shoulder to make sure no one else had overheard. "Please stop. This is not funny. This is my wedding."

"So I see." He rubbed the shadow of stubble on his jawline. "That's a hot dress."

"No, no, it is not. It is elegant and ladylike and it belonged to my fiancé's grandmother." Since she couldn't cross her arms, she settled for putting her hands on her hips. "Hey! My eyes are up here. You know what? It doesn't really matter why you're here. Whatever you're doing, whoever you're with, I hope your whole life turned out great. I hope it's unicorns and gumdrops and fluffy pink clouds every day. But you need to go now. Okay? You, me, this whole thing never happened." She leaned forward just far enough to air-kiss each side of his face. "Mwah, mwah. Take care. Bye-bye!"

His expression went from wryly amused to rankled. "I have news for you. A lot's changed since we were twenty-two. You don't get to send me on my way and forget I ever existed."

She froze, her lips still puckered into a little moue. "I haven't forgotten you ever existed."

If only it were that easy.

Of all the crazy things Emily had done in her youth, marrying Ryan was by far the craziest. And when she'd filed for divorce five months later, she'd been absolutely confident she was doing the right thing for both of them. Ryan Lassiter was not husband material. He was reckless. He was headstrong. He was trouble.

And yet.

He had lingered, in the back of her mind, in the depths of her heart. Even as she plowed forward without him, she had been unable to completely sever the connection between them. The intensity of their chemistry was a byproduct of adolescent hormones, or so she told herself. Their love, although intoxicating and all-consuming, had been shallow and unsustainable. The marriage they'd envisioned as twenty-two-year-olds didn't exist and never could.

And yet.

When she had stormed out of their squalid apartment all those years ago, when she'd bargained her way into business school and bought her first suit, she'd fantasized about the day when she'd run into Ryan again, perhaps at a college reunion. She would be poised, professional, married to a guy like Grant and living in a home that could double as a Pottery Barn catalog. Ryan would still be scruffy, repentant, working at a dead-end job and watching Quentin Tarantino movie marathons on Friday nights. She planned to act gracious, even a bit consolatory about the fact that her life had turned out so much better than his.

The real-life version of events was not going as planned. Ryan didn't appear the least bit broken or despondent.

Instead of sallow skin and dark undereye circles, he sported an expensive haircut and an air of understated confidence. His black leather jacket, artfully aged and distressed, hinted at motorcycling in northern California and first-class jaunts to Europe. She didn't know what he'd been doing for the last decade, but he'd finally put some muscle on his rangy frame, and the frenetic brightness in his hazel eyes had given way to a powerful, purposeful magnetism.

And judging from the way he was looking at her, he knew exactly what she was thinking.

Inhale, exhale. She could handle this.

She would get rid of him, and then she would forget this whole thing ever happened. She would tell no one, especially not Grant, and her world would go back to spinning on its axis.

"You're right," she said. "You're right. You absolutely exist, and you know what? You're probably too good for me now."

"Probably," he agreed.

She ground her molars together in a tight smile. "But I am asking you—no, I am *begging* you—to please not be here right now. Please just move along."

"Can't." He pulled a smartphone out of his jacket pocket and checked the little screen. "I'm scouting some filming locations, and the rest of my production team will kill me if I don't stay on schedule."

Her shock vaulted to new levels. "You . . . you're a movie scout?"

He didn't look up from his phone. "Technically, I'm a production executive, but fancy titles aside, I do whatever needs doing."

"So you make movies? Real movies?"

He seemed amused by her incredulity. "Yeah, I've done a few features. Maybe you've heard of them: *Homework*, *The Tunnels*, *Vespers of Death*."

She nodded, recognizing the titles from cinema posters and television ads. "I've heard of them. But I haven't seen them—horror movies give me nightmares."

"And then you have to sleep with the closet light on." He nodded. "I remember. But you should check out *The Tunnels*. It's got a steamy love scene set in this big, underground tunnel at a college campus."

"A tunnel," Emily repeated. "At a college campus. Sounds vaguely familiar."

"Yeah, there's a very cute heroine who has a thing for bad boys and loud indie rock. We stuck the scene in there during a last-minute rewrite, but it's great. My favorite scene from all the movies I've done."

She finally relaxed a little bit. "Let me guess: The love scene gets interrupted by a chain saw–wielding psycho."

"Nope, the heroine makes it to the end of the movie. The screenwriter wanted to kill her off, but I just couldn't bear to let the psycho dismember her."

Emily laughed. "You sentimental softie."

"It was more about audience test scores." He grinned, and she had to fight a sudden overwhelming urge to reach up and rest her palm on the side of his face.

Ryan must have been experiencing a similar urge, because when a breeze rustled through the pine trees, plastering a few strands of Emily's hair against her freshly glossed lips, he brushed one finger across her cheekbone to tuck the hair behind her ear.

She flinched and backed away.

"Sorry." He crammed his hands into his jacket pockets. "I didn't realize . . ."

Emily cleared her throat and took charge. "So you came to Valentine, Vermont, the week before my wedding to film a movie?"

"To consider movie locations, yes." He opened his palm, the picture of bewilderment. "And here you are. Crazy, right? What are the odds?"

She gave him a look. "The odds are astronomically slim."

"Maybe it's fate."

"It's not fate," she said firmly. "How long are you going to be here?"

"Hard to say. Maybe overnight; maybe a few days."

"And you're staying at the Lodge."

"Yeah, and actually, I have few hours free tonight. We could—"

"Here's what's going to happen right now: I am going to go back upstairs and take off this dress. You are going to go do whatever it is that film producers do. We are both going to stay out of each other's way, and we are going to pretend this whole thing never happened." Her eyes widened as a truly chilling thought occurred. "And if you happen to see my mother, run the other way. Right now is not the time to catch up." She gestured to her gown and pearl necklace. "As you can see, I'm pretending to be a grown-up."

"Got it." He didn't move. "God, you look good, Em."

"Ryan!"

"Right. Okay." He nodded. "The timing isn't good."

"The timing is never good for us." She looked away. "I'd say we've already caused each other enough trouble, wouldn't you?"

"Hold on a second." He started smiling again, but this smile was not entirely genial. She recognized this smile as his let's-make-a-deal smile. God help her. "We've seen each other naked. And now you're saying we can't even have a conversation?"

Annnnnd now she couldn't stop picturing him naked.

She felt the underside of her hair start to grow heavy with sweat. Any second now, Bev or Georgia would come looking for her. And even though it had been ten years, she knew better than to get into a debate with Ryan Lassiter.

So she took the only option left to her—she changed the subject.

Emily turned her attention to the dog sitting patiently behind Ryan. The shaggy retriever had a relatively slight build and graying fur along her muzzle.

"You have a dog now?" she asked.

"I *still* have a dog," he corrected.

"What do you mean?" She rocked back on her heels, wincing as a stray pine needle sank into her bare foot. And then she remembered. The day before she'd left for good. The roly-poly little yellow puppy. The chewing, the howling, the peeing on the carpet.

"This is the puppy?"

Ryan scratched the dog's head. "Lieutenant Ellen Ripley, reporting for duty."

"She grew."

"She did. She's a senior citizen now, in dog years."

"I can't believe you kept her."

Ryan's easygoing grin vanished, but all he said was, "She's been all over the world with me. She's drooled on some of the best agents in the business, played fetch with Oscar nominees."

Which meant that Ryan also spent time with Oscar nominees. Emily couldn't reconcile this with her image of him as a starving young slacker, but judging by his expression, he couldn't reconcile the lace and pearls with his memories of the leather miniskirts and body shots of tequila.

He shook his head, his expression half-amused and half-disappointed. "Look at you. Emily McKellips, what the hell happened?"

"I told you: I grew up, settled down, and became one of those practical, predictable people you hate."

"You did not."

"Oh yes, I did. I have an MBA now. I'm a financial planner. I set the table, I make my bed—"

"You straightened your hair." This seemed to

offend him more than anything else. "So who's this guy you're marrying?"

"His name is Grant, and he's wonderful."

Ryan raised an eyebrow at her defensive tone. "Is Grant a financial planner, too?"

"Surgeon." She took a deep breath. "He just joined the organ transplant team at a very prestigious hospital in Boston. We're moving to the suburbs and buying a house with a white picket fence. And I don't really feel like introducing the two of you so—"

"Too late." Ryan lifted his chin as Emily heard Grant's voice calling her name. "Here comes the groom."

CHAPTER 7

"Everything okay, angel?" Grant sounded worried.

"Angel?" Ryan looked confused for a second, then burst out laughing. *"You?"*

Emily felt Grant's hand on her back and shook him off, covering her face with her hands. "You can't see me in my dress! It's bad luck!"

"Angel?" Ryan repeated.

"Calm down." Grant put his hand right back on her shoulder. "My mom asked me to come down here and make sure you're all right."

"I'm fine," Emily insisted, wishing it were true.

"And don't worry, I'm not looking at you. I'm looking at the classic Triumph Spitfire in the parking lot."

"That's mine," Ryan said. "1968, original chrome work. I restored it myself." As soon as he started speaking, Ripley the retriever inched forward to greet the newcomer.

"Yeah?" Grant gave the dog an absent pat on the head. "How long did that take?"

"Five years, give or take. I had to track down all the engine parts on eBay."

Emily stared straight up into the sky as she introduced her past to her future. "Grant, this is Ryan. Ryan Lassiter. He's, uh—"

"Oh, I know who you are." Grant straightened up and got serious.

Emily stiffened, instinctively hiding the scar on her left ring finger deep within the folds of her frilly skirt. "You do?"

"Sure. You're a horror movie legend." Grant offered his hand to Ryan, who shook it.

"You've seen my work?" Ryan asked.

"Well, no," Grant admitted. "I don't watch too many movies. I don't have much of a life outside the hospital—ask Em, she'll tell you—but I've got this patient who loves you. Amazing kid. He's seventeen, and he's been in and out of the hospital for the last three years. He's on the transplant list for a new heart. Anyway, he loves your stuff. I can't tell you how many conversations we've had about heart valves while he watched that movie about the soul-sucking demon on his DVD player."

"*Vespers of Death*," Ryan said. "That was my first studio picture."

"Yeah. Hey, listen, I hate to be an annoying fan, but is there any way I could get your autograph? It would mean the world to this kid."

"Sure." Ryan's expression changed several times, but Emily couldn't tell what he was thinking. "Tell you what, I have a few DVDs signed by the whole cast. I'll have my assistant FedEx them to you."

"Thanks, man, that would be great." Grant turned to Emily with a huge smile. "How do you two know each other, anyway?"

Ryan looked at Emily, his eyes gleaming. Emily, still light-headed from the constraints of her corset, answered, "Oh, Ryan and I went to college together."

Grant looked even more confused. "You're here for the wedding?"

Ryan shook his head. "Scouting some film locations, actually. Running into Em was a happy coincidence." He clapped the groom-to-be on the shoulder and said, "Well, best wishes, buddy! And best of luck—you are gonna need it."

Before Grant could reply, Emily threw herself between the two men and started dragging Grant back toward the parking lot. "Sweetheart, you have to go back inside! I'm very superstitious."

"Leaving so soon?" Ryan called after them. "I thought we were going to have a drink and catch up."

"*Good-bye,* Ryan," Emily threw over her shoulder as she propelled Grant toward the Lodge.

Grant stopped short at the edge of the parking lot, his gaze ping-ponging between Ryan and the silver Triumph convertible. "You're on," he called back to Ryan. "Meet you at the hotel bar in ten minutes?"

"Last one there buys." Ryan walked off toward the Lodge's lobby with Ripley padding along behind him. As soon as he disappeared around a corner, Grant turned to Emily.

"What on earth is going on with you?" he demanded. "Who was that guy? Why are you so angry? Why are you out here in bare feet?"

Emily slumped back against a thick wooden railing, no longer worried about possible damage to the gown. "I'll explain everything, honey. I promise. But first, I need to unlace this thing and breathe for a few minutes."

"Okay, so the guy you met back there? That was Ryan. *Ryan* Ryan." After she'd replaced the Priscilla of Boston gown with a ruffled black sundress, Emily tried to explain the whole situation to Grant as they headed back downstairs.

"Ryan Ryan?" Grant stopped on the landing. "I thought his name was Ryan Lassiter."

"No, I mean he's *the* Ryan. *My* Ryan." Emily braced herself for Grant's reaction, and when he continued to regard her with a quizzical stare, she blurted out, "My ex-husband."

Grant's expression went from quizzical to dumbfounded. "That guy?"

"Yes."

"Ryan Lassiter, the movie producer, is your ex-husband?"

"Well." She could feel herself blushing. "Yeah."

"But I thought you said your ex-husband was a delusional, irresponsible slacker. I thought you said he had no impulse control. I thought you said he was completely out of touch with reality."

Damn the smarty-pants doctor and his steel-trap memory. Emily shifted her weight from foot to foot. "He was."

"Then how did he end up making a bunch of movies?"

She let her hands rise and fall in large swoops. "Impulse control and a firm grasp on reality are probably a liability in Hollywood. Listen, I completely understand if you're upset."

He blinked. "I'm not upset."

"But, truly, I had no idea he would be here. I didn't invite him."

"Do you want to invite him to the wedding? Because I don't mind."

Now it was her turn to draw up short. "You don't?"

"Not at all. I'm sure one extra guest won't be a problem."

"He's not invited." Emily started back down the stairs. "And I promise you, honey, you have nothing to worry about."

At this, Grant smiled. "I'm not worried."

"Good." She took his hand. "You shouldn't be."

When they reached the ground floor, he kissed the top of her head. "I'm not."

"Okay, then. But I still don't want to go have drinks with him."

"Why not?"

"Because. I know he seems all glib and charming when you first meet him, but trust me, the man is ruthless and conniving when it comes to getting what he wants. And he always has a hidden agenda. *Always.*"

"What, you think he's come to steal you away from me?"

"No, of course not." She managed—barely—not to melt into a puddle of humiliation. "I just meant—"

"Let him try. Mr. Hollywood."

Grant didn't sound the least bit threatened by the idea of another male showing up to challenge him on the eve of his wedding.

And he had no reason to be. He was Emily's dream man and Ryan was just . . . well, he was Ryan.

"I can't believe you two were ever together," Grant continued. "You could never really love a guy like that. It's just not who you are."

He sounded so proud of her inherent goodness that Emily stopped trying to dissuade him. She desperately wanted to be the kind of woman he thought she already was.

"Let's bail." She pivoted and tried to urge him back up the stairs. "Forget Ryan Lassiter. Let's just go back to our room and—"

"Hang on." Grant tapped at the screen of his smartphone. "I'm Googling him right now."

"Don't do that." She grabbed for the phone, but he fended her off with one hand.

He scanned the text on the screen, smirking. "Wow."

"What?" Emily crowded in for a look.

"He's quite the player. Says here he just went to a film premiere with a 'sultry Brazilian designer-slash-model.' "

Emily practically gave herself whiplash trying to see the images. "What?"

"Yeah. And his last girlfriend was an actress who won an Indie Spirit award." Grant headed down the hall toward the bar, chuckling as he went. "Steal you away—come on. What's Mr. Hollywood going to do with a nice girl like you?"

Halfway through the lobby, they spied Mr. Hollywood himself, half turned to the wall with a cell phone pressed to his ear. His demeanor, which had been so flip just a few minutes ago, was now grim and businesslike. Emily had never seen him like this.

"Brokering some multimillion-dollar deal, probably." Grant acknowledged him with a wave, and Ryan waved back and indicated that he would meet up with them shortly.

As Emily followed her fiancé into the bar, she couldn't resist glancing back over her shoulder to marvel at the total transformation of her ex-husband.

Ryan's gaze met hers and he didn't look away. He stared at her with obvious, almost proprietary desire, and she knew exactly what he wanted to do with a girl like her.

CHAPTER 8

"You okay?" Grant placed his hand over Emily's on the bar top, which had been handcrafted out of reclaimed wood from an old barn. "You keep fidgeting."

"I'm fine. Just a little stressed about all the wedding plans." She grabbed the wine list and scanned the text. Her chest felt tight and adrenaline was still surging through her. "Let's see . . . What do I want?"

Grant glanced at the list for all of two seconds. "You want the sauvignon blanc." He signaled to the bartender. "A glass of the Cakebread, please."

The bartender poured the wine and gave it to Grant, who offered it to Emily, who was just about to take it when she remembered.

"Oh, wait." She lowered her hand with a sigh. "What am I thinking? I can't have wine. I'm on the dress diet till Sunday."

Then Ryan ambled in. *Swaggered* in was more like it. He carried himself like a gunslinger looking for a shoot-out, and Emily really, really didn't want to get caught in the cross fire.

When he noticed the glass of white wine in Grant's hand, his grin widened. "You're drinking chardonnay? Bold choice."

"It's sauv blanc, and it's for her." Grant passed the glass to Emily, who decided that if there was ever a time to suspend the dress diet, this was it. She took a sip with shaking fingers, and ended up spilling a droplet of wine on her wrist.

Desperate and distracted, she didn't bother reaching for a cocktail napkin. In a throwback to her college days, she lifted her arm to her mouth and licked off the spillage.

Both men watched her licking her wrist.

Oh God. She closed her mouth and put the glass down. Grant looked faintly amused at her momentary lapse in perfect manners, and Ryan . . .

Ryan was clearly thinking about licking a lot more than her wrist.

Grant draped his arm around the back of Emily's chair as he turned to the bartender again. "I'll have a beer, please."

Ryan took a seat on the other side of Emily and spread his knees apart until the side of his leg brushed against hers. "Glenlivet on the rocks."

Screw the dress. Emily knew she'd need something stronger than sauv blanc to get her through this little tête-à-tête. "I'll have, um, a shot of vodka. Chilled, please, with a splash of grenadine."

Ryan snorted with derision. "You're such a girl."

"Shut up." Emily glared at him as she pushed her still-full wineglass aside. "I am a *lady*."

"Right." The gleam in his eyes was positively diabolical. "My mistake." He leaned forward to address Grant, pressing his thigh against Emily's in the process. "So when did you two get into town?"

"Two days ago." Grant curled his fingertips around Emily's upper arm. "We wanted to get here before the other wedding guests. We've both been working too hard lately."

"He surprised me with an afternoon at the spa yesterday," Emily bragged. "Then we got a couples' massage together."

"A couples' massage? Seriously?" A hint of a smirk played across Ryan's lips as he stared at Grant. "What, are your hands too tired from surgery to rub her back yourself?"

She kicked Ryan's ankle. "Would you knock it off?"

Ryan held up one palm as he lifted his drink. "I'm just saying, if that were me, I'd be rubbing you down myself."

She looked around for a handy steak knife with which to stab him into silence. "Well, it's *not* you, so why don't you just—"

"Excuse me," Grant interjected. "Emily, may I have a word? In private?" He helped her down from the barstool and she trailed behind him to the outdoor patio.

As they stepped out into the sunshine, he asked, "Are you okay?"

She refused to look back at Ryan, but she could feel him watching her. "No."

Grant lifted her chin with his index finger so she wasn't looking at the floor. "If you tell me what's wrong, I can try to fix it."

"I'm drowning in testosterone, that's what's wrong." She threw up her hands.

Grant pulled her into his arms. "Angel, I'm sorry you're uncomfortable, and the next time you want to bail on something like this, I promise to listen to you. But since we're already here—"

"I hate him," she said into the front of his shirt. "Do you hear me? *Hate.*"

"Don't let him get to you. Just laugh it off."

"I can't. He makes me insane." She let her voice drop into a stoned surfer drawl and imitated Ryan: " 'What, are your hands too tired?' *I hate him!*"

Grant smiled as she elbowed her way out of the embrace. "You're the one who married him."

"When I was twenty-two and stupid! You want to know why we got married? Because 'it'll be fun.' Yeah." She raked her fingers through her hair, which had started to frizz in the humidity. "We were idiots."

He reached over and smoothed down her hair. "And this time, you don't expect marriage to be fun?"

"Not all the time, no. Marriage is serious. It's

hard work. It's a lifelong commitment." The grim, hardened edge in her voice surprised her. She sounded like a woman preparing to trek through the Death Zone on Mount Everest with dwindling food supplies and poor weather conditions. But she had a realistic idea of what they would face in the years following the wedding: the challenges, the impossible dilemmas, the doubts. She could never recapture the innocence and enthusiasm she'd had on the eve of her first marriage—and truthfully, she wouldn't want to.

She gentled her tone and turned toward the row of orange daylilies bordering the patio. "Would you mind if I took a minute alone?"

He touched her cheek with the backs of his fingers. "You sure you're okay?"

She pressed her face into his hand, then pulled away when she heard Ryan laughing inside. "I'm fine. I just want to, um, make a call."

Ryan officially proposed to Emily halfway through a kegger, the night after their college graduation. The dorms were about to close down for the summer, so all the seniors had crowded into a fourth-floor lounge to say good-bye and wallow in nostalgia and pretend they weren't petrified about entering the real world. He had to ask her twice, shouting to be heard over the pumping sound system. "Let's get married."

110

Emily almost spit out her beer laughing, then sobered up when she saw the determination in his eyes.

"I'm serious, Em. Let's do it."

"Shut up!" Now they were both yelling. "We're too young to get married!"

He captured both her hands in his and pulled her in until their toes, their hips, their noses were touching. "I love you. I'm always going to love you. We're going to get married someday—it's inevitable."

"Then who cares if we do it now or ten years from now?"

"I care." He moved his hands behind his back so that her arms encircled his waist, then murmured directly into her ear during the two seconds of silence between songs. "Let's do it."

She tilted her head to the side and kissed him. "You're crazy."

"Not as crazy as you."

"True." She paused, stunned to realize that she was actually considering his proposal. "But we can't just—"

"Yes, we can." He dragged her out into the hallway, shut the thick wooden door, and dropped to one knee on the scratchy industrial carpet. "You're the one who always says fortune favors the bold."

"You've been reading that book again, haven't you?" she asked. Ryan had spent the last month poring over *Getting to Yes*, a negotiation guide that he claimed was like the Bible for high-powered Hollywood producers.

He grinned and tugged her down until she was kneeling next to him. "I'm trying to make your decision tree limbless. Is it working?"

"Dude." She winced. "This carpet is like sandpaper."

"Admit it: You know you want me."

She threw herself at him, and they both tumbled down. Then she rolled on top of him, rubbed her cheek against his shirt, and closed her eyes while she inhaled his scent. "I always want you."

He sat up and cradled her head in his lap. "I promise you, I love you more than anyone else ever will."

She gazed into his hazel eyes, then started laughing again. "You're going to harass the hell out of me until you get to yes, aren't you?"

"Yep."

"Okay." She grabbed his shoulders and planted a loud, sloppy kiss on his lips. "What the hell. I'll marry you."

Ryan looked so stunned by her acceptance that for a moment Emily worried that he'd been kidding, that the proposal had been a test and she had failed. But then he scrambled to his feet, yanked her up, and flung open the door to the lounge.

"We're getting married!" he announced. Emily

raised her arms like a prizefighter, and everyone cheered.

Twenty-four hours later, both of them starry-eyed and slightly buzzed from the bottle of champagne they'd splurged on after the five-minute ceremony at city hall, they'd stumbled into a tattoo parlor.

Emily barely even flinched as the tattoo artist's needle pierced the tender flesh on her left ring finger.

"Well, now we're definitely going to be together forever," she told Ryan. "I mean, you can always rip up a marriage certificate or sign divorce papers, but tattoos are serious business." She looked down at the tiny letter "R," fresh and raw on her skin, and started to giggle. "My mom is going to freak out."

"You're lucky," Ryan said. "You got in on the ground floor. Once I get some experience and start my own production company, you'll get to go to premieres with me, walk the red carpet. . . . Being my wife is going to be awesome."

"It's already awesome." She sighed with pleasure, then wriggled in pain as the tattoo artist finished up with the needle. "I want to add something to our vows. Promise me we'll never change."

"Never," he swore. "We will always be in love. We will always have fun together."

"For ever and ever."

"Till death do us part."

They kissed. They groped. They made out in the tattoo chair until the management asked them to leave.

And they lived happily ever after . . . for about five months.

In retrospect, Emily blamed the implosion of their relationship on the dog.

A few months after she and Ryan inked each other's names on their ring fingers, Emily started to have doubts. She loved Ryan. She loved curling up next to him every night; she loved riding on the back of his motorcycle and breathing in the scent of worn leather and freshly mown grass while they cruised around the lake; but when they weren't having sex or breaking the posted speed limit, there were. . . problems.

Like his apparent inability to wash even a single plate or use a coaster under his soda cans.

Like his stubborn, unwavering belief that the path to becoming a big-shot producer involved a series of internships that required ninety-hour work weeks and no paycheck.

Which led to the biggest problem of all:

His refusal to admit that the "cozy" apartment they'd leased after graduation was, in fact, a squalid little rat trap hardly big enough for one person, let alone two.

And these problems grew and multiplied like the spiders in the bathroom and the cockroaches beneath the fridge.

One evening, after a ten-hour shift of typing and Xeroxing for the financial firm she temped for, Emily came home to find food congealed on a stack of dishes next to the sink.

She placed her briefcase on the chipped laminate countertop with a bit more force than necessary. "Little known fact: This handle attached to the faucet? It turns the water on. You can actually rinse out a bowl. Incredible but true."

Ryan, sprawled out on the couch, didn't even open his eyes. "I'll do it in a minute."

"No, you won't." She turned the water on full blast. "You'll be asleep in a minute."

"Baby . . ."

"Don't 'baby' me." She snatched up the dish soap, only to realize the plastic squeeze bottle was empty. "I had a really hard day today, and I don't need to come home and—"

"I had a hard day, too. I've had about sixteen hard days in a row. This film is FUBAR."

"Well, then, may I make a suggestion? Maybe you could get a job that actually *pays* you."

He groaned. "Not that again."

"Yes, Ryan. That. Again. I am sick of being the only responsible one around here."

He lifted up his head and gave her that charming, rakish grin. "You? Responsible?"

"I *am* responsible. You're *making* me be responsible," she accused. "For the bills, for the groceries, for the laundry, for everything."

"It's only for a little while. I'm getting my foot in the door with all these industry people, and pretty soon one of them will hire me full-time. And then we'll move out to California—"

"Define 'pretty soon.' I want an actual date."

"I can't give you that."

"Then get over here and wash your own damn dishes."

"Fine." He struggled to his feet, glaring at her with eyes bloodshot from exhaustion. "Damn, Emily. You used to be fun."

"What's fun about living like this? And PS, we're short on rent money."

Rowf!

The demanding little bark derailed the lecture Emily was about to launch into. "What was that?"

"Yeah, I was going to tell you when you stopped yelling at me," Ryan said. "The script supervisor was giving away a few puppies, and, um . . ."

Rowf! Rowfrowfrowfrowfrowf!

Emily followed the sound of frenzied barking to the bedroom door, which she opened with a mounting sense of dread.

An adorable, fluffy tan puppy crouched on the other side of the door, staring up at her expectantly.

Directly behind the dog were the shredded

remnants of the curtains. The metal rod dangled from the wall at a precarious angle.

"Oh my God." Emily clapped her hand to her mouth.

"You love dogs," Ryan reminded her.

"What were you thinking?" Her eyes filled with hot, angry tears. "We can't take care of a dog!"

"Calm down. It's just a little puppy."

"Who's already mangled the curtains and cost us our security deposit. I can't believe you didn't talk to me about this!" She put her hands on her hips. "Who's going to walk her? Who's going to come home at lunch and let her out? Who's going to take her to obedience classes?"

Ryan surveyed the tangled wreckage of clothes, books, DVD cases, and blankets strewn across the bedroom floor. "Uh . . ."

"You don't even clean up after *yourself.* And what about vet bills? Checkups, shots? We're already living on ramen and rice."

Ryan gaped at her. "What is wrong with you? Can't you just relax? Everything will work out."

For a moment, Emily could see herself through his eyes, and she hated what she saw: a joyless shrew with pursed lips and no sense of humor.

And yet, she couldn't bring herself to relax and relent, because she was already at her breaking point. She was back in her childhood, sick to her stomach with anxiety over debts she couldn't pay and a partner she couldn't rely on.

As much as she loved Ryan, being married to him was not what she'd expected. Probably because she hadn't expected anything. She'd just made a snap decision, and now she was going to have to deal with the consequences for the rest of her life.

For the rest of your life. The words echoed through her mind, punctuated by the pounding of a gavel. A life sentence with a cell mate who left his wet clothes in the washing machine until they began to mildew, and who "forgot" to change the bedsheets, and who left her scrambling to play catch-up with overdue bills and snowballing credit card debt.

Ryan picked up the puppy and tried to get her to hold it. "Look at that face. Come on."

She crossed her arms, refusing to accept the puppy. "Did you even check to see if we're allowed to have pets?"

"Whoops. I knew I forgot something. But don't worry, I'll talk to the building manager. You know I'll get him to yes."

"Because rules don't apply to you."

He nodded. "Rules are for people who don't know how to negotiate." He scratched the dog's ears and asked, "What should we name her?"

Emily stalked out of the bedroom and into the hallway. "Take her back."

"What?"

"You heard me. We can't do this, Ryan. She's

118

cute, and I know you meant well, but I can't handle one more thing right now. And if we give her a name, I'll get attached, and I just . . . Please, take her back."

"How about Mina? You know, like Mina Harker from *Dracula*?"

"Open your ears. We are not. Naming. Her."

"How about Blair as in the Blair Witch?"

"I'm leaving." When she slammed the door behind her, she heard a picture frame fall off the wall.

She walked around the city for hours, hunching into her parka as the night air turned frigid. It felt heavenly to be out of that apartment—away from the clutter and the grimy little shower and the twinges of panic that she would be trapped here forever.

Georgia had often remarked that marriage was hard. "You have to work at it," she'd warned Emily. "You really have to *want* to stay married." Emily had rolled her eyes and chalked up Georgia's serial matrimony to a lack of restraint and patience. She'd vowed that she wouldn't settle for anything less than happily ever after.

Just a few months ago, she'd felt certain she'd found her fairy-tale ending. She and Ryan had promised to love each other forever, and she knew that they would. They'd also promised they'd never change.

And he hadn't—but she had.

• • •

"Thank you so much for agreeing to meet with me, Dean Jacobi." The day after she walked out on Ryan, Emily strode into the business school's administrative office wearing a navy suit, offering a firm handshake to the massive mountain of a man seated behind the wide mahogany desk.

The dean, bald and heavy-browed, barely glanced up from the paperwork in front of him. "My pleasure, Ms. McKellips." He looked down at the note scribbled in his appointment book. "My assistant tells me you'd like to discuss admittance to our MBA program."

"That's right." Emily sat down, crossing her ankles and projecting what she hoped was an air of supreme confidence.

"Our deadline for admission was nearly a month ago."

Emily nodded. "I'm aware of that. But I'm hoping I might still be allowed to submit my application materials." She opened the sleek Italian leather briefcase her stepfather had sent her as a graduation gift. "I brought along my résumé and transcript. I also have excellent recommendations." She slid the papers across the desk.

The dean didn't even glance at them. "Have you taken the Graduate Management Admissions Test?"

"Well. No, not exactly. But I've spent the last

few months"—weeks, really, but who was counting?—"interning at an accounting firm downtown." She made coffee and photocopies as an office temp, but "interning" sounded much more professional.

The dean pushed back his chair. "Our successful applicants typically score above the eighty-fifth percentile on the GMAT. In addition, we give priority to applicants who have at least two years of real-world business experience, including budget management." He stared her down, clearly waiting for her to collect her things and exit gracefully.

But she couldn't go. She had already wasted too much time, made too many mistakes to surrender without a fight. Her job and her relationship were both at a dead end, and she needed a way up and out. "I understand, sir. I do. And I know I'm not your typical applicant."

"Nor did you apply before the deadline," he reminded her. "While I appreciate your enthusiasm and interest in our program, I'd strongly recommend that you spend the next few years getting some more hands-on experience, and reapply when you're ready."

Emily took a deep breath and tried to imagine how Ryan would handle this negotiation. How would he make the decision tree limbless?

How would he get to yes?

She straightened her shoulders and waited until

the silence of his dismissal stretched into a long, excruciating pause. Finally, the dean glanced back at her.

"Ms. McKellips?"

"I'm ready to start the MBA program now, sir."

He finally looked at her, really *looked,* and whatever he saw made his expression switch from mild irritation to the beginnings of amusement.

"You're a tough woman to get rid of."

"You have no idea," she assured him. "I understand that you're busy and that this is a very competitive program, but I can't leave here with a no."

The creases in the dean's forehead deepened. "Excuse me?"

She kept her composure. "I'm willing to do the work, sir—whatever they can throw at me. I'll be the best damn business student to ever come through this program."

A faint smile played on his lips. "Are you trying to negotiate with me? Because I should tell you that I've taught multiple courses on the art of negotiation. People pay me a lot of money to negotiate on their behalf, Ms. McKellips."

She maintained eye contact and repeated, "I can't leave here with a no."

His expression flickered, and she knew she had him. She had gotten to yes.

"You're not getting into this program as an MBA student," the dean insisted. "But, I suppose, if you're willing to sit in as an unofficial post-baccalaureate student, you could audit a few classes."

Ryan's words reverberated in her head: *As soon as you get what you want, stop talking and get the hell out.*

She leapt to her feet and grabbed her briefcase. "Thank you, sir. You won't be sorry. I'm going to impress you so much, I'll defy you not to accept me into the program."

Two and a half years later, Emily graduated from the MBA program with an A in her negotiation seminar and a glowing letter of recommendation from Dean Jacobi.

Ten years ago, she'd been so sure of herself. So confident that she could do anything—talk her way into graduate school without sufficient qualifications, claw her way up to corporate vice president before she'd turned thirty, break up with a guy and know that there'd be a better one along any minute. She'd been fearless.

And now she was afraid all the time: afraid of making another mistake; afraid of letting her emotions overrule her rational mind. She'd literally lost sleep trying to decide if she should carry lilies of the valley or hyacinths in her bridal bouquet.

It was easy to be fearless when you were young and poor and low profile. The stakes got so much higher once you started to succeed.

She stole a peek back into the barroom, where the two great loves of her life were talking and laughing together, getting along famously without her. Grant was falling for Ryan's easy charm, just as Emily herself had when they first met.

"Shots!" Ryan gave the vodka Emily had ordered to Grant and ordered another one for himself. "We're doing shots. Who's with us?"

Emily did the only thing she could do, under the circumstances. She found her cell phone and dialed her maid of honor.

"Summer? Where are you? Yes, I know the bridesmaids' tea isn't for four more hours, but I need you right now. . . . Screw the speed limit. And no bathroom breaks, either . . . I'll tell you what's up: We've got a code-red, man-down, what's-the-number-for-nine-one-one ex-husband emergency happening in Valentine, Vermont."

CHAPTER 9

"Let me guess: You're Emily McKellips, and you'll be our cautionary tale today?" Summer Benson swept into the bridesmaids' tea with her usual flair and gusto. Tall and willowy, with platinum blond hair cut so short it would look masculine on anyone without her delicate bone structure, Summer lived for drama, scandal, and general good times. The daughter of a poet, she'd inherited her father's sense of whimsy and aesthetics without any of his mood swings or misanthropy.

The girl was guaranteed trouble, and Emily had loved her like a sister since the day Georgia had announced her engagement to Summer's father. Though their parents had parted ways, the daughters never had, and Summer knew every-thing—*everything*—there was to know about Emily. She also had a tendency to run her mouth when she consumed so much as a drop of alcohol, which was why Emily had ensured that the beverage menu at the bridesmaids' tea was limited to tea and lemonade.

Emily hugged Summer and laughed, but glanced around the room to ensure that Grant's mother and sister hadn't overheard the "cautionary tale" comment.

"Thank God you're here," she whispered into Summer's ear. "Help me. I'm dying."

"You're not dying. Where's Ryan?" Summer craned her neck, scanning the crowd.

"He's bonding with my fiancé. They're on a sailboat as we speak. Sailing. *I'm dying.*"

Summer unsuctioned Emily's tentacles of despair and turned around, lifting her arms to encompass the Lodge and its surroundings. "The drive up here was marvelous. The pine trees, the mountains, the lakes . . . like Lewis and Clark might go paddling by at any minute."

Emily watched the doorway, waiting for Summer's traveling companion to appear. "Where's Pierre? Did he go up to your room already?"

"Oh, him? He didn't come." Summer flicked at her bangs as though irritated by a blackfly. "We broke up, so I'm all by myself. That's part of what made the drive so marvelous."

Emily's eyebrows shot up. "Wait, wait, wait. You and Pierre broke up?"

"*Mais oui.* And not a minute too soon."

"What happened?"

"What always happens?" Summer put one hand on her hip, taking in the pink and green crepe paper streamers and silver balloons Bev and

Melanie had attached to every available surface. "I came to the conclusion that we were incompatible." In response to Emily's exasperated look, she laughed and elaborated: "By which I mean he was more interested in the allure of free flights than he was in my sparkling personality. And also, he took more time to do his hair in the morning than I did."

Emily clicked her tongue. "Another mile moocher?"

Summer's decade-long career as a flight attendant had provided her with the opportunity to date all kinds of men from all walks of life with only one thing in common: They were good-looking. Really good-looking. Like, stop-in-the-middle-of-the-street-and-snap-a-photo-with-your-cell-phone-and-send-it-to-all-your- friends-with-a-caption-about-somewhere-*GQ*-is-missing-a-cover-model good-looking. And invariably, these good-looking men treated Summer badly. Over the years, Emily had suggested that perhaps her stepsister should set her sights on a guy who was a bit more down-to-earth (with the added bonus that he wouldn't steal Summer's hair products from Paris upon dumping her), but Summer insisted that her spotty romantic track record was the result of bad luck. Bad judgment, she claimed, had nothing to do with it.

"Now don't you worry your pretty little head about me." Summer tugged up the shoulder strap of her Kelly green sundress. "This week is all about you." She held out her hand and flexed her fingers. "Um, why is my hand still empty? I need a drink, stat."

"Let's get you an iced tea." Emily steered her toward the bar.

"I assume you mean a *Long Island* iced tea?"

"No booze," Emily admitted. "But how about some refreshing, ice-cold lemonade? Freshly squeezed!"

Summer's baby blue eyes darkened. "What kind of shameful excuse for a wedding is this?"

"It's not a wedding—it's a bridesmaids' tea on a Monday afternoon. With scones and cucumber sandwiches."

"Which is exactly why I need a Long Island iced tea."

"Here." Emily handed her a dainty little pastry on a paper doily. "Have a cream puff and settle down. Don't worry; the rehearsal dinner and the wedding will both have open bars. Top-shelf liquor. Only the best for my boozy little friends."

"What about the bachelorette party?" Summer demanded.

Emily tried to buy herself some time before answering. "Um, pardon?"

Summer gave her the look she reserved for unruly passengers who refused to turn off electronic devices before takeoff. "I said. What. About. The bachelorette party."

"Ah. Well . . ." Emily almost shoved a cream puff into her own mouth due to stress, but managed to restrain herself at the last second. "We're not having a bachelorette party."

Summer grabbed a fistful of the front of Emily's floral chiffon sundress. "Oh, yes, we are having a bachelorette party."

"Sorry." Emily shrugged. "It's not that kind of crowd."

"I'm here now, so it is that kind of crowd."

Emily pried Summer's fingers off the dress one at a time. "We talked about this when I first asked you to be my maid of honor, remember? This wedding is a family-friendly vacation. No swearing, no fighting, no carrying on like hooligans." When Summer opened her mouth to object, Emily reminded her, "You *promised*."

"When did your wedding turn into the town in *Footloose*?" Summer grabbed the nearest cupcake. "I get time and a half for wearing pastels, right?"

"Your check's in the mail."

Emily braced herself as Georgia swooped down on them with an earsplitting shriek. Across the room, Bev and Melanie put their heads together, whispering and shooting judgmental looks at the Titian-haired party girl, who had decked herself out in a figure-hugging, sequined black dress that was more appropriate for a lounge singer than a mother of the bride.

"Summer! Darling! How are you? Let me look at you." Georgia held Summer at arm's length for a moment before engulfing her in a hug. "More gorgeous than ever. And so chic and cosmopolitan! You get that from me."

"You two aren't actually related," Emily pointed out.

"Beauty like ours can't be contained by biology." Summer laughed and hugged Georgia right back. "Still breaking hearts?"

"But of course." Georgia beckoned her in and confided, "I'm on the prowl for my next victim right now."

"Me, too." Summer's eyes lit up. "I saw a really hot lifeguard down by the lake."

"Ooh! Is he single?"

"Not for long." They both giggled and whispered until Emily stepped in between them.

"Will you girls behave yourselves? Please? Just for a few days?"

"She's such a buzz kill," Summer griped to Georgia.

"Tell me about it. She definitely *didn't* get that from me."

"Shouldn't you be talking smack behind my back instead of right to my face?" Emily said.

Georgia patted Emily on the arm, but kept her attention focused on Summer. "Well? Shall we go and rustle up a proper drink?"

"I thought you'd never ask."

Emily protested in vain as they rushed out the door. "Summer, you just got here! You can't abandon me! We have to talk."

"We'll be back," Summer promised. "Just as soon as I get a look at Brad the concierge."

"Mom." Emily appealed to Georgia. "Don't you want to stay for a super fun game of Bridesmaids' Bingo?"

Georgia made a face. "I'd rather get a root canal."

"Hmmph!" Bev, who had labored for weeks on the lacy, hand-lettered bingo cards, turned up her nose and stalked off to the powder room.

"Apologize," Emily ordered, but Georgia raced for the door as fast as her five-inch heels would allow.

Traitors. Emily scanned the room again, taking in the fruit punch, pastels, and pastries. "Well, bring me back something low calorie. Maybe a vodka tonic?"

"We'll make it a double." Georgia blew her a kiss as she exited in a swirl of silk scarves and French perfume.

After Georgia and Summer made their escape, Caroline Mitner walked in, bumping her head on the doorjamb as she stared at the screen of her cell phone.

"Ow." She winced and pressed her palm to her forehead.

"Are you okay?" Emily rushed to help her. "Let me get you some ice."

"Don't worry, I'm fine." Caroline dropped her hand to the side of her perfectly tailored peach boucle suit. "Wouldn't be the first time I've given myself a concussion waiting for a text from Andrew. Marrying a surgeon ought to come with a yearly CAT scan to check for brain damage."

"Oh, please," Emily said. "You with brain damage still puts me to shame on my best day."

Caroline was the wife of Grant's best friend, Andrew. She was also Emily's personal role model. Caroline had rowed on the crew team at a New England prep school before attending Dartmouth and capping it all off with a master's degree in biology. She could handily defeat her tennis opponent, rebalance her financial portfolio based on the latest reports from the Asian market, and whip up a three-course dinner party for eight without breaking a sweat or uttering a single obscenity.

The first time Emily had met Caroline at a hospital charity event, she'd felt a perverse and childish urge to hate her. The woman had *everything*—perfect body, perfect brain, perfect husband, and perfect house. She sat on the board of a dozen local charities and wielded considerable social influence. But from the moment Grant had introduced Emily as his girlfriend, Caroline had been modest, genuine, and welcoming.

"Grant must be crazy about you," she'd

murmured as she'd shaken Emily's hand. "He's never 'gone public' with a girlfriend before."

Emily had laughed, a bit flustered. "Well, we're having fun. But it's still early days; I'm not sure how serious anything is."

Caroline had stepped back and given her a long, assessing look. "If he makes time to leave the OR and throw on a tux, it's serious. Trust me."

At the end of the evening, Caroline had asked for Emily's contact information and stepped into the role of mentor. She started meeting Emily for lunch, showing her the best places to eat and the best selections off the menu. She helped Emily navigate the quagmire of hospital politics—who should be schmoozed and deferred to, who should be avoided at all costs. Though Emily often felt like Caroline's younger, socially awkward sister, she was grateful for the guidance.

But lately Caroline had seemed a bit distant. Emily wanted to attribute this to her own stress levels and sensitivity, but she couldn't shake the feeling that Caroline had pulled back from the friendship after Emily first flashed her engagement ring. There had been a tiny but significant pause before she said, "Best wishes! I'm thrilled for you both!"

Nevertheless, Emily had recruited her friend as bridesmaid. Caroline had stepped into the role with her customary capability—she arrived at every dress fitting five minutes early, and never uttered a word of protest over dress style or color. "Whatever you prefer is fine with me," she'd assured Emily. "You have great taste."

Emily shifted her weight from foot to foot for a moment before leaning in to give her a hug. Caroline hugged back with one arm while holding up her phone in her free hand.

"Goodness, I'm late. Sorry. I got the car all loaded up with the luggage before I realized I had a flat tire. I couldn't even leave the garage."

"I hate when that happens," Emily said. "But at least you weren't stranded on the highway. Did you call Andrew?"

Caroline looked startled for a moment, then laughed. "Call Andrew? What in heaven's name for?"

"To help you change the tire. I mean, you guys live, what, five minutes from the hospital?"

"Andrew's not going to scrub out in the middle of a procedure to race across town and screw on some lug nuts. When I have car trouble, I don't call my husband; I call Triple-A."

"Oh." Emily wasn't sure how to respond to this. But Caroline didn't seem at all upset, just matter-of-fact, so Emily followed up with, "When will he be joining you this week?"

Caroline shrugged. "He says Wednesday afternoon. Using my foolproof 'Surgeon Decoder Ring,' that means Friday night. Possibly Saturday morning."

"But he's the best man."

"Yes. And with any luck, he'll get here just in time to stand at the altar with Grant."

"Grant's going to be bummed. He'll be surrounded by histrionic women in crinoline and tulle all week."

This got Caroline's full attention. "Grant's here? Right now?"

"Of course. He took vacation time for the week before the wedding."

Caroline tilted her head, as if she couldn't possibly have heard correctly. "The whole week?"

"Mm-hmm. And then we're leaving for Bora-Bora for our honeymoon."

At this, Caroline stopped asking questions and looked at her as though she couldn't tell if Emily were delusional or simply a pathological liar.

"What?" Emily asked, lacing her fingers together.

"Nothing." Caroline smiled a very bland, vacant smile. "Nothing."

Emily cleared her throat and tried to rekindle the conversation. "Where did you and Andrew go on your honeymoon?"

"Oh, we didn't have a honeymoon. Andrew had just started his residency, so we were lucky he could take an afternoon off to get married."

"Well, your tenth anniversary's coming up soon, right?"

Caroline nodded. "Next May."

"Maybe you can take a belated honeymoon then."

There was another little pause; then Caroline's smile fell away entirely. "Let's have a bite to eat."

"Why are you changing the subject?"

"I'm famished. Watching someone else change a tire really works up an appetite."

"No, no, don't do that thing where you're all tactful and polite." Emily blocked the way to the pastry display. "You have something on your mind and I want to know what it is."

"No, you don't."

"Yes, I do. Out with it."

Her friend hesitated. "I don't want to cast a shadow over your big day. My life isn't your life. I know that."

Emily waved her hand in a spiral, indicating that Caroline should wrap up the legal disclaimer. "But . . . ?"

"But I know Grant. I know Grant; I know Andrew; I know how surgeons are." Caroline bit her bottom lip. "And if I were you, Em, I wouldn't get my hopes up for Bora-Bora."

Seeing Emily's stunned expression, Caroline placed a hand on her shoulder and led her into a quiet corner. "You and Grant haven't been together that long; you're still in the courtship stage. But you'll see. Living with a transplant surgeon is . . . Well, it's relentless. The demands on their time, the constant complications in the OR."

"Grant doesn't make promises he can't keep," Emily insisted.

"Maybe he'll prove me wrong. I hope he does. All I'm saying is, it's easy for these guys to make commitments outside of the hospital, but not so easy to keep them. The patients always come first."

"They have to. I mean, Grant saves lives."

"So does Andrew." Caroline's gray eyes darkened. "Over and over, week in and week out. And it's hard to save lives when you're lying on the beach in Bora-Bora." She popped a petit four into her mouth and indicated that, since her mouth was full, she could say no more on the subject.

Before Emily could press for more details, Grant's aunts, Darlene and Rose, arrived with their arms full of shopping bags.

"Good afternoon, girls! Hope we're not too late. Oh, just look at you, Emily: You're glowing with happiness. Look, Rose—isn't she a vision?"

To hear Grant tell it, Bev and her sisters had always been inseparable. Rose and Darlene were both a bit taller and leaner than Bev, but Emily could see a strong family resemblance in their dimples and cute button noses. Back in their youth, the three of them had sometimes been mistaken for triplets. In fact, Grant had shared a story of arriving for a party at his grandmother's house when he was a toddler. When Rose opened the door, Grant had looked back and forth between Bev and his aunt and announced, with bewilderment, "Mom? You're already here."

While Bev oozed down-home sweetness and sincerity, Darlene opted for more fashion-forward hair and wardrobe choices, and Rose tended to be bubbly and a little gossipy. But the three sisters banded together for every holiday. They were now the matriarchs of the Cardin family, and they kept tabs on all the children, grandchildren, and elderly relatives.

"No second-cousin-twice-removed left behind," Melanie had joked when describing the "small family get-together" Bev had hosted for Ava's first birthday.

"We brought tarts." Rose started doling out hugs and kisses to everyone within reach.

"And cupcakes." Darlene patted her wavy brunette bob, then joined Rose in greeting the other guests.

"Bless you, how thoughtful," Bev said. "But you know, we already have plenty of food. Pastries over here and finger sandwiches over there."

"Oh, well. No such thing as too much pastry, right?" Darlene opened the lid of a pink bakery box and started lining up chocolate cupcakes next to the red velvet cupcakes already arranged on the catering platter. "And we certainly don't want to run out."

"No," Bev agreed. "We certainly don't."

"Better safe than sorry," Rose said. "Remember Mel's baby shower?" She turned to Emily and confided, "We ran out of cookies. Poor Bev spent days in the kitchen, but we still didn't have enough macaroons."

"Only because Mom's macaroons are so delicious," Melanie said. "Can you blame the guests for devouring them all before we even opened the presents?"

Emily felt like she was watching a documentary—a documentary on a foreign and exotic tribe, where all the tribeswomen looked out for one another and baked pies from scratch and sang one another's praises.

A functional family. Right here in their natural habitat.

And she was about to become one of them.

"Oh!" Rose clapped her hands, then rummaged through another paper shopping bag. "Wait till you see what we bought downtown."

Melanie looked wary. "It's not more musical instruments for the girls, is it?"

"No. Although I did see a finger paint set that I know they'd adore." Darlene took out three identical lavender angora cardigans. "Look, Bev! Can you believe it?"

"We had a sweater just like this in high school," Rose informed Emily and Melanie. "Of course, back then we all had to share clothes, so we fought over who got to wear it every week."

"When we saw this in the store window, we just couldn't resist. And look—here's the best part!" Darlene unfolded the cardigans and pointed out the initial embroidered on the left lapel of each one. "We had them monogrammed! Now we'll always be able to tell whose is whose."

"All right, girls, let's try them on!"

Rose and Darlene slipped into their fluffy purple sweaters, then started giggling like teenagers when they saw each other. Their merriment faded, however, when Bev struggled to pull the sleeve over her upper arm.

"Let me help you," her sister offered.

"It's too small," Bev whispered.

"It fits," Melanie said, tugging at the neckline. But the loosely knit yarn strained across Bev's back. "It almost fits."

"Too many macaroons, I suppose." Bev blinked several times, then regained her composure as she took off the sweater. "I'll just wear it tied over my shoulders, the way we used to back in school."

Rose and Darlene exchanged stricken glances.

"Oh, dear." Darlene nibbled her lower lip. "We all wore the same size back in high school—"

"We shared clothes, shoes, lipstick—everything!"

"—so we bought all three in the same size, and we just thought . . ."

"Don't worry, Bev," Darlene said. "I'll take yours back and exchange it tomorrow."

"You can't," Rose murmured. "We already got the 'B' embroidered on it."

"Oh." Darlene patted her dark hair again. "I'm so sorry." She put her arm around Bev and gave her a side hug. "I feel terrible."

"Please don't." Bev busied herself with fanning out a stack of paper napkins. "It's the thought that counts."

Emily admired Bev's grace and good humor, and couldn't help imagining Georgia's response to the same situation. Woe unto anyone who dared to imply that anything was too small for Georgia, *ever.* Georgia would have screamed and stomped and—

Right on cue, Emily heard the commotion in the hallway: glasses clinking, music playing, and high-pitched laughter.

The subdued small talk inside the reception room ground to a halt as everyone listened to the party progressing toward them.

"What on earth is that racket?" Darlene asked.

"It's not even five o'clock." Rose sounded scandalized. "Isn't it a bit early for carousing?"

Emily squinched her eyes shut and prayed for a well-timed bolt of lightning.

"We're back!" Georgia trilled as she led a conga line of hotties through the doorway.

"Arriba!" Summer hoisted a bottle of tequila, spilling a few drops as she headed for the antique crystal punch bowl.

141

Three gorgeous, tanned lifeguards followed Summer, one of them shirtless and all of them under twenty-five.

"Everyone, meet Todd, Tim, and Kyle. They're here to spike our drinks and liven up our luncheon!"

Aunt Darlene couldn't have looked more appalled if she'd seen a rabid skunk rampaging through the room. *"Who* is *that?"*

Emily sighed. "That would be my mother and my sister. Well, stepsister. Well, ex-stepsister. It's a long story."

"Come on, girls—fall in line," Georgia commanded. And several of the attendees did just that. The atmosphere grew louder and rowdier as women started laughing, dancing, and flirting with boys young enough to be their sons. Even Melanie slipped off her sandals and started to loosen up.

But not Bev.

Emily's future mother-in-law perched on an upholstered armchair, flanked on either side by an equally prim-faced sister. Clearly, the Cardin matriarchs did not enjoy drunken debauchery, particularly during daylight hours.

So Emily couldn't, either.

Summer bebopped over, holding a cup of spiked punch in each hand. "You know what the *t* in *tea party* stands for? *Tequila.*"

Emily grabbed the drinks and set them down on a table. "This is Summer, my maid of honor. Summer, this is Beverly."

"I'm Grant's mother," Bev informed her icily.

"And this is Darlene and Rose; Grant and Melanie's aunts."

"Charmed," said Darlene in a tone that conveyed she was anything but.

"Rock on!" Summer flashed what appeared to be a gang sign at Mrs. Cardin. "Hey, Em, did you tell her about the time you—"

"No."

"How about the time we—"

"No." Emily followed this with a shut-up-or-else glare.

Bev folded her hands and rested them on her knee. "Your family is certainly . . . vibrant," she said to Emily. Then she addressed Summer with pointed politeness: "Is this your first visit to Valentine? How are you enjoying the hotel?"

"I'm used to overnight layovers at the airport HoJo's in Houston, so this is like paradise!"

"She's a flight attendant," Emily explained. This seemed to thaw Bev's icy reserve a bit, but before she could ask about the job, Summer exclaimed, "This lodge, the lake, the lifeguards . . . This is way better than your first wedding!"

"Shut up," Emily hissed. Summer couldn't hear her over the music.

Bev leaned forward. "Pardon, dear?"

Rose and Darlene circled like hyenas around a fresh kill. "What was that?"

Summer continued, oblivious to the tension.

"Em blew me off when she married her first husband. I didn't even get to go to the wedding. No one did."

"Your . . . ?" Bev's smile flickered on and off. "Your first husband?"

Summer froze, mid–booty shake. "Uh-oh."

"I . . ." Emily's throat constricted. "Grant didn't mention anything about that?"

"No." Bev's pinched, worried face went pale. "Goodness, no. I would have remembered that, I'm sure."

Darlene turned to Rose. "Did you know about this?"

"Sorry," Summer mouthed over Bev's head.

"Let's go somewhere and talk." Emily hustled Bev out to the hallway and tried to explain. She could feel a trickle of sweat run down her back. "It was a mistake. A starter marriage! A tiny little blip!"

"You've been married before," Bev repeated. "And you think of it as a tiny little blip."

"That came out wrong." Emily covered her eyes with her hands. "What I meant was—"

But Bev wasn't listening. The older woman strode toward the lobby in her sensible pumps.

"Grant!" Bev shouted, louder than Emily had ever heard her. "Grant Cardin, I need to speak with you this instant!"

CHAPTER 10

That night, a series of tense negotiations ensued in Emily and Grant's luxurious king-size bed.

"Are you still awake?" he asked. The room was completely dark.

"Oh yeah," Emily said.

He waited a few beats, then asked, "Are you freaking out?"

"Oh yeah."

The sheets rustled and the mattress dipped as he rolled to face her. "What's wrong?"

"Other than the fact that your mother hates me now?"

"My mother loves you." He yawned and rolled back. "You just took her off guard. But I sat her down and talked her through it. She's fine now."

"Ha. You didn't see the way she looked at me when Summer mentioned I'd been married before. Like I suddenly showed up with multiple facial piercings. Or a green-and-purple Mohawk. And your aunts! If you go through with this, you'll never be invited to the family Thanksgiving dinner again. We'll be outcasts."

He stilled. "What do you mean, 'if I go through with this'?"

Emily readjusted the top sheet and blew out a big, nervous breath. "You still have five days to change your mind and go find someone who's *not* damaged goods."

"Hey." He sat up. "Don't even joke about that. You're not damaged goods. You're perfect."

"But that's the thing—I'm not perfect." Her voice quavered a bit. "I've made a lot of mistakes. I have a less than stellar track record."

"Your history has nothing to do with who you are now." His voice was firm. Grant had always refused to get into a detailed discussion of their respective romantic pasts. He subscribed to the "less history, more mystery" school of thought.

"I don't fit into your family. Everyone's so normal and well-adjusted! No one else has to introduce their maid of honor as their ex-stepsister–slash–best friend."

"Give yourself some credit." He settled back under the covers. "You're well-adjusted. Totally normal."

She had to laugh. "See? That you would even say that just goes to show that you don't know me at all!"

"Maybe I know you better than you know yourself." He sounded stubborn now, and determined. "I definitely know you're the only one I want." He paused. "And my family will never ban us from Thanksgiving. If I don't go, my mom won't go, and they'll have no macaroons or pumpkin pie or gravy from her secret recipe. It'll be anarchy. Riots in the streets."

"Somehow, that doesn't make me feel better."

"Mom just wants us to be happy," he said. "She's a little old-fashioned, but she's not judgmental."

"Please." Emily scoffed. "Every mom wants a certain kind of wife for her perfect son the doctor, and it's not some fly-by-night hussy with a starter marriage and a mother who goes through rich husbands like they're free samples from Sephora."

"I'm sure your mother isn't thrilled to be dealing with a woman whose idea of a good time is a trip to the yarn shop," Grant said. "But they're big girls. They'll work it out."

"If we find my mom stabbed to death with a knitting needle, we'll know who did it," Emily said. "Or if your mom is mysteriously strangled with the strap of a Chanel bag."

They lay there, side by side, in silence for a few minutes, before Grant said, "You're still freaking out. I can feel it."

This time, Emily rolled over to his side. "Why didn't you tell her I was married before? Seriously?"

"When you told me about it, you kept saying that it was no big deal and it was hardly worth mentioning." Grant's hand found hers under the soft cotton blanket. "So I took you at your word. I didn't mention it."

"Uh-huh."

"You're the only one who has a problem with the fact that you've been married before."

"Uh-huh."

"I care about *you.* Not your past marital status. You."

Emily knew when she was defeated. "How am I supposed to argue with you when you make such good points?"

"You can't. So stop obsessing and go to sleep."

She gave him a quick peck on the lips, readjusted her pillow, and kept perfectly still for as long as she could bear it.

"What are you worrying about now?" he demanded.

"What? I'm totally sleeping."

"Liar. I can hear the synapses in your brain firing."

"I'm just thinking," she said. "We're going to Bora-Bora, right?"

"Yeah. I booked the tickets myself." He squeezed her fingers. "Why?"

"Well, Caroline says we're not going."

Grant paused for so long that Emily wasn't sure he'd heard her.

"She says you and I aren't actually going to have a honeymoon. Because she and Andrew didn't. She says it's a surgeon thing."

Another endless pause.

Emily scooched over until she was practically on top of him. "Hello?"

"Hi."

"Do you have a rebuttal?"

"Yeah." He looped both arms around her waist. "Never leaving the hospital isn't a surgeon thing; it's an Andrew thing. I love the guy, but he's addicted to cutting. I'm pretty sure he can't even use a regular knife anymore. He asks for a scalpel for his filet mignon at a steak house. But that has nothing to do with us."

"So we're Bora-Bora bound? You promise?"

"Yes. And when we get there, and all this wedding hoopla is behind us, I will cancel your fancy spa massage and rub you down myself."

There it was—the topic they'd been avoiding all day. The dirty little secret from her past who'd resurfaced and refused to go away.

"Don't let Ryan get to you. He's so . . ."

Grant chuckled. "He's fine."

"I can't believe you're okay with all this." Emily raised her head, wrenching her neck muscles. "My ex-husband shows up to torture me—"

"He's looking for places to film."

"My mistake. Torturing me is just an added bonus."

"He can't torture you if you don't let him, right?"

Emily coughed. "Right."

"So why would I worry? In fact, he asked me to go fishing in the morning. He seems like a decent guy."

Emily dropped her head and murmured, "Not as decent as you."

And that, she reflected as Grant settled into slumber, was part of the problem.

Emily had known that Grant was one in a million from the moment she'd met him. Her usual MO with men—flirt, have fun, and break up before things got too serious—hadn't worked on him. Mostly because she hadn't tried it. He took the lead from the beginning, easing them into a slow, sweet romance.

To her unending surprise, she had loved it.

"I need you to slap me," she'd told Summer as they elbowed their way through the Friday evening crowd at an upscale cocktail lounge. "I need you to put down your purse—very cute, by the way, is that new?—and smack some sense into me."

Summer used her pointy-toed stilettos to clear a path through the throng of dark-suited bankers and brokers. "Are you trying to get me tossed in jail for assault? Because that's not going to work. This time."

"Hang on." Emily leaned across the bar and

shouted their order to the bartender. "No. I had a dream about Grant last night."

Summer lit up. "Do tell."

Emily hung her head. "It's embarrassing."

"Ooh, was it steamy?" Summer tossed some cash on the bar and grabbed the two glasses. "I need to hear every inappropriate detail."

Emily opened her mouth, but couldn't force out the confession.

Summer's eyebrows shot up. "Wow, this must be really good."

"I can't even look you in the eye." Emily bowed her head. "You have to look away while I tell you."

Summer did as instructed, turning her gaze toward the restaurant's plate glass window.

"Okay, so last night I had this dream, and in this dream, Grant and I were . . ." Emily trailed off.

"Spit it out already."

"We were at the opera. And he reached over and took my hand."

Summer stopped looking out the window and stared at her. "And . . . ?"

"And we sat there, holding hands, and I felt so happy. Deliriously happy. My heart swelled ten sizes like the Grinch."

"At the opera," Summer repeated.

"Yes."

"And that's it? That was your big dream?"

"Yes."

Summer threw back half her drink in one

gulp. "That's the lamest thing I've ever heard."

"I know, right?" Emily shook her head in chagrin. "I woke up all glowy and smiley, and I wanted to call him right away. But I didn't."

Summer narrowed her eyes. "What is *wrong* with you?"

"I have feelings for him, okay? Warm, caring feelings."

"Ew."

"It's true. In the deepest, darkest part of my soul, I want to hold hands with him at the opera." Emily let out a little squeak of despair. "I told you, I need to be slapped."

Summer put down her glass. "Believe me, it's taking all my self-control to hold back."

"And this is all his fault! The last time we went out, he told me a bunch of stories about how he went to his nieces' ballet recitals and how he hires a snowplow service to make sure his mom's driveway is clear in the winter."

Summer shook her head. "That bastard."

"I don't do relationships," Emily cried. "This was just supposed to be a fun little fling."

"But he refuses to be flung."

"Exactly. He's making me have *feelings*. And now I'm getting attached." She slammed her open palm against her leg. "Damn it!"

Summer regarded her with disgust. "Holding hands at the opera. My God. Someone's seen *Pretty Woman* too many times."

"Take it up with my subconscious."

Summer twirled her straw, considering the options. "Okay, so you have feelings for him. So you're getting attached. So go for it, right?"

"I can't."

"Why not?"

Emily struggled to explain this, as much to herself as to her best friend. "Because he's perfect. Smart and successful and stable and sweet, and I'm . . ." Her shoulders sagged. "I'm me."

"All of a sudden you have an inferiority complex?" Summer demanded. "Knock it off. It's boring, and also, self-doubt is not a good look for you."

Emily took a deep breath and tried to explain. "I don't feel inferior, exactly, but he's always been all about self-control and delayed gratification, and I have not. You *know* I have not. I've tried to tell him a little bit about how I used to be, but I don't think he gets it."

"He probably loves it," Summer said. "Good guys can't resist reformed bad girls. All the naughtiness with none of the drama."

"The point is, I'm not his type."

"Well, you kind of are. He's a surgeon and you're a fancy-pants financial executive."

"Which is why he *thinks* I'm his type."

"And so he keeps asking you out and you keep saying yes."

Emily sighed with resignation. "Yeah."

"Well, what's the worst that could happen? You hold hands for a while? You fall in love and live happily ever after?"

They both laughed, and Emily said, "Now who's seen *Pretty Woman* too many times?"

Grant never actually took Emily to the opera, but they did hold hands a lot: at coffee shops, at hospital events, at Grant's apartment.

One blustery Sunday in April, while the wind blew so hard that the rain seemed to be falling sideways, Grant paused in the middle of getting ready for work and asked her, "If you could go anywhere in the world, where would you go?"

"Right now?" She stopped reading through work e-mail on her laptop and glanced out the window at the dark skies. "Bora-Bora sounds pretty good."

He yanked a blue scrub shirt over his head and started across the room toward her. She moved her computer to the coffee table so he could sit down next to her on the sofa. After he kissed her, he pulled her against his chest and said, "Bora-Bora, huh?"

She rubbed her cheek against the soft, thin fabric. Scrubs felt even more comfy than pajamas, which was why she loved to steal his at any opportunity. Even the faint trace of surgical soap that clung to his skin smelled appealing to her.

"Yeah. Although, to be honest, I'm not even sure where it is." She leaned forward, opened a new browser on her laptop and did a quick Internet search.

"Over by Tahiti, I think," he said.

"You're right; there it is." Emily scanned the Web site of a luxury resort. "Ooh, look at this place. It's got an actual marine biologist on staff to take you snorkeling."

"Let's go." Grant stood up and reached into his pocket.

She blinked. "Right now? I thought you had to go to work."

"No, I mean for our honeymoon." He dropped to the hardwood floor next to the sofa. His knee hit the floor with a thud.

Emily sucked in a breath. "Are you okay?"

"I'm fine," he insisted. "Don't ruin the moment. I'm proposing here."

She stared at him, shocked into speechlessness.

He took her hand in his and offered up a black velvet jeweler's box. "Emily McKellips, will you marry me?"

She couldn't focus on the sparkly diamond ring. She was too busy trying to process the fact that yes, this really was happening. They hadn't been dating that long, and they'd certainly never discussed marriage. She'd had no clue he was even considering it.

He rushed to fill the silence. "Angel, I may not be the smartest man in the world—"

At this, she burst out laughing. "Oh, let's be real. Yes, you are."

"—but I know what I want when I see it. I always said that if I found a woman who is everything I want—who is sweet and selfless and beautiful and brilliant—that I would be smart enough to stop looking and settle down. And that's you, Emily. You're everything I want. You're perfect for me." He appealed to her with earnest blue eyes. "Come to Boston with me. Be my wife."

Reeling with surprise and disbelief, she tried to stay in the moment as he slid the ring onto her finger. "Yes. Yes, I will marry you."

He got back up, but before he could kiss her, she added, "On one condition."

"Anything," he agreed.

"You have to let me ice your knee."

He laughed. "You're a tough girl to sweep off her feet."

"You have to stand at the OR table for hours at a time," she pointed out. "You need your knees." She was filling up a plastic bag with ice cubes when Grant's pager buzzed.

He glanced at it, frowned, and strode toward the door. "Damn. I have to go."

"Wait!" Emily finished assembling the ice pack. "Your knee."

"My knee will heal," he assured her. "I'm more concerned about this guy's heart. I should be home around eight. Make reservations, and we'll have dinner to celebrate." He grabbed a thermos of coffee and his black leather briefcase on his way out. "Love you forever."

"Love you forever," she echoed, and after he shut the door behind him, she had a moment of delicious solitude. She slid the ring between the base and the knuckle of her finger, basking in quiet joy.

She didn't feel like she was in a fairy tale. She wasn't hoping for happily ever after.

Real life—real love—was going to be so much better.

"What the hell?" Summer had gone apoplectic upon hearing the news. "How are you engaged? I haven't even met this guy!"

"Only because you both have ridiculous work schedules. He's always at the hospital and you're always on some flight to Europe."

"But isn't it too soon to be getting engaged? You've only been dating him for . . . ?"

"It's been, like, eight months," Emily said. "Miss Frequent Flier."

"Has it really been that long? Lemme see." Summer grabbed Emily's hand and checked out the ring. "Classic setting, lovely stone. Well done."

Emily helped herself to a bit of Summer's chocolate torte and fanned out her fingers so she could admire the diamond for herself. "It was his grandmother's."

"Of course it was."

"And we're going to Bora-Bora for our honeymoon."

"Of course you are."

"I know, I know, I'm all gushy and obnoxious."

"No, you're just happy." Summer hesitated a few seconds before adding, "Really happy. I haven't seen you this happy since . . ."

"Since when?" Emily prompted.

"Well, since you and Ryan—"

Emily practically spat out her cake. "Don't you even speak his name. I wasn't happy with Ryan. Not really. I was just hopped up on hormones and fantasies."

"If you say so."

"I do say so! Ryan was an immature, delusional jackass, and Grant is—"

"The perfect doctor from the perfect family with the perfect engagement ring. I heard."

"He's not perfect," Emily said. "I don't think that anymore. He's great, and his family is great, but he's not perfect. He's just perfect for me."

Summer leveled her fork at Emily. "Be that as it may, you're not officially engaged until I approve the guy. When are we meeting?"

The three of them had dinner a few days later,

and as the appetizers arrived, Summer pulled an index card out of her bag and began interviewing him like a job candidate. "So, Grant. Did you always know you wanted to be a surgeon?"

"I actually worked as an EMT for a couple of years after college," Grant said. "Our job was to get patients stabilized and drop them off at the hospital, but after a while, I couldn't stand to leave them at the ER doors. I wanted to go in there and finish the job."

Summer scribbled down a few notes. "So you decided to go to medical school?"

"Yeah. I had to go back and take some upper-level science courses, and some math."

"And you kept working as an EMT while you took classes?"

Grant nodded. "Had no life. But it was worth it."

"And what about now?" If Summer had been wearing glasses, she would have been peering over the top rims. "Do you have a life now?"

He grinned. "I'm building one with Emily. That count?"

Emily snatched Summer's index card away. "Will that be all, counselor?"

"No further questions. For now." But when Grant turned away, Summer caught Emily's gaze and mouthed, "I love him."

Emily rested her hand on Grant's shoulder and mouthed back, "Me, too."

• • •

She loved Grant then and she loved him now. She never had doubts about him.

All of her doubts stemmed from herself.

She could hear a dog barking out by the lake, and she imagined that it was Ripley, out for a late-night romp with Ryan.

Unruly, unpredictable Ryan Lassiter with his dark hair and his trusty canine sidekick and her name etched indelibly into his skin.

Why was he here? Why now?

And why couldn't she keep her mind off him?

The barking stopped and she finally fell asleep, but she didn't dream about holding hands with her future husband. Instead, for the first time in years, she dreamed about her ex-husband, and in her dream, she and Ryan were doing a lot more than holding hands.

And when she woke up the next morning, sweaty and shaken, Grant's side of the bed was empty.

TUESDAY

CHAPTER 11

"*Why* are we doing this, again?" Summer huffed and puffed next to Emily as they jogged down the gravel path that led to the lakeside trail.

"I run every morning," Emily said. Unlike Summer, she hadn't yet broken a sweat or started to breathe hard. Instead, her mind started to warm up along with her body. She could feel her fatigue and stress fall away as her leg muscles settled into a steady, familiar stride. Cold speckles of early-morning dew splashed across her ankles as she ran. "It's important for my mental and physical health. And for making sure I fit in my wedding dress."

"Really?" Summer hawked a loogie into the underbrush. "You're going to be one of those distorted-body-image brides? I thought you were better than that."

"This isn't about body image," Emily countered. "It's about a twenty-six-inch waistline. And that's with the side seams let out."

"So why are you torturing yourself into this dress? I'm sure Georgia would have let you borrow her Vera Wang. The one with the little ruffly pleats in the back? That one was gorgeous."

"Don't start with the Vera Wang. I already got an earful from my mom." Emily glanced at the heart rate monitor on her wrist and picked up the pace. "But Grant's mom and grandmother got married in this gown. It's a family heirloom. It's tradition."

Summer grabbed Emily's arm and slowed the pace back down. "Tradition's great, but just remember you have a family, too. I know we're not white picket fence material, but we're awesome in our own way."

"Last Christmas, you were working on a flight to Paris and my mother was in Hawaii with some guy she met online," Emily said. "So sue me if I want a normal family with normal holiday traditions."

"Normal is just another word for boring."

"Not on my wedding day. Not on Christmas. I want Currier and Ives, baby. I want sleigh rides and snowball fights and homemade cookies. I want hot cocoa and marshmallows and chestnuts roasting on an open fire."

"Great." Summer wheezed. "Now I'm starving."

"Just a few more miles," Emily urged. "Then we'll have some egg whites and fresh strawberries at the Lodge."

"A few more *miles?*" Summer slowed from a jog to a walk. "I quit. And let me just say this about your precious in-laws: The only reason they seem normal is because you don't know them well enough."

"That's not true. They're the kind of family I always wanted. Everyone loves one another. They all get along and want the best for each other."

Summer rolled her eyes. "No, they don't."

"Yes, they do."

"Bullshit. Every family has problems."

"Not the Cardins. You saw Bev and her sisters yesterday. They're like the three musketeers. Three jolly little peas in a pod."

"Eh." Summer waved this away. "They're probably just repressing their true feelings of rage and resentment."

"Why is it so hard for you to believe that a healthy, happy extended family exists in real life?"

"Because my job involves taking cross-Atlantic flights with large groups of people. I've seen families just as shiny and happy as the Cardins crack under the pressure: flight delays, sleep deprivation, financial extortion for packets of pretzels. The stress gets to them and they turn on each other two hours before landing. It's ugly."

Emily laughed. "You're crazy."

"I'm telling you, the three musketeers are either hiding something or they're heavily medicated. Wait and see."

Emily tugged Summer back into a run. When they veered right at a trio of pine trees, the shores of Valentine Lake appeared before them. The water was dark and calm, with a heavy gray shroud of fog blanketing the surface. Emily could hear the gentle lapping of the waves between her breaths. "See? Isn't this lovely?"

"It'd be a lot more lovely if my heart weren't about to explode." Summer clutched her chest dramatically. "You know, I don't remember you running in college. Or getting up at the crack of dawn."

"Grant got me started. He runs every morning. He calls it the 'Five at Five'—five miles at five o'clock."

"That's a prison sentence, not a workout."

"You get used to it. He convinced me to give it a try, and now I love it. It helps me stay focused and energized."

But that wasn't strictly true, she realized as she slowed her pace to accommodate Summer's struggle to keep up. She hated dragging herself out of bed while it was still dark outside, and she'd never been able to find "The Zone"—the peaceful euphoria Grant claimed to experience while sprinting through rain and sleet and suffocating humidity. But she always got up, with or without Grant, and she always ran the whole distance without shortcuts or complaints. To prove that she had finally developed discipline. To prove that she had evolved beyond the flighty, fickle girl she used to be.

"Okay, I'm out." Summer grabbed the hem of

Emily's shirt as she sagged against a tree trunk, gasping for breath. "If you need a running buddy, go find Grant. Me? I'm your drinking buddy."

"Come on. Don't you want to push yourself?"

Summer gave her a withering look. "Don't you want to just chill out for once?"

Emily tightened her ponytail and tried to forget about her target heart rate. "Yes. You have no idea."

"Great. Let's start right now." Summer trudged toward the beach. "I hardly even recognize you these days. You're so . . . so . . ."

"So what?" Emily asked, even though she was a little afraid to hear the answer.

"So proper. Serving punch and pastry, wearing your mother-in-law's wedding dress, running five miles every morning . . . Honestly, Em, what *happened* to you? You used to be so happy-go-lucky."

"I was out of control," Emily corrected. "I had no structure, no sense of balance."

"But you were happy."

"I *thought* I was happy."

"Oh, sell that crap somewhere else." Summer collapsed into the damp sand, heedless of her pristine white shorts. "I was there, remember? You were happy, full stop, end of discussion. You were a crazy desperado, but you were happy."

"I'm still happy," Emily said. Yet she seemed incapable of following her friend onto the beach. She couldn't bear to think of all those gritty grains of sand getting into her socks, her shoes, her toes. "Plus, now I have clean baseboards and the cholesterol levels of a teenager."

"Clean baseboards?" Summer made a face. "I wouldn't brag about that." She turned her face into the sun that was starting to stream through the morning mist. "Lord. You and Grant are so perfect, it's a little frightening. Ken and Barbie in their dream house."

"Now, now. I haven't found the dream house," Emily argued. "Yet."

"You know everyone in your new neighborhood is going to hate your guts."

"Oh no, they won't. Not after I bring them all homemade cookies at Christmas."

"Puke."

"Why are you being so negative?" Emily gave up worrying about sand stains and sat down next to Summer. "I thought you liked Grant."

"I do like him. But I *love* you, and I want to make sure you really know what you're getting into."

"Grant is everything I want in a man: He's kind; he's smart; he's family oriented. Our relationship is built on mutual trust and respect. We're adults, you know?" Emily paused. "Plus, he can cook. I really can't overstate the importance of that."

At the mention of food, Summer perked up. "What does he cook?"

"Everything: Italian, Indian, Thai, French. And we set the table every night with china and candles."

"You have dinner by candlelight?"

Emily nodded. "When we're both home. What?"

Summer flicked Emily's forehead with her fingers. "Honey, that's not romantic; that's a cry for help."

"What are you talking about? What's wrong with having a lovely table setting and candles?"

"Do you eat in the dining room when Grant isn't home?" Summer demanded.

"Well. No."

"Exactly. I'll bet when he's not there, you lie on the couch watching E! and eating cereal and then drinking the milk out of the bowl."

"Um, maybe."

Summer nodded. "And let's be honest: He's not there most of the time, right?"

Emily stopped slouching and sat up straight. "What are you trying to say?"

"I'm saying that, candlelight and romance aside, Grant's pretty unavailable. Physically. Emotionally. Whatever." She waited a beat for Emily to respond, then continued. "And I have to ask . . ."

Emily started brushing the damp sand off her bare legs. "What?"

"Isn't it possible that you kind of like it that way?"

"No."

Summer wasn't deterred by this vehement denial. "Look, I know it's scary to be in a real relationship after all you've been through. Your childhood . . . my childhood . . . who can blame us if we have a few intimacy issues?" She shuddered and shook her head. "Ugh. This is why I'm a flight attendant and not a therapist."

"I appreciate your concern, but I promise you, I know what I'm doing." Emily used the same calm, confident tone she used when talking to her clients about short-term corrections in the stock market. "Grant's totally available. We're totally intimate. Everything's great."

"Then I'll shut my mouth." Summer tapped her sneaker against Emily's. "I just want you to be happy."

"I am." Emily stared into the thinning fog. She could just make out the red raft floating at the edge of the lake's swimming area. "I know what you mean, though."

Summer pulled her knees up to her chest. "About what?"

"The candles. All of it. Sometimes, I just feel . . ." *Out of place in my own life,* she wanted to say. But she couldn't give voice to the words.

Before Summer could ask her to elaborate, an exuberant pair of early-morning runners emerged from the mist. Ryan loped along the beach while Ripley splashed in the waves. Although the dog was off her leash, she never strayed from Ryan's side.

Ryan stopped short when he noticed Summer and Emily sprawled on the wet sand.

"Well, looky here," Summer drawled. "If it isn't Ryan Lassiter. I heard you were skulking around the resort."

Ryan rallied from his shock and put on his most charming grin. "You know me. I live to skulk."

Summer tilted her head toward the dog. "Who's your sidekick?"

"This is Lieutenant Ellen Ripley." Ryan rested his palm on the dog's broad furry head. The dog sat down and panted, awaiting further instruction.

"Cute." Summer paused before asking, "So what's up with you these days?"

Dumbfounded, Emily glanced at Summer, then back at Ryan. "That's it?"

Summer's brow creased. "What do you mean?"

"I mean, you two haven't seen each other in, like, ten years, and all you're saying is 'What's up'?" Emily narrowed her eyes as suspicions bubbled to the surface of her brain. "No hugs? No 'You look fantastic'? No questions about who, what, when, where, and how?"

"Hold your horses. We're getting there." Summer brushed back her hair and told Ryan, "You look fantastic."

"So do you." He opened his arms. "Give me a hug."

"Too late." Emily nibbled her lower lip as she

tried to work out what was going on. "I'm onto you."

"No, you're not," Ryan assured her.

Summer sprang up from the sand. "I should really go. Late for a . . . thing."

Emily stopped her with a raised palm. "What's going on?"

"Nothing!" Summer insisted. "Not everybody has to kiss and hug and cry just because they haven't seen each other in years."

"Many years," Ryan added.

"Ten years." Summer inched away from Emily.

"Uh-uh. Not so fast." Emily tried to grab Summer's sleeve, but Summer made a break for it, sprinting back to the safety of the Lodge. "Bye, guys! See you at breakfast!"

"*Now* you want to run?" Emily yelled after her. Summer waved over her shoulder as she picked up speed.

"Wow." Ryan took his hand off Ripley's head, and the dog waded into the surf, barking with delight. "Look at her go. Homegirl's fast."

The more innocent he looked, the more Emily suspected shenanigans. "What was that all about?" she demanded.

"No idea." His thick brown hair was wind-blown and his faded blue T-shirt made his shoulders look broader than she remembered. Dark stubble shadowed his jaw.

Plus, he smelled good.

And just like that, she was remembering the night they'd met, when he'd told her to put her hands up, then given her the shirt off his back.

She closed her eyes, gave her head a quick shake, and forced her train of thought into a U-turn. When she opened her eyes, he was looking at her with a wicked gleam in his eyes.

"Aren't you supposed to be packing up and moving on this morning?" she asked, her voice tight.

From the look on his face, he seemed to be relishing her discomfiture. "Ripley needed her morning walk."

"You don't get up this early."

"Neither do you." He started walking, and Emily found herself falling into step beside him. "And I've decided to stay a few more days. Your fiancé said I was welcome to join in the wedding festivities."

When Emily quickened her pace, so did he. "That's because he just met you. He doesn't know what you're really like."

Ryan didn't take the bait. "He seems like a nice guy."

"He is." She prepared to list Grant's many virtues, but Ryan interrupted with, "Why do they call this place Valentine Lake?"

Emily knew the answer from listening to Bev's exhaustive oral history of Cardin family lore. "Supposedly, the lake is shaped like a heart."

"How romantic."

"It's really not, though. I've seen it on a map, and it's kidney-shaped, at best." She edged away from his side. "But Kidney Lake probably doesn't bring in the tourists the way Valentine Lake does."

He sidled right back up to her. "You're a coldhearted cynic now?"

"Believe it."

He looked at her, his gaze lingering on her bare legs, then shook his head. "Nah."

Emily stooped down to pet Ripley, who had fished a stick out of the water and was offering it to Emily for a game of fetch. "She's so well behaved."

"Best dog ever." Ryan hadn't sounded nearly as proud of his restored vintage car. "I take her to the set with me when I'm working. She's worked with some of the best animal handlers in the business."

"Ah." Emily threw the stick over by the lifeguard's chair, and Ripley raced off in pursuit. "Well, that explains it."

Ryan laughed. "Because I couldn't possibly have trained her myself, right?"

"I didn't say—"

"You didn't have to. I know how your twisted little mind works. You want to keep me locked up in the 'bad boyfriend' box in your head."

"You're insane. I don't have any 'bad boyfriend' boxes."

"Yeah, you do. I've been stuck in solitary for the last ten years, with no chance for parole. But guess what? It's time for a prison break."

Ripley came barreling back with the stick, but perhaps sensing the emotional tension, changed course at the last moment and plunged back into the lake.

Emily crossed her arms. "Enough. Seriously, Ryan, I'm not doing this. In four days, I am getting married to Grant. All our friends and family are here, and I refuse to waste this week bickering with the man I never should have married."

"Ouch."

"Do you disagree?" she challenged. "Do you think we did the right thing, getting married?"

"Maybe we weren't ready at twenty-two," he admitted. "But you never gave us a chance. You just walked away when the going got tough."

"We were both miserable at the end, and you know it." She was determined to disengage, but couldn't resist adding, "And, just for the record, you do not know how my mind works."

His hazel eyes sparked. "Try me."

"Stop it."

They stared each other down, relenting only when Ripley galloped in between them and shook herself off.

Ryan's expression softened as he reached out and wiped a droplet of water off Emily's forehead.

"I don't want to bicker, either. That's not why I came."

"I know. You came to find a filming location."

"And I wanted to see you again."

Emily glanced up at the clouds, down at the sand—everywhere but at the man standing in front of her. She forced her face into an expression of detached disapproval.

But she also felt a tiny, forgotten corner of her heart tug free and unfurl like a ribbon loosening from a knot.

She was so horrified by this internal betrayal that she redoubled her efforts to appear icy and unaffected. "There's nothing to see, Ryan."

That slow, smoldering smile returned. "Oh, I disagree."

"No. No, no, no. Don't get all flirty. It doesn't work on me anymore. This is my wedding." When he glanced pointedly at her ring finger, she corrected herself. "This is my *real* wedding, all right? With gowns and flowers and a reception."

"And a fancy diamond ring."

"That, too. It was Grant's grandmother's."

"Big change from the girl who said diamonds were played out and she'd rather spend the money on a Harley."

"Yes." She nodded. "That's what I'm telling you—I have changed. I'm not the girl you married anymore."

"You're not a temptress in a T-shirt?"

She could feel her cheeks burning. "No. I'm coldhearted and cynical. I go running at the crack of dawn and wear boring business suits to my boring job."

He rubbed his chin. "Good to know."

She splayed open her fingers, wordlessly asking him what more he wanted from her.

"You married me first." He said this as if it made some kind of difference. "I promised to love you forever. I meant it."

"Yes," she conceded. "And then we got divorced."

"That doesn't mean I stopped loving you." He caught her hand. "Besides, I want to know if you still wear black lace under your business suits."

She was stunned to feel the hot prickle of tears in her eyes. "This is just a game to you. You think it's some kind of challenge to show up unannounced and say these things and ruin the most important day of my life."

He let go of her hand. "The most important day of your life? Sounds like someone needs to put down the bridal magazine and go get deprogrammed."

"I don't mean it like that." She could still feel the warmth of his fingers against her palm. "I couldn't care less about the dress and the cake and all that stuff. It's more . . ." She trailed off, not wanting to tell him the truth: that on some level, she believed that marrying a man like Grant would make her a better woman. So she waited until she could suppress the quaver in her voice. "Like I said, I've changed."

"So have I," Ryan said. "Now you're a Stepford wife and I'm Wes Craven. So what? People change. They still love each other."

She stared at him, trying to decide if he was serious. The morning had suddenly gone still—the breeze had stopped blowing, the dog had stopped splashing. She looked at him and all she could hear was the shallow pull of her breath and the rush of her pulse in her ears. And then she did the only thing she could to turn this negotiation around. She got off defense and went on offense.

"Love?" She crossed her arms and let the heels of her sneakers sink into the sand. "So you've spent the last ten years pining away for me?"

A flash of emotion flickered in his eyes. He opened his mouth to speak, then clearly thought better of it and set his jaw.

She pressed on. "You've been lonely and celibate for ten years, and yet you never once called or e-mailed me?"

He shrugged, his cocky grin back in place. "I didn't say I was celibate. Los Angeles is like a magnet for the hottest women in the world. It would be wrong to let them sleep alone."

"Ugh." She turned her back on him and trudged toward the hiking trail. "We're done here."

Ryan moved so quickly, she didn't even realize what he was doing until he'd hooked his finger under the waistband of her running shorts and gotten a glimpse of her underwear. "Stepford wives don't wear neon pink thongs when they work out."

He strode away, basking in triumph.

"I hate you!" She reached down, snatched up a pinecone, and hurled it at the back of his head, missing him by a good ten feet.

Ripley raced over and scooped up the pinecone, ready for another game of fetch. Ryan threw it for her, and as he and the dog loped away, he lifted one hand in a salute to a worthy opponent. "Four days and counting. See you around, Stepford."

CHAPTER 12

When Emily returned to her hotel room, she showered and put on the least alluring white granny panties she owned.

The she slipped into a modest khaki skirt and a blouse buttoned all the way up to the collar and went in search of Grant. She found him in the lobby with his cell phone pressed to his ear and one of his nieces enjoying a piggyback ride.

"Hang on a second," Grant said into the phone when he glimpsed Emily. He covered the mouthpiece with his hand and said, "Sorry I had to miss our run this morning. I got a page from the hospital at four thirty, and I didn't want to wake you up." He staggered as Ava dug her heels into his rib cage. "Oof. Easy, there, you're cutting off my airway."

"Giddyup," Ava commanded.

Grant complied, galloping over to the concierge desk and back, all the while hanging on to the little girl and rattling off a rapid-fire spiel of medical jargon that Emily couldn't begin to understand.

When he clicked off the phone, he gave Emily a kiss and apologized again.

"Everything okay?" she asked.

"Yeah." His gaze slid ever so slightly to the right. "Just following up on a patient."

She touched his arm. "Do you have to go back home?"

"No." He grimaced as Ava threw both arms around his neck, securing him in a choke hold. "It's our wedding. My whole family is here."

Emily tried to loosen the tiny blonde's death grip. "Do you *want* to go back?"

"No." He paused. "Okay, yes. The guy's been my patient for years, and it looks like he might finally have a shot at a new set of lungs."

"The man needs lungs," Emily said. "Go."

"It's our wedding," he repeated.

"Not until Saturday. And I don't want you to stay here with me out of guilt."

"I'm staying here with you out of love, not guilt."

"That's very sweet of you. But lungs trump bridal shower."

"Who said anything about a bridal shower?" He recoiled at the very suggestion. "I'm not going to that. Love only goes so far."

She laughed.

"Anyway, we're still waiting for final confirmation from the donor team. These things can and do fall through. So until I know more . . ."

"Hey!" A shrill little lisp rang down the corridor. "I want a piggyback, too!"

Emily glanced behind her to see Alexis sauntering toward them. She had filched a huge jug of maple syrup from the hotel restaurant and was guzzling down the thick amber liquid like a sippy cup of juice.

"Alexis!" Grant clapped his hands over his eyes. "Don't drink that."

When Emily reached out to confiscate the syrup, the little girl darted around her and starting tugging Grant's pant leg. "My turn! My turn!"

Ava refused to budge, so Alexis grabbed her sister's ankle and sank her teeth in.

Ava screeched like something out of one of Ryan's horror films and kicked her legs wildly. The jug sailed through the air, right toward Emily.

Emily threw up her hands and managed to protect her face. But when the jug hit her forearms, the impact sent a tidal wave of syrup onto her head. She could feel the warm, thick liquid seeping down her scalp and cheeks.

Ava and Alexis stopped wrestling and started giggling. They pointed and laughed until Ava slithered down off Grant's back and collapsed on the floor next to her little accomplice.

Grant shot the girls a stern look and opened his mouth to reprimand them, but before he could launch into a lecture, his phone chirped again. He glanced at the screen, then at Emily.

"I'm so sorry, angel. I have to take this."

"It's fine." Emily stuck out her tongue and licked a trickle of syrup off her upper lip. "I'll go back to our room and get cleaned up." She stared down the flower girls from hell. "As for you two . . ."

"You smell like pancakes," Alexis said. "Yum!"

"Can I taste you?" Ava asked.

"Girls!" Melanie finally arrived, her face spattered with oatmeal and something that looked like strawberry jam. "There you are! How many times do I have to tell you? Polite little ladies don't leave the table until they are excused. And they use silverware. And they don't drink syrup straight out of the bottle. Now come back and finish your breakfast." She gave Emily a distracted apology and herded her daughters back to the restaurant.

On the way back to her room, Emily ran into Caroline, who, as usual, looked crisp, cool, and chic.

And alone.

Caroline was too well-mannered to stare, but she did raise an eyebrow at Emily's state of dishevelment. "Is that syrup?"

"Yes."

Without asking for further details, Caroline unlatched the flap of her quilted lambskin handbag. "Tissue?"

"I think it might make things worse, actually. My only hope is gallons and gallons of scalding hot water."

"Go." Caroline stepped aside and motioned Emily past. "Have you eaten yet? I was heading to the restaurant, and I'd love some company."

"I'll try to hurry, but I can't make any promises." Emily patted the ends of her curls, which felt stiff and crunchy. "This might take awhile. It feels like it's starting to crystallize."

"Don't worry; maple syrup's great for your hair. Some women actually use it as a deep conditioning treatment."

"Really?"

"Really."

Emily stared at her friend in disbelief. "How do you know all this stuff?"

Caroline gave her a serene Martha Stewart smile. "When are you going to realize that I know *everything?*"

Both women laughed and continued on their way, but Emily couldn't help acknowledging that Caroline was right about a lot of things.

Just not about Grant's priorities.

Hopefully.

After twenty minutes in the shower, the top of Emily's hair was indeed shiny and lustrous. The ends, however, had twisted into a Gordian knot of curls.

The snarls merged into one big, dense thicket, and her efforts at detangling only made matters worse. As she cursed and speared a comb through the matted mess, Summer knocked on the door.

"Are you almost ready, Em? The shower starts in fifteen minutes, and Bev's getting antsy."

Emily, wrapped in a towel, didn't bother getting dressed before she yanked open the door.

"Oh my God." Summer stared at the comb sticking out of Emily's hair at a forty-five degree angle. "What happened?"

Emily grabbed Summer's wrist and pulled her in. "I got caught in the crossfire between Ava and Alexis."

"The adorable little flower girls?"

"Ha! Don't be fooled by the ringlets and the lacy dresses. They're demon spawn, do you hear me? They have harmonicas and jugs of syrup and fists of fury!"

"No wonder Melanie looks so tired all the time," Summer said.

"Demon spawn," Emily repeated. "Straight out of *The Omen*. And that DNA is lurking in Grant's gene pool. What if our kids turn out just like them?"

"That'll never happen," Summer assured her. "Even if his gene pool has the demon DNA, your side of the family is so, um . . . Yeah, you're screwed."

"He'll be at the hospital for days at a time and I'll be trapped at home with *this!*" Emily shook a hank of hair at Summer. "There'll be no escape."

"Don't be so dramatic—of course there's an escape. It's called a full-time nanny. Now let's focus on the problem at hand." Summer gave the comb a tentative tug. "Yeah, we definitely need to focus right now."

"Good point." Emily stopped panicking long enough to notice Summer's understated pink sheath dress. "You look very nice, by the way."

"Thanks. I had to buy all new outfits for this week. Blew my whole paycheck at the House of Beige."

"Help me," Emily pleaded. "You're good with hair. Work your magic."

"Does this mean I'm off the hook?" Summer looked hopeful. "For the whole thing with Ryan?"

"Hair first, interrogation later."

Summer sat Emily down at the vanity table and went to work with a hair pick, a blow-dryer, and a spray bottle of leave-in conditioner. After a few minutes, she gave up. "It won't come out." She held up a lock of hair and checked her watch. "Time of death, ten thirty-two."

"We're late for the shower. What am I going to do?"

Summer lifted the top layer of curls, considering. "We're going to have to cut it."

"What?" Emily clamped both hands on top of her head. "No! I've been growing it out all year! Grant loves it long!"

"Don't worry—I'll just trim the part underneath. I'll layer it. It'll be super subtle."

"I don't think so." Emily glanced at Summer's short, sleek pixie cut. "Curly hair is tricky. You really have to know what you're doing."

"I know exactly what I'm doing." Summer dug through Emily's baby blue toiletry bag until she found a pair of nail scissors. "I'm your sister, your best friend, and your maid of honor. Plus, I have a God-given talent for hair and makeup. You can trust me."

"You swear?" Emily closed her eyes as she heard the first metallic snip of the scissors.

"I swear. No one will even be able to tell. Now stop making that face and prepare to be amazed."

CHAPTER 13

"Goodness gracious, you cut your hair." Bev's face blanched as she inspected Summer's handiwork.

"It's so . . . curly. My word, just look how much, er, volume you have!" Rose and Darlene joined Bev in clucking with disapproval. "Well, I guess there's no point in gussying yourself up just for us gals. Although it *is* your bridal shower . . ."

Emily opened her mouth to retort, but Summer cut her off with a swift elbow to the ribs.

"Doesn't she look cute?" Summer asked.

"Very cute," Melanie said. Then she gave Emily an agonized look and mouthed, "Sorry."

"Oh, well, of course." Bev rallied with her usual tact and sweetness. "You'll be a beautiful bride on Saturday."

"Yes, but try to get some extra beauty sleep before then," Rose suggested. "You look a bit peaked."

"Exhausted," Darlene agreed. "Here, dear, we brought you some cucumber undereye cream. It'll help get rid of those dark circles."

"It's organic," Rose added. "Handmade right here in Vermont."

"How thoughtful!" Summer exclaimed. "Thank you so much!" She led Emily away to the huge picture window overlooking the lake.

"Do I really look exhausted?" Emily whispered.

"No, no, I'm sure she didn't mean that. You look great. All you have to do is smile and nod and open presents."

"While everyone silently judges me for being so haggard and frizzy."

"You just need a nap. And I'll make sure you get one, right after you ooh and aah over a bunch of stemware and china."

Emily put on a smile and did her best to shift into bride mode. "Oh, we didn't register for china. We're going to use Grant's grandmother's place settings. They've been in his family for generations."

Summer rolled her eyes. "I should have known."

Georgia glided up, resplendent in a silver ruched cocktail dress and an obscene amount of diamond jewelry.

And just like that, Emily stopped worrying about her untamed frizz and dark undereye circles.

"Mother. What's up with the red carpet gown?"

"I'm feeling extra festive today." Georgia placed her hand on her chest, the better to show off her sparkling rings and bracelets. "Do you like it?"

Summer and Emily exchanged a look. "You're just dressing like that to piss Bev off. Admit it."

"I admit nothing." Georgia frowned as she examined Emily's curls. "What happened to your hair? It looks a little . . ."

"Summer cut it."

Georgia clapped her hands. "Oh, it looks fabulous!"

"Uh-huh."

"You're very talented, Summer." Georgia opened her arms to her ex-stepdaughter, then squinted out the window. "Are my eyes going or is that Ryan Lassiter out there?"

Emily and Summer followed her gaze, and sure enough, Ryan was racing around in front of the sparkling waves, throwing a Frisbee for his dog. He looked so energetic and exuberant that for a moment, Emily felt a pang for what she had lost —for what she herself had been like when she was younger.

"That's him." Summer jumped up and down and waved at him. "He's all rich and famous now. Some kind of Hollywood big shot."

Ryan waved back and started toward the Lodge.

"What are you doing?" Emily cried. "Now he's going to crash my shower."

"But what is he doing here, of all places?" Georgia asked.

"Scouting film locations, I think. And stalking our little Emmy."

Emily pinned Summer with a stare that belonged in a police station interrogation room. "I know you're responsible for this somehow. I know you two are in cahoots."

"You poor thing." Summer patted her head. "The stress is really getting to you."

"I always did like Ryan," Georgia said. "So charming and charismatic."

"Who are we waving to?"

All three of them startled at Bev's voice. No one had heard her approaching—she was quite stealthy for a woman wearing pink pumps with a sensible two-inch heel.

"Emily's ex-husband," Summer answered. "He came out for the wedding."

"The two of you are still friends? I don't believe Grant mentioned that, either." Bev watched Ryan approaching. Between the wind-ruffled brown hair, the tan, and the retriever, the man looked like he'd arrived fresh from the Kennedy compound. "My, he certainly is handsome."

"He's nothing compared to Grant," Emily said a little too loudly.

"Well, obviously, dear. That goes without saying."

Emily turned to Summer and pointed at the door to the reception room. "You go out there and intercept him. I do not need him in here, teaming up with my mother for the toilet-paper wedding gown game."

Summer went, then returned with a little thumbs-up. "All clear. He had to go back to his room and comb out Ripley."

"Now you're on a first-name basis with his dog, too?"

"We'll talk about this later." Summer grabbed Emily's hand and towed her toward the mound of pastel gift bags piled by the window seat. "Right now, it's time for toasters and coasters."

Emily sat on a white wooden folding chair while the guests gathered around in a ring of commingled perfume and high-pitched exclamations.

"How beautiful," she cooed, after sifting through layers of pink tissue to reveal a hideous candy dish in the shape of a squirrel. "It will look darling on the coffee table in the living room."

Then she opened Beverly's gift, a large box wrapped in mint green paper and topped with a silver ribbon.

"What is it?" Georgia asked as Emily peered into the box.

"It's . . . it's, um . . ." Emily pulled out a round, black cooking implement that looked like a skillet with no sides.

"Now we're talking." Summer grabbed the wooden paddle nestled next to the pan and slapped the flat surface against her palm. "Just in case the honeymoon gets boring."

"Wait till you see the negligee I got her,"

Georgia stage-whispered. "No chance of that."

"It's a crepe turner," Bev informed them with crisp formality. "And a crepe pan. So you can make Grant his favorite spinach and bacon crepes on Sundays. I'll give you the recipe, but not until after the wedding. It's a family secret."

"And I'll give you my secret recipe for sour cream pancakes," Rose said.

"Don't forget my walnut coffee cake," Darlene said. "Our mother used to make it every weekend."

"Okay." Emily heard her own voice, hearty and cheerful, as if from the other side of a long tunnel.

"Listen to us, going on about our cooking. What's your specialty, dear?" Bev asked. "You must have a few secret recipes of your own."

"Oh, well, there's . . ." *Do not say Jell-O shots and pot brownies, do not say Jell-O shots and pot brownies.*

Summer must have been thinking the same thing, because she jumped in with, "Bacon crepes and coffee cake sound great. I'm totally coming over for brunch." She thrust another gift into Emily's hands. "Here, this one's heavy."

Emily stared down at the ribbon but made no move to unwrap the box. Her limbs felt leaden, but her head got lighter and lighter.

Summer nudged her, then took over and ripped into the tissue paper. "Ooh!" She held up a pair of brass candlesticks.

"They're antique," said Grant's great-aunt Sophie.

"Thank you so much! They'll go perfectly with the antique china!" Summer gushed.

Emily sucked in a long, shallow breath.

Summer put a hand on her shoulder and tried to shake her back to her senses. "You and Grant like to eat by candlelight, right?"

"We . . ." Emily nodded. Her line of vision tilted as though she'd just stepped aboard a sailboat leaving the harbor. "Right."

"Steady there," Summer muttered. Then she helped herself to a bulky, rectangular package. "Okay, moving right along."

"That's from me." Caroline, resplendent in a collared yellow shirtdress, leaned forward.

Summer tore off the wrapping and examined the maroon box. "It's . . . the complete series of *Buffy the Vampire Slayer*?"

Caroline adjusted her earring, looking self-conscious. "Yes. You can return it if you like. Exchange it for a blender or something."

Emily regained her focus long enough to thank her friend and assure her that no exchanges would be necessary. "I'm kind of surprised, though. You don't seem like a *Buffy* kind of girl."

Caroline shrugged. "I didn't think so, either. But I started watching the reruns on cable one night while I was waiting for Andrew to get home, and I was hooked."

"That happened to me," Georgia said. "I almost

died of sleep deprivation when *Dynasty* came out on DVD."

"I only watch PBS," Bev interjected.

"Anyway, give it a try and see if you like it," Caroline said to Emily. "It's very well-written. It helped me get through a lot of lonely nights."

That's when Emily blacked out.

The world fell away and darkness rushed in so quickly that she didn't have time to say or do anything to help herself. One second, she was watching Summer rip through the rest of the loot ("Food processor! Score!"), and the next she was flat on her back, blinking up at the ceiling beams.

Bev, Summer, Caroline, and Melanie surrounded her, all talking at once:

"She needs some cold water."

"Elevate her feet."

"It's just the excitement."

"Maybe it's the heat."

"Maybe she's pregnant."

"No!" Emily forced out the syllable like a cough. "I'm fine!" She struggled up into a sitting position. Rose and Darlene tried to push her back down.

And then her mother was at her side, taking charge.

"Out of my way," Georgia commanded. She slapped everybody else's hands away and embraced her daughter. "Breathe, baby. Put your head between your knees."

"What's wrong with me?" Emily pitched forward.

"Cold feet." Georgia offered up a glass of lemonade, which she had apparently plucked out of thin air. "Happened to me dozens of times. Perfectly normal. You'll be fine."

A sympathetic murmur rippled through the women. The semicircle of concerned faces was replaced by an array of open palms, each offering up a quick fix for her distress.

"Xanax?" said Georgia.

"Valium?" said Melanie.

"Altoid?" offered Bev.

"Here." Summer pulled a little orange prescription vial out of her straw clutch. "I brought my emergency stash. Want one?"

Emily's jaw dropped. "Since when do all of you take meds?"

"I don't," Georgia said, sounding a bit offended. "It's purely for dental cleanings and bad hair days."

The women's voices blended together in Emily's head until all she could hear was a thick, high-pitched buzzing. She needed air, but couldn't breathe. She needed space, but couldn't escape the crowd.

She needed, desperately, to be alone.

As she closed her eyes again, she felt her mother's hand on her forehead and heard Summer calling, "Emily? Twitch if you're okay."

"We need a man!" Georgia cried. "Ryan! Yoo-hoo! Ryan, over here!"

"Someone fetch my purse," Bev said. "I'm calling Grant. He's a doctor, you know."

Emily jerked back to the here and now when she felt rough, wet pressure against her cheek. The smell of liver assaulted her nostrils, and she could hear a moist snuffling sound.

"Argh." When she rolled to the side, Ripley placed one dainty paw on her bicep.

Then she heard Ryan's voice, laced with both concern and amusement: "Give her some air, give her some air. Getting a waffle maker is exciting enough to make anyone pass out."

Ripley nudged Emily's shoulder blade and barked, then went back to licking off her blush and foundation.

Emily started to gag; then she started to laugh, and she knew she was going to be fine.

"You're fine," Grant pronounced twenty minutes later, after he ran through a quick physical exam in their hotel room. "Your pulse is steady, your pupils look good, your airway is clear."

"I know." She cupped her hand around the back of his neck and gave him a kiss. "Can I wash the dog slobber off my face now?"

"I'll get a washcloth; you stay in bed." After he'd arrived at the bridal shower, Grant had scooped her up and carried her back to their room. "Your mom said you had a panic attack."

"My mom tends to exaggerate." She sat up. "I really feel much better. Want to go for a walk? We can see the town. Pet a cow."

"Absolutely not." He leaned over and confiscated her shoes. "You need to rest. Don't argue; I've got an MD."

"So your mother kept telling us." She settled back into the fluffy down comforter. "How long do I have to lie here?"

"Until I say you can get up."

"God, you're bossy."

"You're just noticing this now?" He smoothed her hair back from her forehead. "I'm going to go get you some food. You need to rest, hydrate, and eat."

"Sir, yes, sir." She gave him a salute.

"I mean it. You need to take better care of yourself." His frown deepened. "I need to take better care of you."

"We take care of each other," Emily said. "And we always will."

"Be right back." As he opened the door to the hallway, his cell phone chirped, and he answered with a terse, "Dr. Cardin here."

Thirty minutes later, he hadn't returned, and Emily felt fully restored. Forty-five minutes later, she was starving and restless.

After an hour passed, she dialed room service

and requested grilled salmon and steamed veggies with no butter, oil, or sauce. She ate her meal and drank her water and waited and waited for Grant.

Then she opened Caroline's gift and slipped a DVD into the room's little media console.

She didn't know what was more worrisome—the fact that her fiancé hadn't come back to be with her, or the fact that she was relieved to be left alone.

WEDNESDAY

CHAPTER 14

Grant waited until the last quarter mile of their five-mile run to break the bad news to Emily.

They'd spent the previous four-and-three-quarter miles chatting about the campfire scheduled for that evening and Emily's plan to help Bev bake sugar cookies to give out as favors to the wedding guests.

"Your mother has a lot of strong opinions on frosting," Emily said. "I mentioned buttercream and she practically had a stroke. Apparently, royal icing is the only acceptable option."

"You don't know the half of it," Grant replied. "She's like a drill sergeant when you put a whisk in her hand. And my aunts are even worse. Watch out for that tree branch."

As they emerged from the forest into a clearing, Grant said, "The hospital called again. We got the green light for the lung transplant. They're doing the surgery tonight, and I want to be there."

Emily never faltered in her stride. "Okay."

"I'll be back early Friday morning. You won't even notice I'm missing."

She could tell from his tone that he expected an argument. "Okay."

"That's it?" He glanced over at her. "You're not upset?"

"Well, this guy's been your patient for years, right? I'm sure he wants you to do the transplant. You're the best."

"You've definitely been spending too much time with my mother." He broke into a sprint as they neared the resort, and she sped up alongside him. "I know the timing's terrible, but—"

"Grant, look at me. It's fine."

"I feel like I'm disappointing you. And to be honest, I'm not used to disappointing people." He said this sheepishly, without a shred of ego.

"This is your calling, and you have to answer," she said. "I get it." She paused. "As long as you're not bailing on Bora-Bora."

He slowed to a walk and held up his hand as though swearing in at a witness stand. "I am not bailing on Bora-Bora."

"Then we don't have a problem." She started to ask for more details on his trip, but the roar of an engine drowned out her words.

A motorcyclist wearing a black helmet and a familiar leather jacket swung a cherry red bike in a swooping arc before parking next to Grant's Audi. Grant shielded Emily from a spray of gravel with his shoulder.

"You're kidding me," Emily muttered.

Ryan pulled off his helmet, shook out his hair, and strode toward them.

"Hey." He nodded pleasantly. "How's it going?"

"Nice bike," Grant said, running his hand along the burnished leather seat and chrome work, so shiny that Emily could see her reflection in it. "Is that a real Indian?"

"Yeah, 1951 model."

"Look at those lines," Grant said in the hushed, reverent tones of an art history major viewing the Sistine Chapel for the first time.

"One of my director buddies just signed a ridiculous three-picture deal, and he asked me to pick out a bike for him."

Grant couldn't keep his hands off the motor-cycle. "Where did you find a 1951 Indian in Valentine, Vermont?"

"Are you kidding? This is rich-summer-people territory. There's a specialty dealer near Woodstock. I drove over there last night and told the guy I'd need a few days to test-drive it and make up my mind."

Emily grabbed her ankle and stretched out her quads. "Let me guess: They don't usually do that, but you got them to yes?"

He winked. "How well you know me."

"You're just coming in from last night?" Grant asked.

"Yeah." Ryan glanced at his watch. "Time got away from me."

Emily wrinkled her nose. "You reek of cigars. What were you doing all night?"

"Do you really want to know?"

"You know what? I don't."

Ryan followed Grant's gaze back to the motorcycle. "Want to take her out for a spin?"

Grant hesitated for a second before shaking his head. "Nah. I've got to run back to the city for a couple of days."

Ryan leaned in, keenly interested. "You're leaving? This morning?"

"He's coming right back," Emily said. "Forty-eight hours."

Grant explained the transplant situation. "The last thing I need is to show up for surgery on crutches."

"Oh, come on," Ryan urged. "The weather's perfect; the road's dry. Just a quick little drive around the lake."

Emily held her breath, hoping that Grant would succumb to the temptation of the spotless red paint and purring engine.

But Grant held firm. "Thanks, but I better not. You work in a hospital long enough, you start to get paranoid about motorcycles."

"Got it." Ryan turned to Emily. "Any chance I can talk you into it?"

If she opened her mouth, he would find a way to get her to yes. So she turned on her heel and strode away as quickly as she could. Grant followed her, obviously confused.

"Good luck with your surgery," Ryan called after them. "And don't worry about Emily, bro. I'll keep an eye on her."

"You." Emily found Summer curled up in a white Adirondack chair, flipping through a magazine and eating a Fudgsicle for breakfast.

Summer looked around, the very picture of innocence. "Me?"

"Grant's leaving. Ryan's staying. Everything's going to hell in a handbasket. And I know you had a part in this."

"I have no idea what you're talking about." Summer removed her flip-flops from the chair next to hers and indicated Emily should sit down. Then she offered her the Fudgsicle. "Care for a bite?"

"Give it up, Benson." Emily remained standing, the better to tower over her friend. "I saw the guilty looks zinging around yesterday morning. I know you sold me out. Do yourself a favor and come clean. Don't make me force you to go running again."

Summer studied a shampoo ad with rapt attention. "What makes you think it's not just a coincidence? Coincidences happen, right?"

"Not like this, they don't." Emily confiscated Summer's magazine. "Come on. Of all the rustic resorts in all the towns in all the world, Ryan has to walk into this one?"

Summer turned up her palms. "I know, what are the odds? It must be a sign."

"It's not a sign. It's a planned ambush with malice aforethought."

"Listen to you. 'Ambush.' 'Malice aforethought.' " Summer slid on her sunglasses to avoid Emily's probing gaze. "You sound like the narrator on one of those true-crime TV shows."

"So you deny you had any involvement in any of this?"

"Em." Summer looked stricken. "I shouldn't have to deny anything. I'm your sister. We've been best friends for years—*decades*—and you have the nerve to accuse me of—"

Emily held up a hand. "Did you or did you not?"

"You're nuts," Summer sputtered. "How would I even get in touch with him?"

"You tell me." Emily watched as Summer hemmed and hawed but failed to issue a flat-out denial. "Oh my God. You did. You set me up. You *betrayed* me."

Summer bit into her Fudgsicle in a show of defiance. "First of all, I would never betray you, and you know it. Second of all, Ryan is not the enemy."

"Oh yes, he is."

"No. He's your ex."

"Which by definition makes him evil."

Summer lowered her sunglasses and gave Emily a look. "He was never evil. He might've

208

been a little immature and a little too intense, but he was always a good guy. And you two love each other like crazy."

"Love*d*." Emily sat down next to Summer. "Past tense."

"And then you broke up, and you pretended he never existed."

Emily nodded. "Just like I pretended none of your boyfriends existed after you broke up with them. So far, I'm not seeing the problem here." She tried to sound upbeat, but the truth was, her breakup with Ryan had been mercilessly swift and strict. Once she'd signed the divorce papers, she'd never contacted him again, by phone, e-mail, or social media. She'd forced herself to look only ahead, never behind. On some level, she knew that one slipup, one brief point of contact, would cause her to relapse and she would succumb to Ryan again—his charm, his enthusiasm, his body against hers.

Like she was relapsing right now.

"Well, here's the thing, Em: He *did* exist. And you can't put him in the same category with any of my ex-boyfriends," Summer said. "Because he wasn't your boyfriend, he was your husband."

"A minor technicality."

Summer made a noise like a basketball buzzer. "Wrong. It's a huge difference, and you know it."

Emily waved this off. "Ryan and I may have

signed some paperwork, but we were boyfriend and girlfriend in all the ways that mattered. We were just playing house. Grant's going to be my husband."

"Well then, what difference does it make if Ryan's here or not? Just ignore him."

"I'm trying. But he refuses to be ignored."

"It's true. The man is impossible to say no to." Summer examined her cuticles. "And that's why, if I did accidentally tell him about your wedding —and I'm not saying I did, but *if*—you should understand that it wasn't my fault."

"Understood." Emily tilted her head back, momentarily indifferent to the risk of sunburn and freckles in her wedding photos. "So what happened?"

Summer let out a heavy sigh of defeat. "We ran into each other a few weeks ago. I was working a red-eye from Los Angeles to New York, and he was sitting in seat 3C."

Emily raised one eyebrow. "First class?"

Summer nodded. "He recognized me as soon as he sat down. He started asking about you before I could even offer him a drink."

"So you ratted me out and poured him a soda. Instead of pretending he didn't exist."

"That's my job." Summer grabbed her magazine back. "And would it make you feel better if I said I spit in his Diet Coke?"

"Ryan doesn't drink Diet Coke." Emily snorted.

"And save those puppy dog eyes for a Humane Society commercial."

"You're right. He just wanted water. He was a great passenger—patient, polite, and low-maintenance. So after the other passengers fell asleep, we got to talking." She shrugged. "What are the odds that he would be on my flight?"

"You're the one who's always telling me that sooner or later, everyone is on one of your flights."

"Not Ryan Gosling. I'm still waiting for him." Summer rubbed her palms together. "But he'll show up one of these days, and when he does, I'll be ready."

"Forget Ryan Gosling. Back to Ryan Lassiter," Emily said. "So you told him I was getting married. And where and when and to whom."

"No! I didn't tell him anything. Every time he asked about you, I changed the subject."

"Then how . . . ?"

Summer bowed her head and muttered, "He took me to breakfast when we landed and plied me with mimosas at the Four Seasons."

Emily clapped her hand to her forehead. "You're killing me."

"I couldn't help it! He kept complimenting me and topping off my glass. And you know how chatty I get when I have champagne."

"Apparently, so does Ryan."

"One thing led to another, and I mentioned a

few details about your wedding. But I had no idea he'd actually show up here! I mean, really, who does that?"

"My ex-husband." She shaded her eyes and looked back toward the parking lot as she heard a motorcycle engine revving. "The lost cause with no boundaries."

"Lost cause?" Summer's jaw dropped. "He matured into a responsible adult who's still fun and funny as hell. He's the Holy Grail of dating."

"Uh-huh."

"I'm telling you, he's like a unicorn. We may never see another one in our lifetime. If I could find a guy like that, I'd marry him tomorrow."

"You're welcome to him," Emily said. "He's showing off his vintage motorcycle in the parking lot right now. Go grab a helmet and some leather chaps, and have at."

Summer made a face. "Gross. He's like my brother. Besides, he only wants you."

"Not according to the World Wide Web." Emily pulled up some Internet photos on her phone. "Here he is at a red carpet event last year. Check out his date—she looks like Gisele's younger, hotter sister. Oh, and here he is at a fund-raiser with some other blindingly hot blonde."

Summer leaned over to inspect the pictures. "I see a trend here." She took the phone and clicked through more search results. "Oh, yet another one that's the polar opposite of you."

"That's what he wants now: physical perfection. I mean, look at her body. And her hair. And her face!"

"Forget her," Summer said. "Look at *his* face. Does he look happy? No. He looks bored. He's all empty inside because his one true love abandoned him."

"You've been watching too many in-flight rom-coms." Emily rolled her eyes. "He's gone Hollywood, and I'm trying to have a real life in the real world. With, you know, yard work and in-laws and dentist appointments."

"Ooh, sounds fun."

Emily laughed. "That's my point. Marriage isn't all wine and roses and sex on the kitchen counter. I'm trying to have realistic expectations this time around."

"I know why you had that anxiety attack yesterday," Summer said. "It's because you can't shut your brain off."

"And that's a bad thing?"

"You know I love you, but sometimes you just need to live in the moment. Having a conversation with you is like playing chess with a supercomputer. Your mind is always, like, twenty moves ahead. And you didn't used to be like that. You were the original fly-by-the-seat-of-your-pants girl."

"True." Emily sighed. "And look where that got me."

"I'd say your life turned out pretty well."

"So did Ryan's. He's got everything he ever wanted."

"Wrong." Summer repositioned her chair to get a better view as a pair of shirtless lifeguards started their morning workout on the beach. "He's got everything he wants except what he wants the most."

CHAPTER 15

Emily made Summer come with her to Bev's baking extravaganza ("All the bridesmaids have to help assemble favors. It's the *law*"), and they ran into Caroline in the lobby.

"Want to come bake eighty million sugar cookies shaped like tiny wedding cakes?" Emily coaxed.

"She has to," Summer said. "She's a bridesmaid. It's the law, remember?"

"I'd be delighted," Caroline said. "I love baking. Are we making the cookies from scratch?"

"It's Bev. What do you think?"

Georgia waltzed through the lobby in a floaty turquoise sundress.

"Look at you!" Emily was impressed. "You're right on time."

Georgia blinked. "On time for what, sweetie?"

"Baking with Bev."

"Oh, that." Georgia made a face. "Maybe later. I've got a hot date!"

Caroline checked her watch. Emily said, "At ten o'clock in the morning?"

Georgia's blue eyes sparkled. "I'm going water-skiing with one of the gentlemen I played tennis with yesterday." She pulled a mirrored compact out of her bag and checked her reflection. "Most men his age are just looking for a nurse with a purse, but not him! I'm telling you, Em, he's a dynamo. Might have real potential."

Summer nudged Georgia's side. "Two dates in twenty-four hours? You vixen, you."

"Oh, and he has a house in the Hamptons. Just think of the parties!"

"So you're bailing on the baking," Emily said.

Georgia wrung her hands in a totally insincere show of distress. "Unless you'll be terribly disappointed."

"No, no. But you know, people might talk."

"The only person who's going to talk is that sourpuss Bev and her sourpuss sisters." Georgia harrumphed. "And girls like them have been talking about girls like me since the beginning of time. Jealousy, pure and simple." She waved like a beauty queen as she headed for the exit.

"Have fun," Summer called after her.

"Oh, I will." Georgia dashed back and confided, "I have a new bikini I've been dying to wear. Black, chic, very European."

Summer wagged her index finger. "Make sure you double knot the strings. We wouldn't want a wardrobe malfunction."

"Wouldn't we?" Georgia laughed and traipsed

out toward the waterfront in five-inch sequined silver stilettos.

Caroline stared after her, wide-eyed and speechless.

Emily extended her right arm. "Ladies and gentlemen, my mother."

"That woman needs her own reality show," Summer said.

"I'm sorry," Caroline finally said. "Did she say 'a nurse with a purse'?"

"She did." Emily tugged the elastic band out of her ponytail. "She and Bev don't really get along."

"I can't imagine why."

"Girls! Stop poking the butter! Girls! Stop throwing the flour! *Girls!* Stop drinking the vanilla!" Bev's placid, sweet veneer was cracking right before Emily's eyes. The Lodge's catering kitchen, which had started the morning as a pristine expanse of stainless steel and marble countertops, had slowly given way to a greasy, sugarcoated disaster area as the flower girls continued their campaign of destruction.

Melanie waded into the fray and warned the girls, "If you don't behave for Grandma, you're both going into time-out."

"Poor little lambs." Darlene clicked her tongue. "They're just hungry and tired."

"Here, who wants a candy bar?" Rose wiped her flour-coated hands on her apron and opened her handbag.

"No!" Melanie cried. "Don't get them all hopped up on sugar!"

"Oh, they'll be fine, won't you, dears?" Rose handed a chocolate bar to each child. "Now run along and find your father."

The girls raced out of the kitchen, yelling at the top of their lungs. Melanie followed, shooting her aunt a look of reproach as she went.

"Hurry up." Summer had retreated with Caroline to the far side of the room. "Put the trays in the oven and let's hit the cooking sherry."

Ava and Alexis's attempts to "help" had hindered the adults to the point that the cookies, which were supposed to be baked, cooled, and ready to be frosted by now, were way behind schedule. Bev was still rolling out rectangles of dough and using a metal cookie stamp to cut out dozens of uniform wedding-cake shapes.

She double-checked the oven temperature, then allowed Caroline to slide in the baking sheets. "We'll rotate the trays after five minutes."

"You know, there's a bakery right down the street," Summer said. "We could just order a bunch of cookies and save some time."

"Shh," Emily hissed.

Bev was aghast. "Homemade cookies are much better than store-bought. And besides, this is my grandmother's recipe. It's a family tradition."

"Isn't everything?" Summer slipped out the door with a suspiciously sherry-shaped lump under her sweatshirt.

While Emily started washing the mixing bowls and the aunts wiped down the counter, the flower girls returned, leading Ripley by the collar.

"What happened to your mother?" Caroline asked.

"Dunno. Here." Alexis grabbed a handful of dough and shoved it in the dog's mouth. "Good doggie."

Ripley thumped her tail against the walk-in refrigerator door and gobbled the scraps.

Bev clutched the tiny gold cross around her neck. "Why is there a dog in the kitchen?"

Emily heard Ryan's voice on the other side of the swinging service doors. "Ripley?"

Ripley responded with a bark, then snarfed down another handful of dough.

"There you are." Ryan walked in and wrestled the dog's collar out of Ava's grip. As soon as he saw Emily, he stopped looking exasperated and turned on the charm. "What are you guys doing?"

"Trying to make favors for the wedding," Emily said.

He jerked his thumb in the direction of the lake. "Hey, did you know your mom is out there water-skiing?"

"You must be mistaken." Emily shot a pointed

look at Bev. "My mother had to miss all the baking fun because she's in her room with a migraine."

"What a shame." Ryan shook his head sadly. "Yeah, it must've been someone else."

Rose and Darlene started whispering by the sink.

Ryan peered into the oven and rubbed his stomach. The hem of his T-shirt rode up and Emily caught a glimpse of bare flesh before she forced herself to look away.

"These smell delicious, Mrs. Cardin."

"Why, thank you." Bev got a bit fluttery. "We're going to use royal icing to make them look like wedding cakes, and then we'll put them in little cellophane bags with ribbons and give them as favors to all the guests." She slid another tray into the oven. "But right now, the staff needs to start prepping for lunch, so I'm afraid we're going to have to clear out. We'll do the frosting tonight. We can stay up late and chitchat. Won't that be fun, girls?"

"Absolutely," Darlene and Rose agreed.

Caroline turned off the hot water and wiped her hands on a dish towel. "I think I feel a migraine coming on myself."

While Ripley endured the children's over-enthusiastic hugs and ear scratches, Ryan showered Bev with flattery about her culinary prowess and questions about her brilliant son.

By the time Emily had returned the bottles of vanilla extract to the pantry, Bev was beaming.

"See you tonight at the fire pit!" Bev practically glowed as she waved good-bye to Ryan and Ripley. "Oh! And here, take a cookie with you. But don't burn your tongue; it's still hot."

"Bye, guys. See you tonight!" Ryan winked at Emily. Emily scowled back.

"What a nice young man. So helpful and polite." Bev linked her arm through Emily's and led the way back to the lobby.

"He's, uh . . ." Emily stumbled a bit. "He's one of a kind."

"Are you all right?" Bev patted her forearm.

"Yes. I just wish I hadn't been married before. I'm sorry I made such a big mistake. I'm sorry I rushed into everything when I was younger." Somewhere back in the furthest reaches of her rational mind, Emily knew she shouldn't be apologizing for who she was and what she'd done before she ever met Grant, but she couldn't stop herself. She didn't want to be the kind of person who had a "starter marriage" in her past. She wanted to be fresh and unspoiled, able to embark on a permanent partnership without having to qualify it as her second try.

"That's all right, dear. It's in the past and it can't be helped." But Bev sounded resigned and determined now, rather than gushy and indulgent. "We all make mistakes."

"The good news is my taste in men has really improved," Emily said. "Grant is so thoughtful and grounded and . . ." She wanted to add "reliable," but her lips rebelled as she thought about how little she'd seen him this week, how many times he'd sworn he would "be back in a minute."

Bev didn't notice her hesitation. "But I suppose he and Ryan aren't really such opposites, under the surface."

"What are you talking about? Ryan's a madman."

"They both have that spark. That passion for what they do." Bev focused her gaze on Emily with sudden intensity. "And they both adore you."

Emily didn't know what to say or where to look.

Bev squeezed her forearm. "I think it's touching that Ryan came for the wedding. He wants you to be happy even though you broke his heart."

Striving for a poker face, Emily asked, "How do you know I was the one who ended it?"

Bev smiled. "The way he looked at you at the bridal shower yesterday. I can tell these things. I'm a woman of the world, you know."

As much as the notion of Bev being a "woman of the world" tickled Emily, she couldn't get past the idea that Ryan's efforts to regain her attention were so obvious to everyone else.

Everyone except Grant.

She cleared her throat and proceeded with

caution. "I don't think he looks at me all that much."

"Well, you were unconscious, dear. You couldn't see anything."

"No, trust me. He dates actresses now. And models."

"A model might look good on his arm, but she can't make a house a home the way you can." Bev kept smiling. "And you know men never really get over their first love. But I think he's truly happy for you and Grant. It's sweet."

Emily threw up her palm. Ryan Lassiter could be accused of many, many things, but being sweet was not—and never would be—one of them. "Don't let the dog and the sweet talk fool you. He's cunning and Machiavellian and relentless."

Bev waved this away. "Who a man is in the boardroom isn't always who he is at the breakfast table. Mark my words, you don't really know a man until you marry him."

Emily forced a laugh. "But what happens if you don't like him once you do?"

Bev patted Emily's cheek. "Well, you don't have to worry about that this time around. You're marrying Grant—what's not to like?"

As she made her way back to her room, Emily glimpsed Melanie standing on the far side of the Lodge's back porch. Melanie gazed out at the lawn, her arms crossed and her right hand moving toward and away from her mouth.

Emily trod heavily on the wooden deck, trying not to surprise her soon-to-be sister-in-law. "Hey."

Melanie didn't turn around. "Hey. Sorry to cut and run like that. I just needed five seconds of peace and quiet."

"No problem." Emily paused. "I didn't know you smoked."

"I don't."

Emily glanced at Melanie's hand, which was indeed empty. "Oh, sorry. The way you were holding your hand, it just looked a little like—"

Melanie half smiled. "I'm fake smoking."

Emily nodded as if this made sense. "Fake smoking."

"Yeah. I used to smoke when I was younger. I gave it up when I got pregnant with Alexis. But I still miss it sometimes." She paused, lifting her fingers to her mouth, sucking in a lungful of fresh air. "So now, when the girls get too wild, or my family's driving me nuts, I just go through the motions. It's surprisingly effective. Must be the deep breaths or something."

Emily joined her in staring out at the lush green foliage. "Whatever gets you through the day."

Melanie forced a thin little laugh. "At these family reunions, I need a fake cigarette break, like, every half hour."

"But why?" Emily blinked. "Your family is so . . . so . . ."

"Crazy? Passive-aggressive?"

"No, they're wonderful! All the hugs and the secret recipes and the singing around the piano! You grew up with it, so I guess you're used to it, but if you'd grown up in my family . . ."

Now it was Melanie's turn to look confused. "What are you talking about? Your mom seems awesome."

"My mom is the second coming of Elizabeth Taylor."

"Yeah, but at least she's not afraid to be herself."

"Your mom is just so . . ." Emily searched for the right word. "Maternal. So nurturing. And she has such an amazing relationship with her sisters. That whole thing with the sweaters on Monday was great."

Melanie snorted. "That whole thing with the sweaters was designed to make my mom feel like crap. And it worked."

Emily's jaw dropped. "No."

"Yes. Come on, look at my mom. She's obviously not the same size as she was in high school. They just did that to point out how much thinner they are than her. And you'll notice that they made sure she can't return it. She has to keep it and be reminded of how much weight she's gained."

Emily could practically hear the sound of her youthful illusions shattering. "Are you sure?"

"My aunts are masters at giving gifts that make you feel bad about yourself. They've been at it for decades. It's pure bitchery with a cute little bow on top."

Emily thought about the undereye cream. "Wow. That's diabolical."

Melanie took a long drag off her fake cigarette. "Yep. They mean-girl everybody, but they really have it in for Mom. They're always making digs about her weight or her clothes or her hair or her cooking. And they've given her dozens of pairs of earrings, even though they know she never got her ears pierced."

"But why? I can't imagine your mom offending anybody."

"Well, my mom was never assertive to begin with. But ever since my dad died, she's kind of turned into a doormat. She's not into stuff like clothes and makeup, and she's an easy target. They know she'll never call them out on it, so they just keep going."

Emily shook her head. "They both seem so sweet on the surface."

"That's why they're the masters. They'll give you candles with scents you can't stand—"

"They gave me a rose candle for Christmas."

"Yeah, and my mom's allergic to roses. Coincidence? I think not. My sweet little aunties will give you ponchos in horizontal stripes, framed photos of family trips they took without you, drum sets for your five-year-old. When they're not pumping my kids full of high fructose corn syrup and artificial colors, they're giving me parenting books on how to 'reform your little rebels.'"

"That's terrible. Your girls are"—Emily coughed—"delightful."

"They'll be coming for you, too, once you're officially part of the family. Don't think they didn't see the tattoo on your finger."

Emily instinctively covered her left hand with her right. "You weren't supposed to notice that."

Melanie turned around and lifted up the hem of her shirt, revealing a little purple flower inked on her left hip. "I have one, too. My mom doesn't know."

"Does Grant know?" Emily asked. Her fiancé had never mentioned anything about tattoos when describing his chummy, old-fashioned family.

"Yeah. But I'm not surprised he never mentioned it."

"What do you mean?"

"Grant views things in a certain way. He has an image of people, and he's really good at not noticing things that don't fit with that image."

"Hmm," Emily said.

"To him, I'll always be his sweet little sister, and my aunts will always mean well." Melanie sighed. "It's not his fault—he always had to be the good kid because I was such a handful growing up."

"You? I can't see it."

"Trust me, I was a hellion and a half. So Grant

had to get straight As and be class president and letter in track and field. He had to make my parents proud. And he did. I used to think that maybe he had a wild side hidden in there somewhere. But he doesn't. He's just *good,* all the way through."

"He is." Emily ducked her head and let her hair shield her face. "I knew that the first time we went out. He's not just a nice guy; he's a good man."

"Yep. He's a good man, and I was a bad girl, and the whole family pretends it never happened." Melanie's smile twisted. "God forbid that anyone think we're less than perfect. Family tradition is very important, as I'm sure you've noticed. We have to keep coming up here every summer, even though my poor husband spends the whole trip in bed with allergies. He has to use up his vacation days miserable and trapped in a hotel room because, you know, it's *tradition.*" She looked over at Emily's expression and laughed. "But don't worry. You're the perfect woman for my perfect brother. You two will fit right in with the traditionalists."

"Except for the tattoo." Emily's stomach clenched. "And my fractured family, my serial-marrying mother, my starter marriage, and my misspent youth."

"Right. Except for that."

Emily mulled all this over for a moment. "Mind if I have a fake cigarette with you?"

Melanie pretended to spark an imaginary lighter. "Smoke 'em if you've got 'em."

CHAPTER 16

The campfire started off innocently enough, with the grownups telling ghost stories and leading sing-alongs, and the children roasting marshmallows in the flames. The starry night was clear and still, and the air was scented with the sharp, citrusy tang of mosquito repellent.

Even Ava and Alexis were on their best behavior, lulled into tranquility by a steady stream of sugar and two-part harmony.

Emily enjoyed the company and abstained from everything else. Every time someone urged her to have a s'more, she took another swig of water from her canteen and said, "I'm on the wedding dress diet till Saturday." Every time someone asked, "Where's Grant?" she answered, "Grant had to run back to the city for the day."

"Don't worry." Caroline gave her a pat on the back. "He'll be back soon."

"I know. Really—I'm fine with it. I try to think of him as Clark Kent." Emily grinned. "He's a great guy just walking around Metropolis, but

229

he's happiest when he's putting on his cape and saving the day."

"Aw," Melanie said. "That's so sweet."

"Didn't Clark Kent have a lot of relationship problems?" Summer wondered aloud.

"Shouldn't your mouth be full of graham crackers right now?" Emily countered. She sandwiched herself between her bridesmaids and spent the night ignoring Ryan, who was schmoozing his way through every man, woman, and child at the resort. He told blood-chilling stories about imaginary zombie invasions and real celebrity meltdowns at some restaurant in West Hollywood. He helped the children toast marsh-mallows and made sure all the great-aunts and -uncles had an extra wool blanket to ward off the chill.

"Ryan's great," Caroline said. "He seems so fun and spontaneous. I can't believe you two used to be a couple." She paused. "Wait. I didn't mean that the way it sounded."

But it was too late—the rest of the women piled on.

"I still can't believe you let him get away," Georgia scolded. "But even if you have no use for him, I do. He promised me VIP passes for his next premiere."

"He had a whole carton of signed DVDs FedExed overnight for Grant's patient," Bev added. "And he promised to take Rose's husband for a ride in that fancy old car of his."

"He's so good with Ava and Alexis," Melanie added.

Summer didn't say anything. She just leaned against Emily, offering silent support.

Emily straightened her shoulders and launched into a loud, off-key version of "The Lion Sleeps Tonight." Ryan immediately joined in, his voice blending perfectly with hers.

Ignore, ignore, ignore.

When Bev suggested "Kumbaya" for the next song, Summer reached into the pocket of her hooded sweatshirt and retrieved a flask, which she offered to Georgia.

As the night wore on and the flames died down, guests started drifting back to the Lodge.

"This smoke is making my eyes water." Bev stifled a yawn as she rubbed at her face. "I know I said we had to decorate the cookies tonight, but maybe we can do it in the morning instead."

"Well," Rose said. "If you're sure."

"It's your wedding," Darlene said.

"Actually, it's Emily's," Summer pointed out. All three sisters ignored her.

"I've got plans tonight, anyway," Georgia said. "My date's picking me up in half an hour."

"That explains the shoes." Summer laughed and pointed out Georgia's fringed magenta booties.

"What? These are my camping shoes," Georgia said. "They're rugged. They have fringe."

"Yeah, you're practically Davy Crockett." Summer took another nip from her flask and gathered up an armful of blankets.

"But we'll have to get started early in the kitchen," Bev warned. "Melanie and I planned a bachelorette party for Emily, and we want to leave plenty of time."

"Wait." Emily didn't dare look at Summer. "I thought we weren't having a bachelorette party."

"Oh, it's nothing fancy," Bev said. "Just a fun little get-together."

"Will this fun little get-together involve naked men?" Georgia asked.

"Goodness, no."

"I don't get up before nine a.m. unless there's a naked man involved," Georgia declared, then strutted back toward the Lodge, cursing as her heels sank into the lawn.

Rose shook her head. "Oh, my."

"Don't worry, Emily." Darlene brushed off her twill capri pants. "We don't hold you accountable for your mother."

"You go on to bed, Bev." Summer linked her arm through Emily's. "We'll get started on the cookies tonight."

"I don't know." Bev fretted. "I think it might be better if I were there to supervise."

"We'll be fine." Summer said this in her most authoritative flight attendant voice. "You showed us the pictures and told us exactly how to make

232

the icing. We'll frost for an hour or two and that way, we won't have to rush tomorrow."

"But I—"

"Nighty-night." Summer smiled brightly. "Remember, you're the mother of the groom and you need to save your strength. Big weekend coming up."

As Bev headed back to the hotel along with Melanie and the girls, Summer jabbed her finger at Caroline and Emily. "Beverly Cardin has no business planning your bachelorette party."

Caroline turned up her palms. "This is the first I'm hearing of it."

"Me, too," Emily said.

"I'm the maid of honor. Planning the bachelorette party is *my* job." Summer's expression grew positively mutinous. "Fine. If she's going to be that way, I'm going to raid Georgia's closet before- hand. I'm going to find something sequined, leopard print, and obscenely low-cut."

"Please don't give the three musketeers any more ammunition," Emily begged. Then she turned to Caroline. "Hey, I watched the first few episodes of *Buffy* last night."

"And? What'd you think?"

"I think I'm going to have to reconsider my anti-vampire stance."

"*Buffy* is a gateway drug." Ryan's voice startled all of them. "Next thing you know, you'll be hitting the hard stuff: *True Blood*, *Shadow of the Vampire*, *'Salem's Lot*. . . ."

Emily whirled around, dropping the empty marshmallow bags she'd collected. "You're still here?"

In the shadows cast by the fire, his eyes looked darker than usual. His teeth flashed white and even. "I'm always here."

"So I've noticed." She leaned down to retrieve the plastic bags.

"Well, we better get cracking on those cookies!" Summer grabbed Caroline and dragged her into the woods. "Adios, you two!"

"Hotel's that way," Ryan pointed out.

"Of course it is!" Summer did a one-eighty and tramped off with a bewildered Caroline asking, "What just happened?"

"You guys are the worst bridesmaids ever!" Emily called after them.

She listened to the rustle of snapping twigs for a moment, then gave Ryan her full attention.

"Okay." She held out her arms. "You did it. You got me here, all alone."

"I did." He sounded pleased, but not surprised. "It's just me, you, and the campfire." He prodded the glowing red embers with a stick. "Old flame's still burning."

She rolled her eyes. "Where's your trusty sidekick?"

"Ripley? Poor pup OD'd on fresh air. She's sleeping it off in my room."

They stood side by side in silence, watching the ash and flame overtake each other.

Finally, Ryan reached down to scavenge through the remaining box of graham crackers. "Have a s'more."

She watched him assemble layers of cracker, chocolate, and warm marshmallow.

"I can't. If I gain so much as half a pound, my wedding dress is going to cut off my circulation."

"Don't be that girl." After a minute, he picked up the s'more and lifted it to her lips. The warm glow of the fire reflected in his eyes. "Take a bite."

She looked at him and realized that one way or another, she was going to give in to temptation tonight, and the s'more was by far the lesser of two evils.

So she leaned forward and nibbled, closing her eyes as she savored the crunch of the graham cracker, the sticky sweetness of the marshmallow, and the gooey richness of the chocolate. She took another bite, then another.

When she opened her eyes, she found him closer than ever, watching her with an intensity that made her throat go dry.

She swallowed hard and put the rest of the treat down. "This s'more has zero nutritional value."

"That's what makes it so good." He stepped closer, gaze fixed on her mouth, and she knew he was going to kiss her.

She waited, barely breathing, while he reached

up and brushed his thumb along her lower lip.

"You had some chocolate there," he said.

Her lips parted of their own accord and when he took his hand away, her tongue traced the path his thumb had taken. She tasted chocolate, along with a hint of smoke. She tasted danger. She tasted possibility.

She forced herself to take a sip of water.

As the cool liquid washed her mouth clean, she edged back until her heel collided with a fallen log. Never taking her gaze from his, she crossed her arms and made her stand.

"What are you doing, Ryan? I want to know. What is it, exactly, that you're trying to accomplish?"

He stopped trying to charm and cajole her. His voice dropped and his expression changed. "I'm asking you if you still love me."

She had no idea what to say to that, and so she clung to the only thing she knew for sure. "I'm getting married in three days."

His eyebrows shot up. "So?"

"So, it doesn't matter how I feel about you."

"Yeah, it does matter. It's the only thing that matters."

"No, Ryan. No." She drew a ragged breath and hugged herself tighter. "You can't just show up out of the blue and sweep me off into the sunset. That's not how real life works."

"You're the expert on 'real life' now?"

"Yes. And here's what else: I am not the girl you married. I have a completely different life, and a lot of responsibilities. I have a great man who loves me."

He took a single step toward her, his hands in his pockets. "You have two great men who love you. Just for the record."

She started to tremble. "If you really loved me, you wouldn't be here. You wouldn't make this hard for me. You'd let me go on with my life."

"Why would I do that?"

"Because . . ." She trailed off, her brow creasing. "Because that's the noble thing to do—to walk away and let the person you love be happy."

"I don't walk away from things, Emily. Never have, never will." His tone hardened, and she remembered how she'd run from their old apartment, slamming the door on him midsentence. "And I want you. Always have, always will."

"You don't want me." She was almost pleading with him now. "You just think you do."

"You're right. I think we'll be happy together. I think you owe it to yourself to give us another shot. And I think, if you loved Grant as much as you say you do, you wouldn't be standing here arguing with me. You'd be curled up in bed, watching *Buffy* and having phone sex with him."

"Stop it."

He continued toward her until she could hear

the creak of his old leather jacket. "I'm not saying Grant's not a good guy. But the bottom line is he's not the right guy for you."

"How can you say that? How can you possibly know?" she demanded. She needed to hear his answer, because she didn't have one of her own.

"He can move on. I can't."

She half laughed, half choked. "You're going to have to move on, because I'm marrying Grant. It's too late for us. Years and years too late."

He didn't argue, just kept studying her with total, unwavering intensity. "Do you love him?"

"Of course I do."

"Do you love him as much as you loved me?"

Emily couldn't answer. She did love Grant—she was sure of that. Their love was the kind of relationship she had always aspired to. Mutual trust and respect. No drama, no surprises, no secrets.

Well, almost no secrets.

Her love for Ryan, on the other hand . . . that had been all-consuming and overwhelming. All highs and lows with no happy medium. Bliss and despair and screaming and sex and never a moment of clarity.

She turned her face away, gazed into the starlit patches of sky between the trees, and said, "I can't compare you and Grant. You two are completely different. And I'm completely different than I was back then."

Ryan laughed softly. "So you can never do anything exciting again?"

She lifted her chin. "I'm not saying that."

"What are you afraid of, Emily?"

Her voice faded into a whisper. "I'm not afraid."

"Then prove it. I dare you." He held out his hand to her. "Let's take a walk."

She turned and ran the other way.

CHAPTER 17

Emily sat on the edge of the dock with one foot tucked underneath her leg and the other dipping in and out of the cool lake water. She felt the wooden boards beneath her sway as someone approached.

"Fancy meeting you here," Summer said. "Mind if I join you?"

"I thought you got lost in the woods after you deserted me."

"I did. And then I ended up here. You know I have no sense of direction. So what're we doing"—the dock creaked as Summer sat down—"howling at the moon?"

"Whimpering at the moon, maybe." Emily turned to her best friend. "We've known each other for a long time, right?"

"Since the days of permed hair and pegged jeans," Summer agreed.

"So I need you to tell me what to do."

"About . . . ?"

"Everything." Emily summed up the conversation she'd just had with Ryan. She left out the part about the s'mores. And the lips. And the tingling. "I'm not thinking clearly right now. I'm not thinking clearly and I'm not seeing clearly, and I need you to straighten me out and tell me what to do with the rest of my life."

"But no pressure," Summer deadpanned.

"Oh, there's pressure. Time pressure, financial pressure, social pressure. Planning this wedding has sucked me dry. And now Ryan shows up, thanks to you."

"I told you, it was entrapment. Entrapment at the Four Seasons."

Emily shook her head. "Why am I letting him get to me? I'm decisive. Fix it or forget it. No second-guessing. So how could I even consider . . . ?" Emily decided it was unwise to finish that sentence. "I am marrying Grant this weekend."

Summer nodded. "So it says on the fancy engraved invitation I got."

"I love Grant and he loves me, and we are good together." Emily clutched the weathered wooden planks with both hands. "*Perfect* together."

"Mmm-hmm."

"That's a statement, not a question."

"I'm not arguing with you."

"Is this a private party, or can I join in?" The dock swayed again as Caroline arrived.

Emily gestured for Caroline to take a seat. "Aren't you two supposed to be decorating cookies?"

"We're waiting for you." Summer folded a piece

of gum into her mouth, then handed a piece to Caroline. "We're telling her what to do with the rest of her life."

Caroline looked at Emily. "You're deciding the rest of your life by committee?"

"Yes. My judgment is faulty. Especially when it comes to men."

"So this is about Ryan," Caroline said.

Emily groaned. "Is it that obvious?"

"Yes." Caroline held up her index finger while she gathered her thoughts. "Here's what I know: I did all the things I was supposed to do. Went to the right schools, landed a high-paying job, found a house in the most desirable neighborhood, married a guy I love."

"And your life is wonderful and you're living the dream?" Emily asked hopefully.

"Wrong. I'm . . . well, you know what I'm dealing with. And I can accept that. I made a choice, and I have to live with it. But do you know what I really *want*?"

Summer leaned forward, eyes huge. "What?"

"I want what Andrew and I had in the beginning. The looks, the butterflies. Making up any excuse to see each other and touch each other." Caroline sighed. "These days, we barely see each other at all. Sometimes, I'll be stuck in traffic or waiting in line at the grocery store, and I'll think to myself: This is it. I'll never have another first kiss. I'll never have that feeling you get when a guy holds your hand for the first time."

Summer clapped her hand to her heart. "I love that feeling."

"It cuts both ways, though," Emily argued. "I left Ryan for a reason. And now that ten years have gone by, it's easy to gloss over all the crap and just focus on the good times. But eventually, every marriage gets to the point you're describing. What if I did get back together with Ryan, and then, in another ten years, all I can think about is Grant and how I should've stayed with him?"

"I would kill for a dirty weekend in Vegas." Caroline wasn't even pretending to listen to anybody else. "In a swanky hotel with nice linens, expensive champagne . . ."

"So basically, you want a fling," Summer said.

"A love affair," Caroline corrected. "With my husband. I want him to actually notice me. I don't claim to know everything about love, Em, but I will tell you this: Ryan notices you. He can't take his eyes off you." She paused. "And also? He's hot like fire."

Emily laughed. "Caroline!"

"What? I'm not supposed to notice? The man is hot. It's an indisputable fact."

"Truth," Summer agreed. "Aren't you attracted to him?"

"I plead the fifth," Emily muttered.

"Oh, come on, you can tell us," Caroline said. "I

just sat here and admitted I want to have an affair with my own husband."

"Fine, I'll say it: I'm attracted to him. I get all blushy and my tender little heart goes pitter-pat when he walks by." Emily shrugged one shoulder. "But so what?"

"Well." Summer snapped her gum. "Surely that means something."

"No, it doesn't. Just because I'm attracted to him doesn't mean we're good for each other. It doesn't mean we're soul mates. *It doesn't mean anything.*"

"But you can't deny that chemistry's important," Caroline said. "You can't have a real relationship—even a friendship—without it."

"Ha. You know what chemistry is? It's a combination of hormones and delusion that strings you out like street drugs and makes you do stupid, stupid things like tattoo some guy's name on your finger." Emily held out her left hand. "Behold—the result of great chemistry."

"Wow." Caroline craned forward for a closer inspection. "That's really carved right in there."

"But you can't read what it says anymore," Summer added helpfully. "It's just a mass of scar tissue."

"Oh, the manicurist at the spa can read it just fine. So can Melanie. So can Grant."

"Do you feel this way about all chemistry? Or just the kind you have with Ryan?" Caroline

244

wanted to know. "Because I feel like you and Grant have chemistry, too."

"We do," Emily said. "But our chemistry isn't all crazy-making and raging out of control. I would never get Grant's name tattooed on my finger, and he would never want me to."

"And that's a good thing?" Summer asked.

"A very good thing. Grant makes me want to be a better person. He helps me focus. He believes in me."

Summer stopped snapping her gum and got serious. "How's the sex?"

"I'm going to pretend you didn't just ask that question."

"Then I'll ask it again: How's the sex?"

"You've seen the man. He's brilliant, he's sensitive, he's great with his hands. How do you think the sex is?"

"I don't know." Summer reached into the water and splashed Emily. "That's why I'm asking you."

"Well, it's great. Amazing. Mind-blowing. Next topic?"

"Is it better than the sex with Ryan?" Caroline pressed. Summer gave her a thumbs-up.

"I . . ." Emily dropped her head into her hands. "I cannot believe I'm having this discussion."

"Well?" Summer and Caroline waited.

"Ryan and I were twenty-two years old. You can't compare sex at twenty-two to sex in your thirties."

"Sure, you can. We'll help."

"You've done enough already." Emily got to her feet, officially ending the interview. "Now get your minds out of the gutter and let's ice some cookies."

Piping icing onto dozens of sugar cookies turned out to be even more tedious—and way more painful—than Emily had anticipated.

"Ow." She took a break after she added the petals to a tiny pink flower. "My hand keeps cramping."

"Push through it," Summer advised. "Eventually, it'll go numb and you'll lose all feeling in your fingers. Sweet relief."

Caroline gave up at ten thirty, yawning and apologizing as she put down her pastry bag. "I can't even see straight anymore," she said. "Let alone make tiny little rosettes on tiny little cookies."

"Go." Emily hugged her and thanked her for her help.

"We're putting these in little gift bags, right?" Summer frowned down at her handiwork.

"Little clear bags with ribbons, yeah. Why?"

"Well, you might want to think about bags that aren't see-through. That's all I'm saying." Summer used a silicone spatula to scoop some more icing into her bag. "There's a reason I didn't go into the visual arts."

"Looks fine," Emily said. The green and pink icing was a bit lopsided, but after months of demanding perfection for every single aspect of the wedding, she found she was willing to settle for "good enough" with the cookies. "It's the thought that counts."

"We've only done, what? Thirty cookies? We're going to be here all night," Summer said.

They heard the clatter of high heels on the stone floor and then Georgia swept in, wearing a backless navy gown and glittery combs in her red hair. "There you are, Summer! I've been looking everywhere for you! You have to get changed and come with me. Chop-chop, right now."

"Where are we going?"

"My suitor has a friend." Georgia sank her pearly pink nails into Summer's sleeve. "I told him you'd be happy to join us all on a double date."

"Whoa, whoa, not so fast." Summer hung on to her chair as Georgia tried to pry her fingers off. "Who is this guy? How old is he? What's he like?"

"Does it matter? It's just a few hours."

"Help me," Summer begged Emily as Georgia led her away.

"Wear your work uniform," Emily advised. "No man can resist a sassy flight attendant."

"I want a new family!" Summer howled, and then the kitchen doors swung shut behind her and she was lost to Georgia's machinations.

Emily sat back, assessed their progress, and looked at the mountains of cookies still left to ice. She could quit, she knew. Bev would take over in the morning. The finished products would look better. No one expected her to tackle this monumental task by herself.

But if she went to bed now, she would have to lie there in the darkness and think about all the things she was trying so hard not to think about. She would have to feel all the feelings she didn't want to acknowledge.

So she picked up her pastry bag and resumed piping. The kitchen felt cool and peaceful. She could hear the low hum of the refrigerators and the lights overhead. She didn't have to make any decisions right now. She didn't have to think at all. She just had to make tiny pink flowers.

And she did—for forty-five minutes. Then she ran out of icing and realized, when she attempted to make more, that she didn't know where to find the rest of the confectioners' sugar Bev had bought. Her hands were aching, her mind was churning, and now she had nothing to do with them.

She checked her cell phone. Still no texts or calls from Grant.

Something inside her snapped, and she started crying. She was shocked at her own reaction, but she couldn't stop. A silent, steady stream of tears rolled down her cheeks while she cleaned up after herself and started back to her room.

As she crossed through the hotel lobby, she heard Ryan's voice out on the front porch. She knew she should keep moving. She should retreat, the way she had at the campfire.

Instead, she pushed open the huge double doors and headed straight for him.

He was pacing and yelling into his cell phone: "The reception out here sucks."

As soon as he saw her, he hung up. "Hey. Are you okay?"

She nodded. "I'm out of sugar."

"And you're crying about that *why?*" His tone was gentle, indulgent.

She buried her face in her hands, knowing as she did so that she was ridiculous. She was a caricature of every histrionic bridezilla on cable TV shows.

She was also about to have her second official panic attack.

Ryan didn't say anything else. He guided her to one of the wide wooden benches, sat down next to her, and waited while she struggled to regain her composure.

He didn't ask what the problem was or how he could help. He simply put his arm around her and pulled her against him.

She closed her eyes and let him hold her, feeling completely safe and knowing that feeling this way was incredibly dangerous.

The knots in her stomach loosened and the adrenaline surge drained away. As she came back to herself, she became aware of the crickets chirping and the luminous glow of the moon. She could smell the sharp, clean scent of the pine trees mixed with . . .

Her eyes flew open. "Are you wearing Drakkar Noir?"

Ryan grinned and gave her a squeeze. "You noticed."

"Are you kidding me? You're a grown man. Who lives in LA and goes to fancy red carpet events. Might be time to upgrade to cologne that you don't buy at the drugstore." She laughed. *In middle school.*

"When I'm working the red carpet, I wear designer aftershaves that I can't even pronounce." He pressed her closer. "I save the heavy artillery for you."

"Drakkar Noir is the heavy artillery?"

"You know you love it."

She did. Damn him. The scent was evoking total recall of that night they'd first met and all the nights afterward.

She forced herself to ease away from him. "You're evil."

"I'm strategic," he corrected her. Judging by the way he smiled at her, he knew his strategy was working. "And solving problems is my job. If you need more sugar, I'll get you more sugar."

"You really want to talk about sugar right now?"

"No." And he gave her a smoldering look that made her turn away. "But you're having a nervous breakdown over it, so right now I'm on sugar detail."

"It's almost midnight," Emily pointed out. "We're in the middle of nowhere."

"I have a GPS and an iron will. I'm your guy."

"Ryan." She got to her feet. "You're not my guy."

"There's a twenty-four-hour grocery store ninety minutes away. Come on—we'll take the motorcycle."

And just like that, Emily McKellips, level-headed MBA, was replaced by Emily McKellips, cautionary tale.

CHAPTER 18

Emily knew, even as she pulled the sleek black helmet over her head, that this was a bad idea. More than that, it was *dangerous*—on every level.

Grant disapproved of motorcycles. Most physicians did. They saw the carnage and casualties in the ER and on the operating table. Emily had once asked, "But doesn't wearing a helmet protect you?" and Grant had laughed and explained that his team referred to bikers' helmets as "brain buckets."

"Besides," he'd added, "maintaining brain function is a small comfort when your entire body is shattered from the neck down."

Grant would not like the idea of his future wife on a motorcycle. Not that they'd ever discussed it—the Emily he knew would never do such a thing.

She stood next to Ryan, one hand resting on the restored bike, and told herself that this was her last chance to back down and back out.

But when she opened her mouth to explain that she couldn't do this, the words that came out were, "Promise me you won't go too fast."

Ryan held up his palm like a boy scout. "I solemnly swear I will not go fast."

"And no hairpin turns or sudden stops."

"You got it."

"And if the road is wet or it starts to rain—"

"We'll be fine." He stepped in front of her and checked the fit of her helmet. "I won't let you get hurt, Em. You know that."

"Yeah, but there are so many factors out of your control," she argued. "Potholes and fog and, like, oil slicks that you don't see until it's too late."

Ryan straddled the bike. "You coming or not?"

With a final, guilty glance back toward the Lodge, Emily climbed on behind him. He turned the key in the ignition and the cycle rumbled to life. She could feel the slow, steady thrum of power beneath her, and as he swung the bike out of the gravel parking lot, she knew she had to hang on to him.

Her grip was tentative at first, barely clasping the side seams on his worn black leather jacket. But as he accelerated, she tightened her grip, inching her fingers toward his waist.

Ryan captured her hand in his and pulled her right arm firmly around his waist. Her palm slipped under the flap of his jacket, against his soft cotton T-shirt. She could feel his abs, firm and warm, underneath her hand.

This was a bad idea, she thought.

But then she stopped thinking and started to enjoy the ride.

She couldn't hear anything beyond the rush of the wind and the roar of the engine. She couldn't feel anything besides the pounding of her heart and the warmth of Ryan's back against her chest and the cool, damp evening air on her bare fingers as she clutched him. She wasn't worried about upcoming potholes or devastating car accidents.

Between the passage of time and all of Grant's horror stories about "brain buckets," she had forgotten the sense of freedom that came with riding a motorcycle. The sense of immediacy and the certainty that some things in life were worth the risk. She leaned into Ryan as he leaned into a turn.

Her arms were wrapped around him now, but it didn't feel sexual or inappropriate. She was just hanging on to him for a little while, reconnecting.

Remembering.

By the time they returned to the Lodge, Emily felt energized and bubbly. Ryan carried the bags full of confectioners' sugar to the kitchen for her, then glanced at Bev's recipe.

"Oh, you don't have to stay." She gave up trying to straighten her windblown curls. "I can take it from here."

"No way." He dumped some sugar into a measuring cup. "If you're going to stay up all night, so am I."

"Really?" She portioned out the water and handed it to him. "You'll help me?"

He shrugged one shoulder. "As Val Kilmer said in *Tombstone*, 'I'm your huckleberry.' "

"But you hate girly stuff like this."

"I'm a producer. Which means I do whatever needs doing." He turned on the mixer. "So if what we're doing involves pink frosting and edible glitter, then pass the frosting bag."

She arched one eyebrow. "You're not even going to make a suggestive comment about edible glitter?"

He peered into the big metal bowl. "Not right now. I'm in work mode."

"I can see that." While Ryan made the icing to Bev's precise specifications, Emily prepped pastry bags for each of them.

He pulled up a chair and started icing the cookies with the same grim concentration she imagined he'd use in the film editing room. She tried to keep up with his swift, steady pace, but her eyes fluttered closed and she let herself doze for a moment, startling awake when she pitched forward.

"Sorry." She reached for her pastry bag, but Ryan grabbed it away.

"Don't be sorry. Take a break." His tone

brooked no refusal. "You do sloppy work when you're tired." He got up, found a stack of folded cloth napkins in a cabinet, and placed them on the counter in front of her. "Just put your head down for a minute."

She did, planning to rest her eyes for five minutes.

When she woke up, the overhead lights were turned off and the golden glow of sunrise illuminated the kitchen.

Ryan was gone. But the pile of naked sugar cookies had been replaced with stacks of beribboned cellophane bags, all of them containing precise, identically decorated little wedding cakes.

THURSDAY

CHAPTER 19

Emily skipped her five-mile run the next morning. For the first time in months, she slept in. Her slumber was deep and dreamless, shattered only when insistent pounding on her door jerked her back to consciousness.

She threw on her robe and cracked open the door to find Summer standing in the hallway, quaking with rage.

"An ice-cream social?" Summer held up the calligraphy-scrolled invitation for Emily's bachelorette party. "*That's* Bev's big surprise?"

"Oh dear." Emily scanned the invitation and nibbled her lip. "But you like ice cream, don't you?"

"I like ice cream when I'm hanging out in my pajamas watching *Clueless* for the seventy-third time. I do not like ice cream when I'm forced to socialize with a bunch of buzz kills who keep giving me pitying looks and telling me not to worry, it'll be my turn next."

"Give it a chance. Maybe it'll be fun."

"Unless the ice cream is made out of White Russians, it'll be hellish, and we both know it."

"Summer, come on. Be a good sport. Bev and her sisters have been planning this for weeks."

"I have been a good sport. I've taken a week off work, I've gone along with all the guitar strumming and Kumbaya-ing, I bought a dress that breaks all of my personal style rules—bows, pastels, and tea-length hemlines—and I choked down the cucumber sandwiches and crumpets. I even went on a double date with my ex-stepmother and a pair of guys she barely knows."

"Hey, how did that go?" Emily asked.

Summer was too worked up to deviate from her rant. "But I am drawing the line at an ice-cream social bachelorette party. Do you hear me? The line has been drawn!" She ripped up the invitation, threw the pieces on the floor, and stomped off toward the lobby.

Emily pulled on jeans and a tank top, gathered up the pieces of invitation, and hurried after her friend. She caught up with Summer on the front porch of the Lodge.

"Don't freak out," Emily pleaded. "I understand why you're on edge. I know this is not your scene. And I deeply, truly appreciate everything you've done for me this week. But—"

"No buts!" Summer was practically frothing at

the mouth as she marched down the steps and across the vast, grassy lawn. "Georgia's right—Bev is taking over the whole wedding. And you're letting her. What's wrong with you?" A family of ducks changed direction and waddled away from Summer.

"I just wanted everyone to be happy."

"It's impossible to make everyone happy," Summer decreed. "Case in point: me, right now."

"I'll make this up to you after the wedding," Emily promised. "Whatever you want. My treat. You name the time and place."

"No!" Summer raised her fist. "The revolution has begun. I demand a bachelorette party worthy of the name. I want booze, I want boys, and I want blackmail material."

Right on cue, Ripley bounded up to see what all the screaming was about. Ryan followed, leash in hand. He looked rested and relaxed, despite the fact that he'd just come off an all-night cookie-icing marathon. As soon as she saw him, Emily wished she'd taken the time to fix her hair and put on makeup. Or at least a bra.

"What's the problem?" He glanced at the fleeing ducks. "You're scaring the wildlife."

"It's her." Summer jerked her thumb at Emily in disgust. "She let Bev plan the bachelorette party."

"It's more of a general girls' night out," Emily hedged. "We're all grown women. *Ladies,* actually. This isn't a sorority kegger."

"It's an ice-cream social and I'm no lady." Summer sounded on the verge of tears. "Ryan, help me. Make her see reason."

"I already had a swing and a miss with that," Ryan said. He found a stick on the ground and tossed it for Ripley. "But I might be able to shut down the ice-cream social."

"Too late—it's already planned," Emily said. "Bev and her sisters have been talking about it since yesterday."

"Only because they don't have anything better to look forward to." Ryan pulled out his smartphone. "I can fix that."

"I want booze, boys, and blackmail material," Summer informed him.

"Done."

"No, no, no. I'm going to have to veto this," Emily said.

"You're overruled," Summer said.

"It'll hurt their feelings," Emily argued. "And besides, look at the time. You'd have to reschedule everything in a matter of hours."

Her objections seemed to galvanize Ryan. "Luckily, I live for difficult decisions and impossible deadlines."

"I don't want some big production," Emily warned.

Ryan's grin was positively wolfish. "Too late, baby. That's what I do."

Rose and Darlene delivered the ultimate passive-aggressive present at high noon.

"Hi, Georgia." Clad in straw sunhats and sensible shoes, they sidled up to the restaurant table where Emily, Summer, Georgia, Bev, and Melanie were finishing up their lunch. "We've been looking all over for you!"

"Yes." Darlene simpered. "We checked the bar first, of course."

Rose pulled a box out of her tote bag. "We brought you a gift."

"For me? Oh, girls, you shouldn't have!" Georgia looked both flattered and confused as she accepted the pink-ribboned package Darlene offered.

Bev's fingers moved in helpless flutters around her throat. Melanie caught Emily's eye and pantomimed strapping on a crash helmet.

Georgia waited until she had everyone's full attention, then made a big display of opening the present. She peeled back layers of white tissue paper to reveal . . .

"Tights?" She held up the folds of magenta fabric with a bewildered smile.

"Stockings," Rose corrected, sweet as pie. "Special stockings. We noticed you had a few, ahem . . ."

"Blemishes," Darlene supplied.

"On your calves."

Georgia's smile morphed into a rictus of horror. "I beg your pardon?"

But the aunties remained oblivious. "We noticed a few little spider veins in your legs yesterday," Rose whispered.

"When you were wearing that cute little miniskirt." Darlene pronounced the word "cute" with a little too much emphasis.

"And these are supposed to be excellent for your circulation."

"We thought you'd like the color, too. Since your personality is so very vibrant."

And then Emily saw it: the malicious glint in Rose's big brown eyes. The shared smirk between two sisters teaming up against the newcomer who didn't know her place.

Bev stared up at the ceiling, probably praying for divine intervention. Melanie stuck out her index and middle fingers in cigarette-smoking position and sucked on a nonexistent Marlboro Light.

And Georgia . . . Georgia was about to blow.

She tweezed the offending stockings between her thumb and forefinger and held them at arm's length. Then she took a huge breath and prepared to open fire with the verbal equivalent of an assault rifle.

Summer sprang into action. "Let's go."

Emily took Georgia's right arm, Summer took

the left arm, and Bev trailed behind them while they hustled Georgia out into the hallway.

As they went, they could hear Rose and Darlene exclaiming:

"Well, goodness, I never! I put a lot of thought and effort into picking those out. A simple 'thank you' wouldn't go amiss."

"Hmph! She's just jealous that she's not part of the three musketeers. It's no wonder she doesn't have any girlfriends."

"Calm down, Mom," Emily instructed. "Deep breaths."

"Compression socks?" Georgia's complexion looked splotchy and mottled under layers of powder, blush, and foundation. *"Compression socks?"*

"They're pink," Summer pointed out. "That's kind of fabulous, right?"

"Compression socks are for *old people,*" Georgia spat. "Old people with varicose veins. Why didn't they just stab me in the heart with a butcher knife?"

"Heavens," Bev said. "I'm sure they didn't mean—"

Georgia whirled to confront Bev. "How did you feel when they deliberately gave you a sweater that was too small?"

Bev stared at the ground. "I'm sure it wasn't deliberate."

"How did you feel?"

Bev's voice was barely audible. "Like they stabbed me in the heart with a butcher knife."

"There you go!"

"Bev?" Rose's voice drifted out from the dining area. "Bev, dear, we need you!"

"Coming." Bev shuffled back to her sisters.

Georgia turned back to Summer and Emily. Her eyebrows drew together in an angry, auburn V. "Allow me to set the record straight: I am not old."

"We know, Mom."

"I am ageless. Men flock from miles away to pay court and take me to dinner."

"We know," Summer said.

"I am pure glamour and elegance. My skin is clear and pristine. Look!" Georgia yanked up her skirt hem. "These are the legs of a twenty-year-old."

"You're gorgeous," Emily assured her.

"A knockout," Summer said.

"And let me tell you something else." Here she raised a lacquered pink nail. "I have been nothing but agreeable and accommodating this week, while the 'three musketeers' run rough-shod over me. Now, I grant you, I may not be the matriarch of some huge extended family. I may not send out foil-lined Christmas cards every year with boastful family updates. I may have been married four times and have only one child, so my opinions don't count. But I am still the mother of the bride, and I deserve a little respect."

Emily frowned at her mother. "Of course your opinions count."

"Ha! As much as Bev's?"

"Yes! You two just have very different—"

"Whose wedding gown are you wearing?" Georgia demanded. "Whose engagement ring? Whose favorite hotel are we staying at?"

"Bev's!" Summer answered for Emily.

"That's right. The Cardins are trying to poach you and suck you into their family. But you were my daughter first. You and me, Emmy. We are a family, too."

"Uh, hello." Summer wiggled her fingers. "Don't forget me."

"And you, too." Georgia pulled both girls in for a jasmine-scented group hug.

"You guys." Emily huddled closer. "I'm not jumping ship. I just . . . I always wanted the fantasy, you know? Security and stability and good, clean fun where everyone gets along."

Georgia's entire face puckered. "Ick. Sounds dreadful."

"Right?" Summer laughed. "I'm bored already."

"Now, if you'll excuse me, I'm going to go find some brawny, handsome man to build a fire so that I can burn these." Georgia gathered up her gift.

"Try not to take it personally," Emily said. "Melanie says that's their way. They mean-girl the other women in the family with gifts that point out everybody's shortcomings."

"Hang on." Summer feigned disbelief. "They're *not* all healthy and functional every minute of every day?"

"Turns out you were right," Emily admitted. "There is no such thing as a perfect family."

"Well, that's just vindictive." Georgia sniffed. "Not to mention childish." The auburn eyebrow V deepened. "Bev might tolerate that nonsense, but not me!"

"Oh boy." Emily rubbed her temples. "Here we go."

"Hide the firearms," Summer said.

"I didn't start this, but I will finish it!" Georgia waved the magenta compression stockings like a battle flag. "They will rue the day they tangled with me, because mark my words: I'm the meanest mean girl who ever lived."

CHAPTER 20

"I've never been in a limousine before." Beverly's voice was a mixture of excitement and worry.

Ryan waved off the chauffeur and opened the car door himself. "Ladies."

"Tell me where we're off to." Georgia minced down the uneven stone walkway toward the car. Her heels were so high, her ankles wobbled with every step. "The suspense is absolutely killing me."

Ryan took her arm and helped her navigate the path. "Not to worry; the champagne should take the edge off."

Emily froze, one foot on the pavement and the other inside the limo. "Champagne?"

"I stocked the wet bar with a whole case." He leaned closer and whispered into her ear, "The good stuff. Your favorite."

As one woman after another ducked inside the stretch limo, Emily heard high-pitched squealing and laughing, popping corks and the clear, ringing chime of crystal flutes being toasted.

She looked at Ryan. "You know I don't drink champagne anymore."

"I figured you'd make an exception for Dom Pérignon."

When she turned around, his shoulder and bare arm brushed against hers. She hadn't realized how close he was. "You bought an entire case of Dom?"

"Why not? Keep up, Em," he chided. "I'm not an unpaid production assistant anymore."

"But you're still insane, obviously."

"I prefer 'spontaneous.' " He held out his hand to help her into the car.

She brushed him aside and clambered in by herself. "Well, thank you. I appreciate the effort, and I'm sure the girls will savor every sip. But I'm not drinking tonight."

"Oh, yes you are." Summer materialized behind her and assured Ryan, "Yes, she is. I'm on it."

"I have every confidence."

"Stop conspiring against me." Emily bristled. "You're wasting your time."

Ryan leaned over and called into the limo, "Have a good time. Call me if you need bail money."

"Don't worry," Beverly piped up from the depths of the black leather interior. "We'll all behave ourselves."

"Speak for yourself," Summer muttered.

"If she makes us play the license plate game, I'm throwing myself out the window," Georgia said.

"Be nice, you two," Emily said. She glanced back at Ryan. "Aren't you going to come with us?"

"My role is strictly behind the scenes." Ryan grinned as he closed the door on them. "Besides, I'd say there'll be more than enough testosterone already."

"You've got to hand it to Ryan." Summer's eyes glazed over with a mix of lust and amazement. "The guy knows how to pick a male strip club."

"I will *kill* him," Emily hissed. She had to admit, though, her friend had a point. When she thought "strip club," she envisioned a dark, dingy hole-in-the-wall with deafening music and cigarette smoke. But the all-male nude revue Ryan had selected was more refined country club than seedy strip joint. The atmosphere was almost spa-like, cool and clean and teeming with beautiful, genteel men in various states of undress.

"Who knew places like this even existed? And right by the Canadian border?" Summer wondered. "How does he do it?"

"He has minions." Emily sighed. "Many minions. And no shame whatsoever."

"I had no idea men could look like this," Caroline marveled. "Every guy here looks like he's trying out for the Olympic swim team."

The muscular, well-mannered males mingling -

with the female patrons boasted sculpted jaw-lines and cheekbones, dazzling white teeth, and smooth skin tanned to perfection.

"What kind of hair removal methods are these guys using?" Summer asked. "I need to get in on that."

"It's like they're not even human," Caroline agreed. "How can no one have a pimple? Or even a freckle?"

"Okay, okay, gather round. You can all go back to drooling in a second." Summer motioned everyone in. "I just need to make a quick announcement. Ryan called ahead and arranged for all of us to have an open bar."

"God, I love that boy," Georgia said.

"And we have the limo as long as we want, so no hurry." Summer dismissed everyone, grabbed Emily, and made a beeline for the bar. "I'm having about five more glasses of bubbly. You?"

"Just some water with lemon, thank you."

Summer shook her head. "Unacceptable. You're in a strip club."

"I'm at a strip club with my mother and my future mother-in-law."

"All the more reason why a real drink is in order," Summer said. "We can do this one of two ways, Em: Either you get yourself a proper drink and start enjoying the beefcake buffet here, or I will order you the Four Horsemen and pour them down your throat."

Emily sucked in her breath. The "Four Horsemen" was a series of shots comprised of Johnny Walker, Jim Beam, Jack Daniels, and Jameson. "You wouldn't."

"Oh, yes, I would. I already have. Remember your twenty-first birthday?"

"No."

Summer nodded. "Because of the Four Horsemen."

"Fine. *Fine.* I'll have one glass of champagne."

Summer gave their order to the bartender (who bore an uncanny resemblance to Jon Hamm) and sat down on a velvet-upholstered circular banquette in the center of the room. "Stop sulking and enjoy the view."

Summer practically purred as one of the men took her hand, lifted it to his lips, and maintained steady, intense eye contact as he murmured, "You're beautiful."

When another guy approached Emily, she motioned for him to keep moving. "I'm good, thanks. And I'm engaged."

"This was completely worth canceling my date for!" Georgia sidled up to them with a crystal champagne flute in one hand and a stack of dollar bills in the other. "Come on, girls, let's go have some fun."

"Can't." Summer batted her eyelashes at the shirtless Olympian. "Your only child has signed up as the chief of the Fun Police."

Georgia tsk-tsked. "Darling, this is your bachelorette party. You might not get another one for a very long time."

"Or ever," Emily said.

"Of course, sweetie. So come along and set the tone. It's what Emily Post would want." Georgia handed her a stack of money and started toward the back of the club.

Emily dug her heels in. "Mother, I am not going to stuff dollar bills into G-strings with you. Do you hear me? There is not enough therapy in the world."

"Fine." Georgia tossed back her hair. "If you're going to be a prude, I'll have to go back to the VIP room by myself."

Emily surveyed the scene, assuming her role as hostess. "I'm going to go talk to Bev. She doesn't look like she's enjoying herself at all."

"That woman needs a lap dance more than anyone I've ever met," Summer said. "With the possible exception of you."

Both of them approached Bev. "Hi, Bev. How're you doing?"

"Just fine, dear." Bev clutched the top button of her blouse with both hands, and her gaze bounced around the room as if she didn't know where to look. "You know, this is all very . . . lovely, but I think I'll wait in the car."

"Don't do that." Summer steered her back toward the bar. "Stay. Sit down. You'll get used to everything in a few . . . Damn, look at that guy's abs."

"No, I'm going to excuse myself." Bev's face had gone pale. "You girls are from a different generation; I know that. But women my age aren't used to all this."

Right on cue, Georgia yelled, "Take it off!" at one of the strippers.

"It's okay." Emily put her arm around Bev. "You're a lady through and through, and there's nothing wrong with that. But I don't want you to sit out in the car by yourself. Tell you what: You and I can—"

"Come with me." Georgia materialized next to Bev with a fizzy pink cocktail in hand.

"Where are we going?" Bev sounded terrified.

"You'll find out in a minute." Georgia wrapped Bev's fingers around the glass. "Have a sip. Tastes just like pink lemonade, doesn't it?"

Emily rounded on Summer. "You and my mother are like peer-pressuring middle schoolers on an after-school special."

"Just wait. Next we're going to spray-paint the girls' bathroom and terrorize the sub in home-room."

"Right this way." Georgia hustled Bev toward the back room. "I've got a delightful surprise for you."

Emily trailed after her mother, protesting, "I don't think this is a good idea."

Georgia swatted her away with a sleek silver evening bag. "I'm the mother here. I'll decide what's a good idea and what's not."

"This isn't going to end well," Emily predicted.

"That's the point, sweetie."

A few hours later, everybody was tipsy and out of dollar bills.

"Now this is a proper bachelorette party," Summer said with great satisfaction. "Although it's pretty much ruined me for all other men for the rest of my life."

"You guys ready to go?" Emily asked.

"Yes." Caroline's complexion looked a bit fevered. "Let's hit the road before things get any more out of hand."

They had all left the club and crowded into the waiting limo before Emily realized they were missing a few members of their party. "Wait a minute. Where's my mom? And where's Bev?"

Melanie's mouth formed a perfect O. "They must be back in the VIP room."

"What?"

Rose and Darlene practically tripped over each other in their haste to be the first to deliver the scandalous news. "Yes, Emily dear, we didn't want to put a damper on your special evening but *your mother—*"

"Bless her heart."

"—hired some hulking Nordic man to sexually

harass poor Bev. I believe his name was Sven?"

"He had no shirt," Rose added. "And very tight pants."

Darlene nodded. "She's probably catatonic by now."

Summer checked the time on her cell phone. "Yeah, they've been back there for a while now. They must be spending a small fortune."

"Oh my God. We have to go rescue her." Emily grabbed her maid of honor and headed back into the club. "We could be at an ice-cream social right now."

"I know! Isn't this so much better?"

It cost them another fifty bucks just to get into the club's VIP area (or, as Summer insisted on calling it, "the champagne room"), and Emily braced herself for the worst:

Full frontal male nudity.

Georgia getting arrested for solicitation.

Bev calling Grant and whimpering while Georgia held her captive in the vicinity of some man's crotch.

But while they saw a parade of well-built men and many woo-hooing women, they didn't see Georgia and Bev.

Then Summer nudged Emily and pointed out a little table in a dark corner. "There they are."

Emily breathed a sigh of relief. "No strippers, no trauma . . ." She squinted into the shadows. "But why are they crying?"

When they approached the table, Bev blew her nose and took a sip of her cocktail. "I had no idea your mother was a widow, Emily."

"*Twice,*" Georgia said. "The second time—that was Walt—I knew it was coming. Walt was older and he had some health problems. But Cal was young, in the prime of his life. Head-on collision on his way home from work one night."

"I'm so sorry for your loss." Bev opened her embroidered handbag and pulled out a photo of her late husband. "I can't imagine how awful it must be, losing your husband in your twenties like that, with no warning. My Stephen died just last year. Pancreatic cancer."

"Oh, honey, that is awful." Georgia rubbed at her eyes, heedless of her makeup.

"He died three months after they diagnosed him." Bev traced the edges of the photo with her fingertip. "We'd been planning a trip for our fortieth anniversary. An Alaskan cruise."

"The first year is so hard," Georgia said. "But it gets easier."

Bev drew in a shaky breath. "It does?"

"I promise. But you have to go through all the stages. First the shock, then the annoyance of all the chores you never had to worry about when you had a man around the house."

"The gutters!" Bev cried. "And raking the leaves."

Georgia nodded and gulped her drink. "I thought I'd have a nervous breakdown when the pipes under the kitchen sink started leaking."

"And the holidays." Bev sighed.

"First Valentine's Day after Cal died, I spent the whole morning lying on the bathroom floor."

"I cried buckets when I was peeling sweet potatoes last Thanksgiving," Bev confided. "They were Stephen's favorite."

"But you make it through the first year, all the crises, and the shock." Georgia shooed away an approaching stripper. "And then reality sets in. That's when you do your true grieving."

"That's where I am now," Bev said. "I try to stay busy—I have my book club and my bridge group and my quilting circle and my church—but at the end of the day, I have to come home alone."

Georgia dabbed at her cheeks with a paper cocktail napkin. "To an empty house."

"Exactly." Bev signaled to the shirtless bartender for another drink. "It's just so lonely. Even when I turn on the TV, it's just so *empty*. And I miss my Stephen."

"I miss my Cal."

They leaned in on each other, weeping.

Summer and Emily looked at each other, then back at the older women.

"Well," Summer finally said, "your mom and Grant's mom are finally bonding."

"Bev's drinking *alcohol*," Emily whispered. "And my mom's not even *looking* at the half-naked men."

Melanie joined them, hiccupping and slurring just a little. "Everything okay?"

Summer jerked her thumb toward the table for two. "Her mom and your mom are about to go out to the parking lot and pour one out for their fallen homies."

Bev was on a roll. ". . . and then you look at other men and think, 'How could any of them possibly compete? I'd rather be alone for the rest of my life.' "

This jolted Georgia out of her teary-eyed reverie. "Let's not get carried away. Not every man is going to be your soul mate, but there's no reason to rule them out altogether. You know what they say: 'The best way to get over a man is to get under another man.' "

"Oh, I could never." Bev waved both hands. "Stephen will always be my one and only. He was my first date, my first kiss—"

"You've only kissed one man? Ever?" Georgia put down her drink. "Beverly Cardin, time's a-wasting! You need to get out there. Right now. I'm going to help you."

"That's sweet of you to offer, but really, I'm not ready."

"Oh, it's not an offer; it's an order. You!" Georgia snapped her fingers at a brawny young hunk. "What's your name? Thor? Thor, this is my friend Bev. I want you to show her a good time." Georgia opened her wallet and pulled out a fistful of cash.

Emily stepped in before the money could change hands. "Hey! Mom! Time to go!"

"So soon?" Bev asked.

"We're just getting started," Georgia protested. "Bev here has a lot of living to do."

"Sorry." Melanie helped Bev to her feet. "Limo's leaving."

"That's all right!" Georgia said. "We'll take a cab. Or better yet, one of these gentlemen will give us a lift home."

Summer shook her head. "Do not make me give you the 'taking rides from strangers' lecture tonight. Move it, ladies. Hup two."

"These heels are ridiculous. My feet are killing me." Georgia held up her sandals, which she'd already taken off. "Give us ten more minutes and an Advil?"

"Right. Now."

Heaving loud, put-upon sighs, the mothers complied.

"Here's to best friends in the making." Summer whispered to Emily, "Score another win for Ryan Lassiter."

"This has nothing to do with Ryan," Emily replied. "It has to do with the fact that my mother is a terrible influence."

"A cautionary tale, would you say?"

"You can ride in the trunk on the way home."

"As long as you give me a bottle of Dom and a straw, I'm happy."

CHAPTER 21

By the time the limo pulled up to the front entrance of the Lodge, half the bridal party members had lost their voices from laughing and singing Tina Turner's "Private Dancer."

Over and over and over.

Bev, whom Emily had never once heard raise her voice, belted it out the loudest. She wasn't a demure, levelheaded mother and grandmother and widow at the moment.

But she was happy.

Ryan was waiting at the front steps to help the chauffeur unload the passengers, most of whom had followed Georgia's lead and taken off their shoes.

"We're outta booze," Summer announced as she spilled out of the car.

"So you had a good time, then?" Ryan replied.

Summer glanced at Caroline and both of them burst out laughing.

"I'll take that as a yes." He put one arm around Georgia, one arm around Bev, and hauled them bodily up the stairs.

"Ryan! Such a gentleman!" Bev gave him a kiss on the cheek. "Speaking of gentlemen, wait till you hear what we did tonight. Georgia and I met a dashing young man named Sven, and he—"

"Discretion, please," Georgia trilled. "A lady never kisses and tells."

Rose sniffed. "Don't talk to us about what a lady would or wouldn't do."

Darlene chimed in with, "We tried to stop them. But you can't stop someone who has no shame."

"Good night." Ryan handed them off to the concierge, who was staring at Bev with a mixture of amusement and astonishment. "See you at breakfast."

"We'll be sleeping in." Georgia flung herself into the concierge's arms. "Brad, darling! How are you? Care to indulge in a nightcap?"

"Great idea!" Summer exclaimed.

Caroline and the others whooped in agreement, and they trooped inside, chattering and laughing and blowing kisses at Ryan as they went.

"Emily!" Melanie called as she held the door. "You have the best ex-husband ever!"

Emily waved until the door closed behind them, leaving her and Ryan alone in the dark. The only sounds were the crickets and the steady lapping of lake water on the shore.

She couldn't see his face beneath the shadow of the pines, but she could hear the smile in his voice. "You're back."

"Yes."

"You all had fun."

"Some of us more than others."

"You had champagne."

"Half a glass." She tilted her head. "How can you tell?"

He didn't answer her, just waited her out until she took off her heavy drop earrings and admitted, "It was the perfect bachelorette party. You accomplished the impossible. You made me break all my rules. My mom and Grant's mom actually bonded. Happy?"

"Not yet."

She threw up her hands, even though he hadn't taken a step toward her. "We had a nice night. Let's leave it at that and not ruin it, with . . . you know."

He let her words linger between them. "I do know."

A glint of silver caught her eye in the moonlight. The thick, tarnished skull ring on his left hand. When he noticed her looking at it, he tucked his hand into his pocket.

"Why do you still have it?" She knew he knew she was referring to the tattoo. "I thought for sure you'd have it removed by any means necessary."

"I tried." For once, he wasn't looking at her. "I went to the laser clinic three times. The first time I made it to the waiting room; the next time I made it to the exam room. But in the end, I just couldn't do it." He laughed softly. "And it made me even more pissed at you."

"Well, that was always our specialty. Driving each other crazy. That's why I left, Ryan."

He shook his head. "You left because you thought I wasn't good enough for you. And all those years in California, I kept thinking that one day, I'd track you down. I'd track you down and show you who I was, what I'd done. But then I saw Summer on the flight to New York and I knew I had to make my move. Now or never."

Emily's heart ached at the pain and reproach she heard in his voice. "I didn't leave because you weren't good enough."

"Then why?"

"We just . . ." She tried to explain, as much to herself as to him. "It wasn't the right time. We were so young, so intense about everything. We weren't ready."

"And now?"

"Now it's the week before my wedding."

A cold wind blew off the lake, making her shiver. Then everything went still except the sound of a car passing in the distance.

"If this were one of your movies," she said, "this would be the moment when the crazed ax murderer runs out of the woods to dismember us both."

There was a spurting sound behind her. The

lawn sprinklers gurgled to life, drenching them both in a shower of icy water.

She shrieked and turned to run back to the hotel, but Ryan ran forward, caught her hand in his, and charged directly into the spray.

"What are you doing?" As the water surrounded her, she felt her senses sharpening. Her heart pounding in her chest, her skin soaking up the shower, her sandals sliding through the newly slick lawn. "We're going to get soaked."

"We're already soaked."

Emily's hair was plastered against her cheeks and her delicate high heels sank into the ground. "Hang on." She clutched his arm with one hand, reached down with the other, and pulled off her shoes. Barefoot and dripping, she had the sudden urge to throw out her arms and spin like a child.

So she did. She made one complete revolution before her feet slipped out from under her. As she caught herself with her palms, the hem of her new silk dress got caught between her knees and the mud.

Emily started laughing and sat down, ruining the back of her skirt as well. She laughed until her chest ached and tears mingled with the sprinkler water.

Ryan watched her, shaking his head. "How much champagne did you drink?"

"I told you, half a glass," she said. "I'm not

drunk. I'm just . . . I'm just . . ." She couldn't stop laughing. She couldn't stop crying.

The sprinklers shut off as abruptly as they'd turned on, and in the lull that followed, Emily could hear how hysterical she sounded.

She felt giddy and terrified and free and alive. For the first time in recent memory, she couldn't pry apart her heart and her mind.

"On your feet." Ryan grabbed her elbows and pulled her up. "I know what you need."

He steered her toward the lake, which reflected the huge white moon in its silver ripples.

"Where are we going?"

"In." He paused on the beach long enough to shuck off his shoes and socks.

She dropped her sandals next to his sneakers, wiggling her toes as the grit of the sand coated the blades of grass on her feet.

"I am not skinny-dipping with you," she warned.

"No one asked you to take your clothes off."

Oh.

Good.

"This is crazy." She hesitated by the waterline. "We're not in high school."

"We're not dead yet, either." He plowed into the lake, yanking his shirt over his head as he went.

She waded after him, trying to focus her gaze on the stars, the sky—anything except the bare skin of his shoulders and chest.

When the water came halfway up her calves, she stopped, cinching her skirt hem around her knees.

Ryan splashed ahead and didn't look back. "What are you waiting for?"

"I don't know." She peered down at the dark water. The farther in she went, the less she could see. But she took another step forward. The bottom of her foot brushed against something slimy, and she shuddered. "There better not be leeches in here."

"I doubt there are any leeches. But that reminds me of a shoot I was on in North Carolina. We were setting up for a scene right by this pond that was famous for having these giant, swimming snakes—"

"I forbid you to tell the rest of this story."

He stopped talking and so did she, and instinctively, as the water submerged her thighs and waist and chest, she moved closer to him.

She couldn't decide what posed the greatest threat to her right now—bloodthirsty leeches, swimming snakes, or a very charming, persistent ex-husband.

"Okay." Ryan stopped just as the water lapped against her shoulders.

Emily looked around. "Now what?"

"Now, we peace out." He inhaled slowly and let his body relax until he was floating under that huge white moon.

She frowned. "That's it?"

"Try it," he commanded. So she did. She let her muscles slacken, one by one, until she sank in up to her chin and the natural forces of her body took over, keeping her afloat under the stars.

In the back of her mind, she registered the thought that the water was cold and she'd probably catch pneumonia and it would be a shame to be sick on her wedding day and *blah blah blah*. But then a sense of tranquility seeped into her soul.

She wished she could stay here forever, suspended between earth and sky. Between single life and marriage.

Between Ryan and Grant.

But if Grant was an anchor, Ryan was a buoy, and she couldn't have both. She couldn't bob on the surface and still be tethered to the sand.

A sharp tug on her scalp jerked Emily out of her little moment of Zen.

"Ow!" She struggled to regain her footing, but she couldn't lift the back of her head out of the water. Her curls had gotten tangled in a length of rope that marked off the hotel's swimming area. Every time she tried to stand up, her hair yanked her back down.

"A little help, please," she called to Ryan, who immediately started swimming her way.

He stood up and took stock of the situation. "Wow. You're really roped in like a filly outside a saloon."

"Thank you for the colorful analogy. Can you please get me out of this?"

"In a second." He studied her face but made no move to free her.

"What? Are we going to have to cut my hair?" she asked. "Again? Summer just chopped it this morning."

"No, I can get it."

"Well, then?" She flailed her arms. "Go ahead."

"I want you to answer one question for me first."

"Are you serious? You're going to make me do a Q and A while I'm trapped and about to drown?"

"We're in five feet of water," he pointed out. "And I prefer to think of it as a friendly exchange of information."

"Screw that." She redoubled her efforts to free herself, but since she couldn't see what she was doing, the tangle got even tighter and her hair started to rip. "Ow."

"I am going to help you," he said, his tone both soothing and amused. "Right after you help me."

"This is why we didn't work, you know. Marriage is not some business deal with wheeling and dealing and constantly getting to yes."

"Sure it is," he replied. "It's a legal contract."

"Not the love part. Love is selfless and generous and . . . and . . . not subject to terms and conditions."

"Duly noted." He stood there and waited her out.

"Fine." She set her jaw and glared up at the stars. "What's your question?"

"What do you see in Grant?"

She struggled so hard she almost tore out a chunk of her scalp. But this bought her some time to consider her answer.

"I'll tell you what I see in him: everything. He's sweet and smart and strong and honorable. He's loving and thoughtful and sentimental and romantic. He's handsome and dashing and chivalrous and—"

Ryan interrupted with an eye roll. "You're engaged to a guy, right, not a thesaurus?"

"He saves lives, Ryan. And he saved me."

"From what?" he challenged.

From myself, she wanted to reply, but stopped herself in time. "From making another mistake. From spending my life with the wrong man."

Finally, she'd found a chink in his cool, casual façade. His expression flickered for a split second before he followed up with, "What did you see in me?"

"You said one question."

"It's one question with two parts." His smile, usually so bright and carefree, had darkened. "What did you see in me?"

"I don't know," she said slowly. "With us, it wasn't about *seeing* anything. It was just about *feeling*. Fitting together."

"We did fit together very well."

She ignored the sexual undertone and steered the conversation back to safer territory. "When I was twenty-two, I didn't have a checklist for potential partners."

"And now you do?"

"Of course. I made a spreadsheet in Excel. For real."

"So you have a lot of rules." He reached over and started to untangle her.

She closed her eyes as his fingers sifted through her hair. The sides of his hands brushed against her cheek as he worked. Then, when she was free, he backed away from her and announced, "I have rules, too, you know."

She stood up, wrung out her hair, and smiled. "Rules for wrangling all your models and actresses?"

"Oh yeah. You have to. Hollywood's very big on dating rules. Haven't you ever seen *Swingers*?"

"Okay, so what are the rules?"

"You're supposed to keep communication at a two-to-one ratio."

She blinked. "I'm not following."

"If I text a woman, she has to text me back twice before I'll text her again," Ryan explained. "If I call her twice, she has to call me four times before I call again. If I—"

"That's appalling."

He shrugged. "Don't hate the player; hate the game."

"It's so adversarial. It's psychological torture." She knew he was teasing her, but she still felt outraged. "If some guy tried that crap with me, I'd dump him."

"I would never try that crap with you."

"I cannot believe you have a dating ratio. The Ryan Lassiter I knew would never have a dating ratio." Of course, the Emily McKellips he knew slept with hot men on the first date. Within the first fifteen minutes of meeting them.

"Yeah, well, after my wife walked out on me, a lot of things changed." His voice roughened. "But other things never did. And let me ask you something: If Grant's so great, where the hell is he?"

"He'll be back first thing in the morning." Emily sounded more than a little defensive. "He's giving one of his patients a new set of lungs. It's literally a life-or-death situation."

"So he left you alone here to deal with your crazy family and his crazy family and your ex-husband who's still in love with you?"

Emily opened her mouth to argue, but Ryan cut her off.

"I don't care how smart and honorable and successful he is. Fact is, it's crunch time, and I'm here and he's not."

"It's just a wedding," Emily shot back. "The

marriage is what matters—the wedding's just a party."

"It's *your* wedding. In thirty-six hours. So why are you spending tonight with me instead of him?"

"Enough, Ryan. This is not a debate. You cannot get me to yes on this."

"Enough," he repeated.

"Yes. Enough. It's too late. We need to stop whatever it is we're doing here." She pushed a wet lock of hair out of her eyes and adopted the detached, professional tone she used with difficult clients. "I'm asking you to please leave."

"But we—"

"Good-bye, Ryan."

Before he could reply, she turned and splashed away from him, back to the safety of the beach. She left her shoes abandoned on the sand and dashed back to the Lodge.

Ryan didn't try to follow her. He let her go, and she didn't look back, but she could feel the bond between them strengthening and stretching, pulling her heart back to his like the tide.

CHAPTER 22

Naked and trembling, Emily wrapped herself in a fluffy white robe and stared at her face in the hotel room mirror. Her cheeks looked pale and her eyes were feverishly bright.

She sank down to the floor, resting her back against the wall as she dialed her phone and held her breath through one ring . . . two . . .

"Hello?" Grant sounded tired and cheerful and impossibly far away.

She braced one hand on the doorframe and got to her feet. "Thank God you picked up."

"Perfect timing. I'm just about to go back into surgery. I know I was supposed to be done by now, but—it's a long story."

"I'm so glad to hear your voice." She walked toward the bed, reeling with a mixture of relief and guilt.

"What's wrong? You sound upset."

"I just . . . I need you here." She cleared her throat. "I need you."

"I know, all the wedding stuff is crazy." She

could hear the bustle of the hospital on the other end of the line, and knew he was only half listening to her. "How's everything going?"

"Well. I went swimming tonight." She took a deep breath. "With Ryan."

He laughed. "You make it sound so ominous."

She dug her fingernails into her palm and tried to be honest. "I don't think it was appropriate."

She heard more rustling on his end of the connection. Then he asked, "Were you two skinny-dipping?"

"No. I had all my clothes on, actually."

"So what was the problem? I understand you have exes, Em. It's fine. I trust you."

She brought her knees up to her chin. "Please come back here."

"Right now?"

"Yes. Tonight." She bowed her head and pressed her forehead against the rough nubs of terry cloth. *"Please."*

"Take it easy. I'm coming, angel. I promise."

"Okay." She felt her world come back into focus. "Okay."

He waited a beat. "As soon as I can. The minute I'm done here, I'll get in the car."

"Tonight?" she pressed, hating her wheedling, needy tone.

"Love you, angel."

She let him go and slipped into a blue silk baby-doll. After three more episodes of *Buffy*, she called Grant again. He didn't answer and she didn't leave a message.

He'll be here. Any minute now, she'd hear his key in the lock.

In the meantime, she listened for the rumble of Ryan's car engine in the parking lot. Once he left, her life would return to normal. *She* would return to normal.

She waited for him to go. But all she heard was a faint, muffled *woof.*

FRIDAY

CHAPTER 23

Emily slept until seven, slogged through a three-mile run, then made her way to Summer's room and knocked until she finally heard sounds of life.

Summer opened the door with the demeanor and hairstyle of a possum trapped in a Dumpster. She squinted out at Emily. "This better be good."

"Rise and shine! Let's go grab some coffee."

"Come back in about five hours." Summer started to shut the door, but something in Emily's expression stopped her. "What's up?"

"Oh, nothing." Emily leaned against the door-jamb. "I just wanted to talk."

Summer matched her air of exaggerated casualness. "About anything in particular?"

"Not really. Just the fact that I'm worried I'm about to make the biggest mistake of my life."

"Oh." Summer rubbed at her eyes. "Just that."

"Yeah. You know, the usual."

"Come on." Summer ushered Emily inside. "But before we get started, I'm calling room service and ordering Belgian waffles, a wading pool of orange juice, and, like, four croissants."

"Allow me." Emily picked up the phone and placed a carb-centric order, charging everything to her room number and requesting a veggie egg-white omelet for herself.

"Veggie omelet," Summer scoffed as she fired up the coffee-maker in the corner. "How many times do I have to tell you, you can't make it through an existential crisis on lean protein. You need butter and refined flour."

"Ryan already plied me with s'mores and booze," Emily said. "My self-discipline is shot to hell. More butter is not the answer."

"Butter is always the answer."

They ended up on the small screened porch attached to Summer's suite, bundled up in the bedclothes against the mist blowing in from the lake. The morning breeze was laced with the smell of dew-drenched grass and the ashy remnants of extinguished campfires.

Just after the room service order arrived, Emily noticed a woman in a red anorak power-walking by on the dirt path, headed for the beach.

"Caroline!" she called out and raised her arm.

Caroline jogged over, looking sporty and refreshed. "Morning, ladies. You're up early."

"So are you." Summer took a slug of OJ. "Ugh, my throat still hurts from singing last night."

"I'm going to do a quick loop around the lake. Care to join me?"

Emily considered this for a moment. Summer did not.

"What is *with* you people and the cardio and the egg whites? We're on vacation!"

"Exercise is great detox," Caroline said.

"It's not time to detox. It's time to nurse our hangovers. Lord. I can't handle this nonsense this early in the morning. Both of you—sit down and eat some waffles." Summer unlocked the screen door for Caroline. "And take off that windbreaker. It's making my eyes hurt."

"But—"

"Argue with me and I'll force-feed you a croissant."

"She's not bluffing," Emily said. "Do as she says."

Caroline gave in with surprising speed. She unzipped her crimson jacket, grabbed a throw pillow from the rattan sofa, and curled up on the floor. "What are you drinking?" she asked Emily.

"Earl Grey," Emily said. "Straight up."

"Hitting the hard stuff, huh?"

"Hot water's over there. And some tea bags from the late nineties." Emily nodded toward the carafe warming in the corner.

Summer patted Emily's ankle. "So what's wrong, puddin'? Spill your guts. Make this headache worth my while."

"Well." Emily listed to the side until her cheek was plastered against the wicker sofa's armrest. "I had a long talk with Ryan last night while you hooligans closed down the bar."

"And?" Summer prompted. "Did he give you a one-man sequel to the strip show? Did you get to guzzle his six-pack?"

Emily appealed to Caroline, who was settling into an armchair with a plastic mug and a little bag of lemon tea. "You see what I have to deal with?"

Caroline looked rapt. "We're waiting. Did you guzzle his six-pack?"

"Of course not!" She held up her hand, displaying her diamond ring. "For heaven's sake, I'm engaged!"

"So you keep saying."

Emily tried to shut up, but the verbal floodgates were open. "It might have been easier if he had ripped his clothes off, actually. Instead, he kept *talking*."

Summer stuck out her tongue. "Boo."

"And the thing is . . ." Emily wrapped both hands around her warm, flimsy mug.

"What?" Summer and Caroline chorused. "What's the thing?"

She couldn't bring herself to divulge this next bit until she'd taken a nibble of croissant. "The thing is, I'd forgotten. I'd forgotten how much I loved him."

Summer turned to Caroline and explained, "Think Bella and Edward from *Twilight* and then dial it up a few more notches."

Caroline's eyes got huge. "Wow."

"Yeah. You could power a small city."

Emily took another, slightly larger nibble of croissant. "We had such a bad breakup, and then I refused to see him again. When I thought about him, I just remembered the end. The fighting. The pettiness. But talking with him last night made me remember the beginning."

Summer snatched up a croissant for herself, then passed one to Caroline, who took a big bite.

The three of them chewed in silence for a few moments.

"I forgot I was even *capable* of that kind of love." Emily sipped her tea. The hot liquid burned her tongue and the roof of her mouth. "I don't think I have it in me anymore."

Caroline put aside her croissant with the care and deliberation she'd show a loaded handgun. "Well, love is different at thirty than twenty. You're more mature. More self-aware."

"You wear skirts with hemlines lower than your fingertips," Summer added.

"You were right, Summer, when you said I'd lost my spark." Emily sighed. "But it's not Grant's fault—I lost it long before I met him. The whole time we've dated, I've been worried about doing the right thing and getting to the next level. Like it's a game of Tetris or something. Will he call? Will he ask me out again? Does he want to be exclusive? Will he propose?" She tucked the blanket around her feet as a light drizzle started to patter on the roof. "I never used to worry about getting hurt. But now I worry constantly. I'm so afraid I'll mess everything up."

"You've got a lot more to lose than when you were right out of college, though," Caroline reminded her. "The stakes get much higher as you get older and more established. When you broke up with Ryan, what did you lose?"

Emily mulled this over. "A few CDs and text-books I'd never read again. Particle-board furniture from Goodwill. Oh, and a puppy I never wanted in the first place."

"Heartless wench," Summer said. "Ripley is pure canine perfection."

"Can we please not have the dog discussion again?"

Caroline refused to be sidetracked. "So you didn't lose anything of real value."

"Just my dignity," Emily said. "And my sense of youthful idealism."

"Your dignity you built back up over time. Your youthful idealism you were bound to lose anyway. A breakup used to mean you were out a futon and a Dave Matthews box set. But now . . ." Caroline settled back on her cushion. "If you get married and it doesn't work out, you'll lose a lot more. Your house, your family, your money. Love's not a game anymore."

"No, it is not." Emily nibbled her lower lip.

"Let me ask you this," Caroline said. "Do you love Grant?"

"I do. But I don't love him the way I loved Ryan."

Caroline nodded. "And that's okay. Nuclear-reactor chemistry is not what sustains a marriage. Respect, integrity, and simple good manners go a long way."

"Listen to you two." Summer's gaze ping-ponged between them. *Good manners?* I don't know what's scarier—the prospect of being alone for the rest of my life, or the prospect of being married with only good manners to keep me warm at night."

"My grandmother used to say that the most important decision I'd make in my whole life was choosing a husband." Caroline put down her cup, her expression pensive. "She said it was more important than where I went to college or what career I chose. I used to roll my eyes and blow her off as hopelessly old-fashioned. The thing is, though, she was right. You see your husband every single day. First thing in the morning, last thing at night." Here, she smiled wryly. "Well, unless you marry a workaholic surgeon, obviously. But when you spend every day of every month of every year with someone, they start to shape who you are."

Summer shivered. "This is scarier than a Stephen King novel. Hold me."

"I've changed my eating habits and sleeping habits to accommodate Andrew. I've put off having children because he wants to wait. I've moved across the country for his job. But, you know. We made a commitment."

Emily and Summer exchanged a look.

Caroline caught them staring and drew herself up. "What?"

"Nothing," Emily said. "It's just, well, you and Andrew seem to be going through a bit of a rough patch."

"We are." Caroline sighed. "A rough patch the length and width of our entire marriage."

Summer passed the pastry. "Who wants another croissant?"

Caroline's cool composure cracked just a little. "I know how it must look—that I don't love him. I'm always complaining that he's late, and then nagging him when he finally gets here. I'm the high-maintenance wife who's never satisfied."

"No, no!" Summer exclaimed. "She just meant that, you know, the way you feel about your husband after ten years of marriage is not the same way you feel on your honeymoon."

"I know how it looks," Caroline repeated. "I know how it sounds. But the thing is, I do love him. And it would be so much easier if I didn't. Because I am never, ever going to be his priority."

She gave Emily a sharp, pointed look. A look that said, *Don't let this be you.*

Emily tried to muster a smile. "There's always retirement, right?"

"His first love will always be his work. That's who he is. My whole marriage has been about waiting. First, I was waiting for him to finish his internship, and then his residency, and then his fellowship."

"And now?"

Caroline glanced down at her phone. "I'm still waiting. For a text, for a phone call, for my husband to actually show up. And I wish someone had told me that the waiting never lets up. If you think that it will get better, and that all you have to do is hang on for another year or two . . ."

"Yes?" Emily asked, as a tendril of dread coiled in her stomach.

"The engagement, these past few months of planning the wedding together? That *was* your honeymoon period."

"We didn't plan it together," Emily said. "I did most of it myself."

Caroline nodded. "That's what I'm saying. You're the support staff. So am I. And we're great at it. But the waiting, the disappointment . . . it wears you out."

"So you're saying Bora-Bora is going to be the only tropical vacation we'll ever take together."

"I'm saying try to lower your expectations and

cultivate your own interests. Make lots of friends."
Caroline glanced out at the sky, where the rain
clouds were starting to clear. "Some of the women
I know have affairs."

Emily threw up one hand. "Whoa, there. I'm not
the affair type."

Caroline turned back and regarded her with
steady discernment. "You just spent last night
with a man who's not your fiancé."

"She didn't do anything wrong!" Summer practically spat out her croissant. "There was no kissing,
no canoodling, no guzzling of six-pack abs!"

Emily had to interject. " 'Canoodling'?"

Summer shrugged. "I read a lot of British
tabloids when I fly to London." She bristled at
Caroline. "It's not her fault that Ryan showed up.
She didn't ask him to come."

"*You* did," Emily reminded her.

"Exactly! You're an innocent bystander here."
Summer addressed Caroline again. "She was just
trying on her wedding dress, minding her own
business, and Ryan—"

"He left," Emily said. "I asked him to go last
night."

"So now Ryan's not here because you asked
him to go, and Grant's not here even though you
asked him to stay," Caroline said.

Emily's mind immediately flashed back to
Ryan making the same point. *If Grant's so great,
where the hell is he?*

"Let's not overthink this," she said. "We're talking about one week. One super-stressful, overscheduled week."

"That sets the tone for the rest of your life," Summer said. Caroline nodded in agreement.

"Wrong. This week is a one-off. A freak of nature. The rest of my life is not going to be spent fending off my MIA ex-husband and wearing corsets and watching my mother corrupt my mother-in-law." Emily paused. "I hope."

And she made up her mind, then and there, to be happy with what she had. She would behave like the responsible woman she had become instead of the reckless girl she once was. She would stop asking dangerous questions and sabotaging her future. And she would stop wondering about what could never be.

"Where *is* he?" Emily fastened and unfastened the clasp of her black patent clutch while she paced between the bed and the bathroom door in Georgia's suite.

"Don't worry, Em. He'll be here," Summer said. "And PS, your hair looks great."

Emily looked to her mother. "Mom?"

Georgia never took her gaze from the lighted magnifying mirror, which she was using to apply false eyelashes. "Grant's a man of his word. He'll be here."

Emily glanced at Caroline, who was too busy texting on her phone to provide any reassurance.

Then she heard Bev's voice behind her: "Don't worry. My son would never disappoint the love of his life on the night before their wedding."

When Emily turned around, her shock at Bev's appearance wiped out her anxiety about her absent groom. Bev's sensible gray-streaked bob had been cropped into sassy, choppy auburn layers. Her modest pink sweater had been replaced by a tailored emerald green suit with a nipped-in waist and a diamond-studded brooch on the lapel.

"My goodness, Bev!" Emily said. "You look stunning!"

"Mom!" Melanie grinned. "You vixen, you!"

"Thank you." Bev ducked her head, embarrassed by all the attention. "Georgia dragged me into town this morning and convinced me to try something new. I can hardly walk in these shoes, though—maybe I should go change into something a little more sensible."

"Bite your tongue!" Georgia stood up, makeup brush in hand. " 'Sensible' is a filthy word around here. And there'll be no need to walk once we're at dinner. You just sit pretty in your chair all night long and let the gentlemen fetch things for you."

Emily noticed a pendant around her mother's neck. "Do my eyes deceive me, Mom, or are you wearing some new jewelry?"

Georgia patted the silver and pink enamel necklace. "Oh, Bev insisted. Isn't it cute?"

"Very cute." Emily tried to downplay her amazement. Georgia had a long-standing policy against any "cute" jewelry. ("I wear only three types of accessories: classic, art deco, and high carat.") Anything featuring flowers, teddy bears, or hearts went straight to Goodwill.

"I wanted to give her a present—a nice present—for all her help." Bev beamed. "She really does have an eye for style."

Georgia fluffed her hair. "What can I say? It's a gift."

Bev beckoned Emily in. "Your mother has a real joie de vivre. I feel better than I have since . . . well, since Stephen. I feel kicky. You're lucky to have her."

"Hear that?" Georgia crowed to Summer. "Who has the perfect family now?"

Bev pulled a box with a matching necklace out of her bag. "I got one, too. We're twinsies!"

"So you're friends?" Emily grinned at Summer. "You have an actual girlfriend? Oh, Mom, I'm so proud of you."

"Shoo, darling, I'm working here." Georgia brushed off Emily and focused her attention on her new protégée. "Now sit in front of the mirror; your cheeks need a little color."

Summer checked the time. "It's nearly seven. We should probably go."

"Yes, the hostess and the bride should be there to greet the guests," Bev said.

Summer shot Emily a sympathetic glance. Caroline kept her eyes on her phone, her expression completely neutral.

"He's not coming," Emily murmured.

"Don't say that." Bev fastened her new friendship pendant around her neck. "He'll be here. He will. He's just—"

"Busy," Emily murmured. "I know." Grant was always busy, always had been, and always would be.

And wasn't that part of his appeal? She remembered what Summer had said about the candlelit dinners and the myth of the "perfect couple." Her fiancé was brilliant, handsome, and doting—when he was around. But he was so often absent. And she loved him in spite of it.

Or maybe because of it?

She turned to Caroline, but before she could utter a syllable, she heard a knock on the door and Grant's voice, clear and steady on the other side of the door:

"I'm here, Em. I made it. I'm here."

CHAPTER 24

"A toast." Grant lifted his crystal champagne flute, and all of the guests followed suit. "To my beautiful bride."

Emily took his hand and stood up beside him. They held on to each other and faced the sea of familiar faces—the friends and relatives who had banded together to witness the creation of a new family.

"I had to run back to the city for a few days, but it sounds like you guys have been having a great time without me."

Everyone clapped in assent.

Grant pressed the back of his fingers against Emily's cheek. "Thank you for being my angel. Since the day I met you, you have been patient and selfless and incredibly supportive. You managed to pull together this whole wedding in two months while I bailed on appointments at the last minute. Which is probably for the best— I have terrible taste in flowers."

Someone—probably Melanie—tossed a lily from one of the table vases at him.

Grant put up his hand for quiet, then continued. "You never complain when I show up late and leave early. You put my needs ahead of your own. You're sweet and sophisticated all at the same time."

Emily heard an outbreak of coughing from the back of the room, and shot a death glare Summer's way.

"I don't deserve you, but I'm hoping you won't figure that out until it's too late."

The crowd *awwww*ed when he kissed her. Emily prepared to launch into an equally gushy reply, but broke off when she saw the thin, rectangular blue box in his hands. "What's that?"

"Your something blue." He pressed the box into her hands, watching every flicker of her expression. "Open it."

Emily froze for a moment, overwhelmed by emotion. She could feel life unfurling before her, wide and fresh and clean like the rolling green hills surrounding them. "Oh Grant, you didn't have to."

"I know. I did, anyway. Open it."

"Yeah, open it!" Georgia yelled. "Don't keep us in suspense!"

The crowd took up the chant: "Open it, open it . . ."

Emily tugged on the end of the white satin ribbon and lifted the lid of the cardboard box to reveal a velvet jewelry case. She ran her fingertips along the top, wishing she could stop time right here and preserve this moment.

But she could sense Grant's excitement and realized that for him, the payoff would come with the presentation rather than the anticipation. And this moment was as much about him as it was about her.

So she opened the hinged lid. Inside was a beautiful bracelet, a delicate chain of white gold interspersed between bezel-set dots of diamond, dark blue sapphire, and light blue aquamarine.

"You don't have to wear it tomorrow," Grant said. "I know you're already wearing my mom's pearls. But I figured—"

Emily wanted to laugh and cry at the same time. "Shut up. Of course I'm wearing it. It's perfect."

"I love you."

"I love you, too." She held out her arm. "Would you please help me put it on?"

He encircled her wrist with the bracelet and fastened the clasp with sure, deft hands.

She kissed him again and prepared for the onslaught of female attention swarming her way. Everyone had to inspect the bracelet and swoon over Grant's romantic sensibilities and tell Emily how lucky she was to be marrying such a catch.

When she disentangled herself from the throng, Grant was turned toward the corner of the room, huddled over his phone. As he walked back to her, she caught a flicker of guilt in his eyes.

"Oh no," she said.

He glanced behind him, then searched her face for clues. "What?"

"I recognize that look. You have something horrible to tell me."

"Nothing horrible," Grant assured her. "Just a little . . . hiccup."

Emily gripped the back of a white wooden chair. "Hit me."

He fiddled with his cuff links and looked around the room, smiling absently at the well-wishers.

Emily quaffed the rest of her champagne. "Do I need to sit down for this?"

He finally returned his full attention to her. "You know how we're supposed to go to Bora-Bora?"

"Oh, *no*."

"We're going! Don't worry, we're still going. I want to make that clear. We are going to Bora-Bora."

Emily lowered her chin, trying to decipher his expression. "But?"

"But we might need to postpone it. Just for a little while. My patient is experiencing some complications."

"The lung guy?"

He nodded. "The lung guy. I know you're disappointed—"

She tried to tell him that she wasn't disappointed, that she understood, that she could be as selfless and willing to sacrifice as he was.

But she couldn't. The best she could muster was a calm, quiet appeal to his emotions. "Grant, this isn't just some last-minute weekend getaway; it's our honeymoon. You proposed to me using Bora-Bora as bait."

"And we are still going to go." She could tell from the look in his eyes that he absolutely believed this. "We'll still be in the honeymoon phase a few months from now. Heck, it'll actually be better because you won't be so frazzled from all the wedding prep."

She sank into the chair, crossing her ankles and arranging her hands in her lap. "There has to be a balance. I'm worried that if you can't find that balance now, you'll never find it."

"Be fair." He crouched down next to her. "You want me to find a balance between saving someone's life or kicking back on a beach drinking Coronas? That's not even a choice."

"Well, that's the thing, isn't it? It's not a choice, for you. It's the choice *I* have to make." Intellectually, she knew that saving a life should win out over beachside Coronas every time. But why couldn't it ever be enough? Why did it have to be either/or?

Surgery or beach? Work or vacation?

Grant or Ryan?

She flinched at this thought, and Grant was right there to comfort her. "I know it's hard, Em.

But you always make the right decision. It's part of why I love you."

"Please don't say that." She laced her fingers together and squeezed. "What if I'm not as selfless as you think I am? What if I'm impulsive and conflicted?" She forced herself to look up and meet his gaze. "I wish I could be that perfect paragon you described in your toast tonight. But I'm not. Full disclosure: Before I met you, my life was a little bit of a train wreck."

"Stop." He rested his index finger against her lips. "It doesn't matter what you were like before you met me. Give us another fifty years like the one we just had, and you'll make me the happiest man on earth."

Scenes from the last year flashed through her head: scenes of courtship and romance, team-work and tenderness. But also bouts of incredible stress and loneliness.

He seemed so confident, so certain that they were doing the right thing. "Be patient, angel. Have faith in me."

"I do have faith in you." Her voice came out clear and firm. "I believe in you one hundred percent."

"Then you know I'll make this up to you. We will get to Bora-Bora if I have to paddle you there in that leaky canoe by the boathouse."

"That thing is a death trap." Emily shook her head. "The hotel's going to get sued."

"If the canoe sinks, I'll swim the rest of the way. I'll drag you along. Dead man's float."

"Dead man's float." Emily batted her eyelashes. "The words every new bride aches to hear."

"You. Me. Bora-Bora. It's happening." Grant wrapped his arms around her.

"It's happening," she repeated into his shirtfront. "Just not next week."

"It's happening. Do you believe me?"

She wanted to. She really, really wanted to. "I do."

After the rehearsal dinner, the guys went off to smoke cigars on the porch, the ladies congregated in the bar, Georgia and Bev slipped off to do God-only-knows-what with God-only-knows-who, and Emily tried to sneak away without anyone noticing.

Summer, of course, noticed. And had apparently sneaked away herself for a little rendezvous with the dark side.

"Here." She pulled Emily out to the patio adjoining the bar and pressed a brown paper bag into her hands. "You look like you need this."

Emily opened the bag and almost shed a tear of joy at the scent of grease and ketchup.

"You know that guy I went out with the other night? I had him make a run into town. You looked like you needed a double cheeseburger and a vanilla shake. It's not fast food, exactly—

it's the Vermont version of fast food, so it's all grass-fed and free-range."

"I love you."

"I know." Summer started to walk away, but Emily caught her arm.

"Not so fast. This guy, does he have a name?"

"Yep."

"Care to share?"

"Nope." Summer surveyed the crowd. "Now get while the getting's good. I'll cover for you."

Emily hurried along the flagstone path and made her way around the corner to the side of the Lodge, where mosquitoes swarmed beneath a pale sodium light and the view was limited to the cars in the parking lot.

Including a painstakingly restored silver Triumph Spitfire.

She froze, burger halfway to her mouth, as she heard the metallic jingle of Ripley's tags behind her.

"I told you to leave," she said.

Ryan's voice warmed her from the inside out. "You did. But I'm not finished with what I came to do."

"Well, I am." Her own reaction to his presence infuriated her, and she forced herself to remain chilly. "We're done."

"I'm not running away this time, Emily. And neither are you. When you divorced me, you said I had no follow-through, no sense of responsibility.

Well, now I do. I set goals, and I achieve them."

She crumpled up the top of the paper bag and turned to face him. "Listen to me, Ryan. I'm not a goal to be achieved. I'm not achievable."

He didn't argue with her. Instead, he leaned back against the split rail fence bordering the forest and motioned for Ripley to sit down next to him. "Let me tell you a story."

She tilted her head back toward the Lodge. "I have guests waiting."

"I'll make it snappy. When I was trying to get my first film made, it was the middle of the financial crisis. Funding had dried up. Investors were nonexistent. So I ended up talking to some Russian guys who were a little on the shady side."

She rolled her eyes. "A little?"

"Allegedly." It was too dark to see his expression, but Emily could hear the smile in his voice. "Anyway, I pitched the film to them and they said no. So I set up another meeting with them the next week, and I told them that my last project had won a bunch of awards. They still said no." He paused. "I'm not going to lie—I was pushy."

"That is shocking. I am shocked."

"Next day, I showed up at their offices again. Kind of uninvited. And the head guy—he was like six-five with a big purple scar on his cheek—he said if I ever came back, they'd cut off my finger."

Emily sighed and dug the milk shake out of the bag. "So of course, you came back."

"Hell, yeah. I wanted to get the project made. I had to come back. And I brought my buddy Joe— big, burly camera guy I'd met on the last shoot. When we knocked on the door, the Russian guy couldn't believe it. He said, we warned you once and now we're going to cut off your finger. I said, I know. He said, your friend here's not going to be able to save you. I said, yeah, that's why we brought a tripod instead of a weapon. You guys are gonna cut off my finger and we're gonna film it. It'll be great for the opening scene." He reached down and scratched Ripley's ears. "And the guy laughed and they bankrolled the picture."

Emily squinted through the darkness at him. "You're insane. Like, certifiable. You know that, right?"

"I wanted to make that film more than I wanted my finger. And I want you more than I want my pride. You want stability? Commitment? Great. I can give you that now."

"Ryan, stop. You're not making a movie against all odds here. You're messing with real people with real lives."

"Yeah, including mine. Including yours."

"You don't want me," she told him. "Not really. You have this image of me, but—"

"I do want you," he shot back. "And you want me."

They lapsed into silence for a moment, staring each other down while the fireflies blinked and the sounds of the party drifted out from the hotel.

Finally, he pushed off the fence post and started back toward the parking lot. "If you don't want to talk about it, we won't talk about it. But we both know."

Emily's heart slammed in her chest. "What do we know?"

"People who aren't having second thoughts don't hang out in parking lots talking to their exes on the night before their wedding."

There was nothing she could say to this. The truth—that she'd weakened in the face of temptation—was too obvious to deny and too painful to acknowledge.

"I'll be there in the morning," he said.

"You show up at that church tomorrow and you really will lose a finger."

"Fine. You can take the one that already has your name on it." He held up his left hand. "And if you marry that guy, I will let you go. I'll be out of your life forever. But I don't think you will."

She swallowed hard, grateful for the shadows that hid her face and her shaking hands. "You're wrong."

"We'll see."

As Emily crept back to her own room, she heard footsteps and feminine laughter around a corner. Before she could duck into an alcove, she found herself face-to-face with Georgia and Bev. Both of them were shushing each other and carrying armloads of what appeared to be . . .

"Shoes?" Emily stopped in her tracks. "Why do you have all those shoes?"

This set off a fresh round of hysterical giggles.

"We're punking Rose and Darlene." Georgia snorted. "I stole their room key out of Rose's purse at the bar. We took all of Rose's right shoes and all of Darlene's left shoes." She collapsed against Bev. "They'll have to wear mismatched shoes to the wedding tomorrow. Although since we know they're the exact same size, that shouldn't be a problem!"

Emily surveyed the assortment of pink flats, black pumps, and tan sandals. "You're nothing if not thorough."

Bev motioned her in and confessed, "And we short-sheeted their beds."

Emily started laughing, too. "Are you twelve? Is this summer camp?"

"Wait, wait." Georgia dropped a few shoes as she held up her hand. "I didn't even tell you the best part."

"Let me guess: You put Saran Wrap on the toilet seat."

"No," Bev said. "But I'll have to remember that for next Christmas."

"We hid five travel alarm clocks all over their room," Georgia crowed. "Under the couch cushions, in the drawers, on the top shelf of the closet."

"Don't forget the one I taped to the back of the nightstand."

"Yes, they'll have to hunt for that one. Genius, I tell you!"

"Five alarm clocks," Emily repeated.

"And they're all set to go off at different times tonight." Bev chortled. "Two thirty-three a.m., three eighteen a.m., four forty-eight . . ."

Emily shook her head. "Remind me never to cross you two."

"They started it." Georgia shook her fist, dropping the rest of the shoes. "You give me compression socks, *you will pay*."

"You can't tell anyone." Bev, crying from merriment, wiped her eyes on the shoulder of her shirt. "Grant's not with you, is he?"

"No. No, I was just, um . . ." Emily felt a blush seeping into her face. "You better hurry back to the bar and return Rose's key before she figures out it's gone."

"First we have to hide all the shoes! But where?"

"Ooh, I know! How about the Dumpster?"

"Now run along, sweetie." Bev dismissed Emily with a little flick of her wrist. "You've got a big day tomorrow, and you need your beauty sleep."

"We know Rose and Darlene won't be getting theirs!" More convulsive giggles.

"You can't tell anyone about this. Ever."

"I saw nothing. I heard nothing."

"Good girl." Georgia gathered up the fallen shoes and turned to Bev. "Let's go. The night is young! And I believe Brad the concierge mentioned something about strip poker."

Emily put her hands over her ears. "I'm not hearing this."

"Don't be such a prude. It should be a crime for that boy to wear a shirt!" Georgia all but purred. "I tell you, Emmy, I've been to the Louvre, the Met, the Tate Gallery, and I've never seen a torso like that."

"We could play cards," Bev agreed. "Or we could just go cow tipping."

"Ooh, that's so rustic!"

"*Aaand* I'm going to bed." Emily resumed walking down the hall. "Try not to break any more laws before sunrise."

"We'll try," Bev said.

"But we make no promises," Georgia added. "Either way, I'll be at your door bright and early to make you beautiful."

"And smile, little lamb!" Bev beamed. "In less than twelve hours, you'll be Mrs. Cardin!"

SATURDAY

CHAPTER 25

Grant was MIA.

Again.

Emily blinked against the bright morning sunlight streaming through the blinds and frowned at the empty side of the bed. She had no idea where he'd gone or when he'd left.

Last night she'd felt sure she'd be tossing and turning with anticipation. But by the time she slipped into bed, Grant was already deeply asleep, and she'd synchronized her breathing to his: slow and steady and peaceful.

But now he was gone.

She fumbled for her phone on the nightstand and started dialing his number, imagining endless medical catastrophes that might have called him away in the middle of the night. But before the call went through, Grant strode through the door, exuding confidence and vitality in his running shorts. He carried a cup of coffee in each hand and gave her a dimpled grin when he saw her.

"Good morning, angel. Happy wedding day."

How many women would kill to be in her

place? On the receiving end of a heart-stopping smile from the man about to pledge his life to her?

He sat down on the bed and kissed her forehead. "Sorry I stink. I did a few extra miles."

"You don't stink; you smell good." Emily stretched her arms over her head and yawned. "What time did you get up? You should've woken me. I would have gone running with you."

He shook his head. "No way. Your mom and my mom pulled me aside last night and gave me some dire warnings about what they'd do to me if you tripped on a root and twisted an ankle before you walked down the aisle." He paused. "When did those two get to be best friends, anyway? Don't get me wrong—I think it's great. My mom has always been so caught up with me and my dad and taking care of the house that she never had time for book clubs or girls' nights or any of that. But when those two get together . . ." His eyes took on a haunted, hunted look. "They're kinda scary."

"You're telling me." Emily sat up and took a tiny sip of coffee. "I still can't believe you went running. You've been going nonstop for the last few days. Aren't you exhausted?"

"I spent the last twelve years sleeping in fifteen-minute increments in an on-call room. I can survive indefinitely on caffeine and adrenaline."

Emily laughed. "I don't know that weddings and adrenaline really go together."

"They do," he assured her, peeling off his sweat-soaked T-shirt. "I feel like I'm a Navy SEAL ready to go into enemy territory."

"That's so romantic."

"Hey, I'm a surgeon, not a poet." He walked to the bathroom and turned on the shower. "How about you? How do you feel?"

She did a quick gut check as she mulled this over. "I feel good." *Surprisingly so.* "Great, actually."

"No jitters?"

"None." She could see her wedding dress, freshly steamed, hanging on the back of the door in a clear plastic garment bag.

"No more panic attacks?"

"I'm not panicking. I kind of expected to be nervous, but I'm not." She climbed out of bed. "We've got this. I am locked, loaded, and ready to go."

"Like a Navy SEAL."

"Exactly." She opened a drawer and pulled out a clean shirt for him. "Now shower and get out. It's all kinds of bad luck for you to see me right now."

He chuckled. "You sound like my mom."

Emily clutched the shirt to her chest in mock horror. "That's it—the wedding's off."

"You say that now." He pulled her close and kissed her neck. "But I have ways of changing your mind."

"You're going to make my decision tree limbless?" The words were out of her mouth before she could stop them.

He froze, his expression puzzled. "What?"

"Nothing." She coughed. "Never mind. It's just this stupid thing Ryan used to—"

"This is about Ryan? Again?" But before she could respond, he stepped back and ran his hand through his hair. "Don't answer that. That was an unfair question."

"No, I think we should talk about it." She reached out to him.

"It's fine, angel. We're both on adrenaline overload."

"But—"

He crossed back to the bathroom and turned off the shower. "I think I'll do one more lap around the lake. Want to come?"

She dropped her arms and let him go. "Yeah, but I have to do hair and makeup and basically pretend I'm getting ready for the Oscars."

"It's good to be a guy. See you in a few hours."

"I'm back. I'm back but I'm not looking at you. Forgot my suit." Half an hour later, Grant reappeared, even sweatier than before. He kept one hand over his eyes, the other outstretched for the hanger.

Emily, half in and half out of her bridal underwear, located his charcoal gray suit in the closet. "Don't leave. I need help. My mother is supposed to be helping me, but she's late. Probably sleeping off strip poker with your mom."

Grant dropped the hand from his eyes. "What?"

"Nothing. Can you give me a hand for a second?" She turned around to show him the foundation garment with all its crisscrossed ribbons. "I can't fasten this thing by myself."

Most men would have been flummoxed by the intricate web of lacing, but Grant was used to working with the thinnest strands of filament and tying complex knots. He set his suit aside and got down to work with brisk efficiency.

"This looks uncomfortable."

"Not really." Emily gasped as the boning cut into her waist. "Maybe a little."

"How tight does it need to be?"

"Tighter than that." She held on to the doorframe as he cinched her in. "Tighter. Tighter." She couldn't help laughing at her reflection in the mirror over the dresser. "This is so not hot. This is the opposite of hot."

He laughed, too. "Lacing you into a corset? It's a little hot."

"*Un*lacing my corset so you can ravish me would be hot," she countered. "Trussing me up in this god-awful contraption is—oof!" She blew out her breath as he cinched the closures at the bottom.

"Almost done." He stepped back, assessing their

335

progress. "Can you suck it in a little bit more?"

"I am sucking it in." But she redoubled her efforts, exhaling and lifting her breasts and squeezing her torso until she swore she heard her rib cage crunch. "This thing fit five days ago."

"Almost there." With one final, intestine-twisting yank, Grant secured the hook and eye closure at the base. "Okay. You're good to go."

"You're sure?"

"We could secure it with a few loops of duct tape," he offered. "But I think it'll hold."

They heard the click of the doorknob turning, then Georgia's voice, high and breathy. "I'm here, Emmy. I'm here. Don't fret. I just got caught up—" She gasped in horror when she glimpsed the groom and the bride together. "Grant, what on earth are you doing in here? Skedaddle!" Georgia shoved him out, slammed the door, then rounded on her daughter.

"You were supposed to be here twenty minutes ago," Emily said by way of defense. "I don't want to be late for my own wedding."

"Have I taught you nothing?" Georgia demanded. "Your husband should not be helping you finagle your way into that girdle. That's no way to entice a man."

"Well, he did manage to get it closed, which is more than I could do." She beckoned her mother closer, then confided, "I gained two pounds."

Georgia gave her a critical once-over, then gave

a satisfied nod. "Don't worry; it doesn't show."

"It's because I ate cookies and s'mores and champagne. With Ryan. And then Summer brought me a milk shake."

"As long as all the buttons button, we don't have a problem." Georgia unzipped the garment bag and pulled out the delicate froth of tulle and lace. "You're going to look perfect, baby girl."

Emily held up her arms and tried not to move while Georgia arranged the gown around her. She watched their reflections in the mirror, a mother and daughter completing a timeless ritual, and was filled with a sharp, sudden ache for her father.

"I wish Daddy could be here," she said softly. "To walk me down the aisle."

"Me, too." Georgia stopped fussing with the shoulder seams. "He'd be so proud of you." She paused, her glossy pink lips parted, and Emily knew she was searching for words that she would never find. Words to explain and apologize for her decisions since Cal died.

In a rush of love and gratitude, Emily took both her mother's hands. "Thank you, Mom. Thank you for everything."

Georgia extricated one hand and fanned her face. "Don't you dare make me cry. I don't have time to redo my makeup."

Emily felt tears welling in her own eyes. "Don't make *me* cry."

They both tried to hold it in, sniffling and laughing and admonishing each other, and they were still trying to wipe off the mascara smudges under their eyes when Bev walked in.

"Are you girls all right?" Bev asked.

"Oh, we're fantastic as always." Georgia dabbed on some concealer. "Just got a little emotional."

Bev touched the strand of pearls at Emily's throat and smiled. "Honey, you look breathtaking. Just breathtaking."

"You're looking pretty good yourself," Georgia said to Bev. "You're going to hook yourself a hottie at the reception, mark my words!"

Bev gave Emily a look. "Your mother certainly has a wild imagination."

Emily grinned. "She certainly does."

Georgia put down the concealer and picked up her eye shadow. "Did either of you happen to see Rose and Darlene this morning?"

"They were late for breakfast, believe it or not." Bev winked. "But Melanie saw them heading into town. Something about an emergency shoe-shopping trip?"

Georgia's smile was positively sharklike.

Bev tried—and failed—to hide a little smirk. "Mel said they both looked exhausted."

"They should have come to me," Emily said. "I'd be happy to share my cucumber undereye cream."

"Mission accomplished." Georgia moved on to

the next order of business. "Did you invite Brad to the reception?"

Bev went all fluttery. "Yes, I did. And I made sure the wedding planner seated him at our table. Right between you and me."

"You're learning, Grasshopper." Georgia went to work on Emily's face for a few minutes, then stepped back to assess her artistry. "Almost ready to get married?"

"Ready as I'll ever be." Emily leaned forward to slip on her shoes, and felt something in the corset give way. "Uh-oh."

"Hold on." Bev flexed her fingers. "I'll get it."

Emily saw spots for a moment while Bev cinched in the corset with surprising strength for such a wee woman. "There." Bev refastened the gown's delicate pearl buttons with mind-blowing speed and precision. "All fixed." She leveled her index finger at Emily. "Just take it easy, now. That's the secret to this dress. Don't move, don't breathe, don't bend. Just smile and look beautiful."

Emily ran her fingers along the whisper-thin silk around her waistline, checking to make sure everything was intact. So far, all the seams were holding. "I'm trying."

"Dude, let's get this show on the road already." Summer paced the vestibule of the tiny white clapboard chapel and dabbed at the nape of her neck with a tissue. Between her mint green bridesmaid dress and the fresh flowers in her hair, she looked every inch the refined lady. She still sounded, however, exactly like herself. "I'm dying of heatstroke over here."

"I cannot believe this church doesn't have air-conditioning." Georgia opened the jacket of her magenta silk dress suit. "My makeup is running." She craned toward the doors separating them from the sanctuary, where a string quartet was finishing up a tasteful selection of Mozart and Bach.

Caroline managed to look regal and refined despite the perspiration dotting her upper lip. "How are you holding up, Emily?"

Emily forced herself to loosen her death grip on the lily-of-the-valley bouquet. "I'm fine." She hadn't even noticed the heat until Summer mentioned it—in fact, she felt a bit chilled. Numb, even.

"I'm hot!" Ava and Alexis flung fistfuls of wilting flower petals at each other. "I'm thirsty!"

"Girls!" Melanie scooped petals off the floor and back into the beribboned baskets. "Save some for the aisle." She sidled over to Emily and murmured, "Meet me out back for a fake smoke break after the ceremony?"

"I'm there," Emily murmured back.

Bev smoothed her hair. "I know it's a bit warm, but this chapel is so quaint and picturesque."

"A bit warm?" Summer blew back her bangs. "It's got to be a hundred and five in here!"

"Patience, please." Bev adjusted her gardenia corsage. "It'll be a short ceremony, and the reception room at the Lodge will be nice and cool."

"My mascara is melting," Georgia said. "I'll look like a raccoon in the wedding photos."

Bev ignored the complaining and lined everyone up. "Places, girls. The wedding planner is going to open those doors in two minutes. Is everybody ready?"

"Yes," they all chorused.

"Good. And don't forget to smile."

When Emily glanced down to make sure that her bouquet was facing the right way, she noticed that her wrist was bare. She snapped out of her daze as anxiety surged through her. "My bracelet fell off. I have to find it!"

"Not now." Bev shook her head. "We're starting in two minutes."

"I promised Grant I'd wear it for the wedding." Emily closed her eyes, trying to retrace her steps. "I know I had it on when I left the Lodge. It must've fallen off on the walk over here. Go tell the musicians to play the Bach piece again." She tossed her bouquet at Summer and headed for the exit.

"You stay here," Melanie said. "I'll go find it."

"No, I know exactly where to look." She jostled

past the human wall of bridesmaids. "Don't start without me."

"Emily!" cried Bev. "Wait!"

Summer strode toward the sanctuary. "Extended remix on the Bach. Got it."

"Be right back!" Emily dashed out of the chapel and scanned the flagstone path. It was only a few hundred yards from the Lodge to the church, but the lawn stretched out before her like an ocean. Desperate but determined, she bent forward to peer at the grass.

"Dry heaves," drawled a familiar male voice. "Classic symptom of second thoughts."

Emily looked up to find Ryan approaching. She'd never seen him in a suit before, and she was shocked at how imposing he looked. He wore the tailored twill with the same self-assurance he exuded in jeans and a leather jacket. Something about the cut of the fabric made him look even taller and his shoulders even broader. But his hazel eyes were flecked with gold in the sunlight, and she caught a glimpse of the boy he'd been beneath all that authoritative masculinity.

"I am not dry heaving," she informed him. "I dropped my bracelet in the grass and I can't find it and it's supposed to be my something blue, and everyone's waiting for me and—"

"Whoa. Slow your roll, there." He rested his hand on her shoulder, but she shrugged it off.

"I need to find it right now!" She dropped to

her knees, heedless of her hose and her gown, and raked her fingers through the grass. "The wedding's starting in two minutes!"

"Stop." Ryan moved his hand to her elbow and lifted her back into a standing position. "I'll find the bracelet. You start breathing."

"You don't even know what it looks like. And it could be anywhere." She knew she was babbling. "It could be over there by the porch steps, or over here by the church or—"

"Inhale. Exhale." He waited until she made eye contact, then demonstrated. "You can do it."

"No, I can't! This stupid dress is like a boa constrictor, and it's all your fault."

He crouched down, scanning the lawn for a shimmer of gold. "I will accept blame for many things, but your wedding dress isn't one of them."

"This thing fit last Sunday," she shot back. "I've been counting calories and avoiding carbs for months, and then you come along with your chocolate and your champagne. Do you know how many calories are in a glass of champagne?"

He didn't look up from the grass. "You needed champagne, I got you champagne."

"No. Wrong. I didn't need champagne. What I needed was to eat clean, and be good, and then you . . . and I . . ." She trailed off, trying to steady her voice and her heartbeat.

As if by magic, Ryan plucked a strand of gemstones off the ground. "Here."

"You found it." Her anxiety ebbed away as she stared at the diamonds and sapphires gleaming in his palm. "I can't believe you found it."

"You're welcome." He lifted her wrist and fastened the clasp. When his fingers brushed the sensitive skin above her pulse, he caught her gaze and held it. She looked down, flushing, and when she raised her eyes, he was still watching her.

They stood in the middle of the manicured lawn, so close but not touching.

And then she heard the pop of her corset giving way.

"Oh no."

He shifted back into producer mode. "What do you need?"

She tucked a strand of hair behind her ear. "Okay, listen, this is awkward, but I need you to undo the back of my dress and fix my corset." She turned around to give him access to the row of pearl buttons. "Something just popped back there, so you have to cinch me up—"

"No." His tone was final.

She turned back around to face him. "What?"

"No."

"Oh right, I forgot the magic word. Okay, will you *please* unbutton my dress and fasten the—"

"No."

She drew up short. "Why not?"

"Because you're standing there panting like Ripley after a run."

She gasped in outrage, and another hook and eye gave way at the back of her bodice. "I *know* you didn't just compare me to your dog."

"And I know you don't need me cutting off your circulation any more than it already is."

"Look at me, Ryan." She grabbed the lapels of his suit jacket. "I'm asking you this as a favor. Tighten my corset."

He shook his head. "Fuck that noise."

"I won't look right!"

"You look great. You always look great." As he stepped away, his devil-may-care grin vanished. He looked almost angry. "Sometimes you just can't force things to fit." He gave her a look that was clearly a dare, then headed for the church without a backward glance.

CHAPTER 26

Despite all the bridesmaids' complaints, Emily hadn't noticed how hot the church was.

She noticed now.

The interior of the little white chapel was stifling, almost suffocating. Sweat poured down her back. The cloying perfume of wilting flowers filled the air.

Her fingers clutched the cool green stems of her bouquet and the straps of her sandals started to bite into her toes. She could feel the whisper of Grant's bracelet sliding up and down her wrist. But inside, she felt only pressure. Her lungs and heart and stomach were compressed to the limit, thanks to Bev, who had readjusted the corset when Emily raced back into the church.

"Now." Bev took her place at the head of the bridal processional. "Are we finally ready?"

Emily held her head high and took her mother's arm. "Ready."

Georgia sneaked one last glance in her mirrored compact, then pulled Emily close. "Listen, honey. I've made this walk . . . how many times?"

"Four," Emily said.

"Four. Right. And during some of those walks, I knew in my heart I was making the wrong decision. Your heart never lies." She shot her daughter a sidelong glance. "So if you're not absolutely positive about this . . ."

"No chitchat," Bev admonished. "We're up."

"We can leave right now," Georgia whispered. "I've got my car keys in my bag."

"Everybody's waiting, Mom. Let's go."

The doors swung inward and the bridesmaids started their right-together-left-together march in single file. Georgia had informed everyone that she preferred *gliding* to marching, so Emily glided alongside her, trying to appear serene and angelic.

She kept her gaze on Grant, who waited at the end of the white satin runner. He looked heart-breakingly handsome, but his expression was tinged with an emotion she couldn't immediately identify. He seemed . . . nervous? She'd never seen him nervous before.

Although she tried to stare straight ahead, she recognized Ryan in her peripheral vision. He waited in the very last row, arms braced on the back of the weathered white pew. While everyone else strained forward to ooh and aah over her gown, he turned away. But in the sunlight streaming through the stained-glass window, she thought she saw his face soften.

She gripped her mother's arm and made a conscious effort to be present in the moment, to smile at the guests, to hear the violin music, and most of all, not to trip.

Were his eyes glinting?

She made it halfway down the aisle, halfway between the only two men she'd ever loved, before she gave in to temptation and looked back.

Ryan had loosened his grip on the pew. His lashes were spiked, his hands were stacked, and he brushed the thumb of his right hand over the ring finger of his left.

And she knew.

All her doubts drained away and certainty flooded in, along with overpowering heat and humidity and the sound of tulle ripping as she slumped to the floor.

CHAPTER 27

Emily didn't open her eyes at first. She remained still, drifting back into consciousness layer by layer. The voices around her sounded distant and blurred, as though she were underwater.

She waited. She breathed.

She recognized her mother's voice first. The high-pitched, dramatic feminine lilt followed by a low male murmuring.

That was Grant.

Her groom. The guy who'd been waiting for her at the end of the aisle.

Everything came rushing back and her eyes snapped open as she gulped in a lungful of air.

"I can breathe," she marveled. She turned her head on the pillow and surveyed a hotel room that looked similar to her own. "Where am I?"

"Oh, baby, thank God you're awake." Georgia dabbed her forehead with a cold, damp washcloth. She looked alternately relieved and enraged. "I've never been so scared in my life."

Emily wet her lips. "What happened?"

"You went down like a sack of wet cement,

that's what happened," Georgia said. "Half an inch to the right and you would've cracked your head open on the pew."

"But she didn't." Grant took the washcloth from Georgia and studied Emily's face.

"I can breathe," Emily repeated. The details of the room slowly came into focus. She was lying in an unmade bed, surrounded by tabloids and candy bar wrappers. "What am I wearing?"

"One of Summer's T-shirts," Georgia said. "This is her room. It was the closest to the lobby."

"We took off the wedding dress and the corset," Grant said. "Your color improved right away." He paused. "Although I think this is about more than the dress."

Her mother heard the undertone in his voice and picked up her purse. "I'll give you two a moment to talk." She leaned over to kiss Emily's cheek, then whispered in her ear, "Ryan's out there pacing like a tiger at the zoo."

Georgia flung open the door with gusto and announced to the populace of the hallway, "She's going to make a full recovery. Just needs ice water and a little TLC."

Emily propped herself up on her elbows and regarded Grant, feeling the same way she had when he'd arrived to pick her up for their first date. This sudden shyness surprised her, and she had no idea what to say.

He sat down in the wooden armchair next to

the bed. Although his suit jacket was unbuttoned and his bow tie had unraveled, he still looked completely calm and controlled.

She studied his face for clues, but his expression remained unreadable.

The chair rungs creaked as he settled back. "We're not getting married, are we?"

Before Emily could reply, he pushed up from the chair and turned his back on her. His shoulders hunched up around his ears, and for a moment, she thought he was pointedly ignoring her.

Then she realized he was answering his phone.

"Uh-huh," he muttered. "Okay. Well, try increasing the dosage and keep me updated. Thanks."

Her mouth dropped open.

He clicked off the line and turned to her with a rueful smile. "I know, I know. I get left at the altar and I'm still distracted with work stuff."

"You know what? You've earned the right to blow me off for work." She sat up all the way. "You've earned the right to say and do whatever you need. Go ahead—yell. Curse my name. Punch me in the face. I can take it."

He looked taken aback by the passion in her voice. "I don't yell; you know that. And I'm certainly not going to punch you in the face."

"Well, you must be feeling *something*. I know I am. So whatever it is, go ahead and unload."

The more she urged him to open up, the more he shut down.

"I can't tell what you're thinking at all," she said. "This was supposed to be our wedding day. This is a big deal. Are you angry? Sad? Frustrated? All of the above?"

He paused, creasing his brow. Finally, he replied, "I don't know."

Her eyebrows shot up.

"What would you like me to say?" He asked this in the same tone he might use to ask her what she'd like for dinner.

"I don't know, either," she said. "But after the week we've just had, you'd think we'd have a few things to talk about."

"There were definitely some surprises," Grant admitted. "I did not see this coming."

She waited.

He cleared his throat and for the first time seemed uncomfortable. "I guess I thought that you were more . . . or I was more . . . or we were more . . ."

"Selfless, sweet, patient, and perfect?"

He shrugged.

"I am so sorry, Grant. About everything." Emily noticed the antique wedding gown draped across the sofa, and glanced down at the diamond ring. She slipped off the delicate gold band and offered it back to him.

He tucked the ring into the pocket of his trousers and reached over to recapture her fingers. He leaned down, and she thought he might be about to kiss her hand.

Then she realized he was studying the faint white scar that etched out Ryan's name.

He lifted his gaze to meet hers. "Still there."

"Yeah." She pulled her hand away and tucked it under the comforter. "I always tried to convince myself you hadn't noticed."

His smile was wry. "I noticed."

"I tried to have it lasered off. But it didn't work. I'm scarred for life." She pulled her knees up to her chest. "I've made so many mistakes. I tried so hard to be someone I'm not."

"Hang on." He started to sit down again, then opted to remain standing. "May I say something first?"

"Absolutely." She braced herself for the barrage of criticism coming her way.

"My patient isn't doing well." His face was etched with tension and worry. "He's got a fever and his lung function is nowhere near where we want it to be at this point."

"That's awful." She closed her eyes as another wave of guilt crashed in. "And for you to be here—"

"Well, that's the thing." He smiled again, this time earnest and generous. "I'm here, but I'm thinking about him. You're here, but you're thinking about someone else, too."

"Grant—"

He shushed her with a slight lift of his palm. "There are some things we can't understand. In life. In medicine. This patient I've been monitoring all week, he . . ." He let out a long, weary breath. "Transplants don't always work. Patients die. We know that going in; it's part of the job. I still remember one patient I saw in residency. He was in great shape. Mid-thirties, former marathoner, ate well, completely healthy. Except for his heart."

"Which is kind of an important organ."

"Right. He wasn't on the wait list that long before we got a donor match. And I mean, this was a perfect match—same tissue type, same size, young, athletic donor. Smooth surgery, no complications. We're talking best-case scenario coming in and out of the transplant."

He paused for a moment. "He should have recovered and gone on to run another marathon. But he didn't. His body rejected a perfectly matched organ. It's rare and incredibly frustrating, but it happens."

Emily peered up at him. He was looking through her now, beyond her. As he continued his story, he walked over to the window. "And then there are cases like the one I saw last year. Guy had smoked for twenty years before he finally quit for good. He had to plead his case to three surgical teams before he could convince one to take him on as a candidate for a kidney transplant. The donor was an okay match, but just okay. We warned him that the outcome probably wasn't going to be all that great."

"It worked out," Emily said.

"Perfectly. Seamlessly." Grant opened and closed his hands. "It's like this guy had been born with this kidney. We'll never understand why some matches work and some don't. It's not right or wrong; it's not good or bad. It just *is*."

He looked over his shoulder at her. "This morning, when you wanted to talk about Ryan?"

Her chest tightened. "Yeah?"

"Maybe that would have been a good idea."

She tilted her head and blinked up at him. "Are you joking?"

"A little bit."

Even in this, he was a true gentleman. He was willing to bow out gracefully.

He was willing to move on.

Emily covered her heart with her hand and spoke softly. "This doesn't mean that I didn't love you. I hope you know that."

He walked back and stood at her side. "I know."

"Because you're a great guy. You are *perfect*. But we . . ." She trailed off, unable to find the right words.

He picked up where she left off. "We probably would have been married a long time, and it would have been fine."

"Fine," she echoed.

"Yes. A long, pleasant marriage. But not a love story."

"Well, of course not." She straightened her shoulders. "Love stories are for fairy tales and sappy movies."

He shook his head. "Not true. My parents' marriage was a love story. Right up until the day my father died."

"My parents, too," Emily admitted.

"You deserve that, Em. So do I." He leaned down and rested his head on top of hers, and even as he held on to her, she knew he was letting her go.

In the silence that followed, they heard an empty glass rattling against the bathroom counter. Loud music started to vibrate through the walls.

"Sounds like they started the reception without us."

"Oh God." Emily twisted the bedsheet with both hands. "The reception. Should I go make the rounds? Or would that be too awkward? I don't think Miss Manners covered this situation."

"Forget Miss Manners. We wrote the check; we don't have to go. Just think of it as sponsoring my family reunion." His phone buzzed again. "I'm heading back to the hospital."

She had to laugh. "You look pretty excited about that."

"I am. Is that wrong?"

"Not at all. You shouldn't feel guilty about what you love."

He kissed her on the forehead and gazed down at her. She looked into his eyes, and this time, finally, she recognized the emotion in his blue eyes:

Relief.

His phone buzzed again, and he hurried out, and before the door could latch behind him, Ryan strode in.

CHAPTER 20

Ryan was smiling when he entered the room, but Emily could sense a restless, almost predatory intensity just beneath the surface. She could see why her mother had compared him to a tiger at the zoo.

He didn't have to say a word. One glance, and she knew exactly what he was feeling.

She climbed out of bed and stood to face him, realizing as his gaze lingered on her thighs that Summer's baggy old T-shirt barely covered her panties.

"Grant looks like a man with a new plan," he finally said.

She tugged down the hem of her shirt half an inch, which of course only drew more attention to it. "He's on his way to the hospital."

"So the wedding's off?"

"The wedding's off."

"Well, the guests started the reception anyway." He tilted his head toward the wall-shaking bass out in the hall. "Bev's leading a conga line out there."

Emily laughed. "You lie."

"She practically had to hip check your mom out of the way, but she's the ringleader now." He moved closer, stopping when he reached the tapered spindle of the four-poster bed.

"At least they're having a good time."

"Everyone seems to be getting along just fine." His expression sobered. "How are you feeling?"

She considered this for a moment, sifting through all the relief and regret. "I'm overwhelmed. I'm everything at once."

"Me, too."

"So here we are again, right back where we started." She glanced down at Summer's shirt. "Wearing clothes from college, even."

"I noticed." He waited, thrumming with anticipation in his expensive, tailored suit.

She wrapped her hands around the spindle on her side of the bed. "Where do we go from here?"

As always, he had a ready answer. "You, me, and Ripley ride off into the sunset in a silver Triumph Spitfire."

Once he said it, she couldn't get the image out of her head. She trailed one finger along the sleek, varnished bed frame as she took a step toward him. Then another and another. "I need you to be serious."

He watched her every move. "I'm very serious."

"I've been trying to figure us out since you showed up on Saturday."

"Did you make an Excel spreadsheet?"

"I tried." She inched closer to him. "But it turns out we defy mathematical formulas."

"So what are you saying?"

"All I know is this: We're not done."

"We're never going to be done." His eyes darkened in the sun-dappled shadows. "I want you in my life. I always have. I always will."

She took a deep breath, aware that she was poised on a precipice. He reached out and pulled her to his side.

"It's your line now," he prompted.

She reached up and adjusted the crisp white pocket square peeking out of his jacket. "I love you. And your little dog, too."

He flattened his hand over hers. She could feel his heart beating under the thin layers of wool and cotton.

"I love you, too. My temptress in a T-shirt." This time, his smile was a slow, wicked grin that robbed her of thought. "Put your hands up."

CHAPTER 29

One year later

"Honey, I'm home."

Ryan's voice echoed down the hall to the master bathroom, where Emily reclined in a bathtub brimming with bubbles.

She listened to the scrabble of Ripley's paws against the hardwood floor as Ryan greeted the dog, then heard the distinctive pop of a cork. A minute later, Ryan appeared in the doorway carrying two flutes of champagne. "Got room for one more in there?"

"Always." She slid over to one side.

"I've been meaning to talk to you about this bathtub." He rested the glasses on the ledge of the tub and sniffed the air. "Peach?"

"Hibiscus."

"I didn't want to say anything at first, but you need a bathtub intervention." His voice was muffled as he stripped off his shirt and jeans. "This is serious, Em. I want you to admit you have a problem."

She laughed and turned on the faucet to add more hot water.

"That sounds like denial."

"Denial and hibiscus," she said. "And don't pretend you're not my enabler. You saw how I was with this bathtub the very first time the Realtor showed us the house."

"Your reaction to this tub is the reason we bought the place." He sloshed in beside her, heedless of the water spilling over the rim. "There's a lot to be said for getting you naked."

"So what's the problem?" She gave him a long, slow kiss. His hands skimmed over her body under the bubbles.

"What problem? What are we even talking about?"

When they came up for air, he handed her a champagne flute, and she took a sip. "Yum. What are we celebrating?"

"We wrapped the shoot today. Right on schedule. And under budget, thanks to our genius line producer."

"Like, two dollars under budget." She feigned modesty.

He nibbled her earlobe. "You're so hot when you're beating studio financial targets."

"I try."

He glanced at the screenplay pages stacked on top of her folded bathrobe. "Did you read the latest rewrite?"

"Almost done. This version's great. Really scary and gross, but great. That scene with the demon-hybrid thing and the vampires? I may have to sleep with the closet light on tonight."

He leaned back against the cool white porcelain and stretched out his arms. "If I hire the right director, you may never sleep again."

"Get me some numbers and I'll start putting a preliminary budget together." She rested her head on his shoulder. "You're so much more comfortable than one of those inflatable bath pillows. Oh, and speaking of vamps, my mom called today. Bev's getting married."

He wrapped his other arm around her. "Let me guess: Brad the concierge?"

"No, some guy she met on that Alaskan cruise they took in September. A widower. Mom says he's lovely. Well, her exact words were, 'A little stodgy for my taste, but perfect for Bev.' She says they're blissfully happy together. They're having the wedding in Valentine, Vermont."

"Is Bev going to wear the boa constrictor dress?"

"It's not that kind of wedding. They're keeping it low-key."

"Are we invited?"

Emily lifted her head and gave him a look. "I left her son at the altar. What do you think?"

"Technically, you passed out halfway down the aisle," Ryan corrected. "And Grant seems to have recovered."

This was true. Six months after the Wedding

That Wasn't (as it came to be known), Grant met a sweet and ruthlessly efficient hospital administrator named Heidi, and the two of them had been inseparable ever since. Even the tickets to Bora-Bora had not gone to waste—Andrew had surprised Caroline by whisking her away for a belated honeymoon in paradise. ("I think you scared him straight," Caroline confided to Emily. "He saw what happened to Grant's relationship, and he figured he might be next.")

Ryan plucked Emily's champagne glass out of her hand and took a sip. "Ask me what else we're celebrating."

She reclaimed the glass and took a retaliatory sip. "Do tell."

"I have a week off before I head to Vancouver to start preproduction on *Dark Matter*."

"Seven whole days?"

"Seven whole days. I was thinking we could do something fun."

"Ooh, like what? We keep saying we're going to drive up to Carmel." She passed the champagne back to him.

"I was thinking something a little crazier."

Something in his tone made her sit up straight, her pulse picking up. "How crazy?"

He set the empty glass aside. "Will you marry me?"

Both hands flew to her mouth. Hibiscus-scented bubbles flew everywhere. "Oh my God."

"I was going to wait until tomorrow to ask you. I was planning to whisk you away to a suite at the Ritz and do flowers and candles and the whole nine yards, but you know I have no impulse control." He watched her face expectantly. "So?"

Her cheeks actually ached from smiling. "Ask me again."

"What? Why?"

"Two-to-one ratio, remember?"

"Are you kidding me?" More bubbles flying. "That doesn't apply to you!"

"Hey. If it's good enough for a bunch of models, it's good enough for me."

He dropped his head back and appealed to the ceiling. "You're killing me here."

She cupped her ear, waiting.

"Fine." He grabbed the other glass of champagne and took a swig. "Will you marry me? Or do I have to make your decision tree limbless?"

"Yes. Yes, yes, yes." She cupped his face in both hands and kissed him. "That's four yeses to your two proposals, thus preserving the two-to-one ratio."

"As long as we're all squared away, mathematically." He pulled her onto his lap and kissed her back. "You know, there's a twenty-four-hour tattoo parlor down on Sunset."

Her eyes widened. "I don't know if I can see myself doing the ring tattoo again."

"I can. It's very cinematic. Opening scene: Hot young thing walks into a tattoo parlor. Right behind her is our hero—brilliant, talented, and ridiculously good-looking."

"And reeking of Drakkar Noir."

Ryan ignored that. "Our heroine can't contain her desire for him. They nauseate even the grizzled, chain-smoking tattoo artist with their public displays of affection."

Emily held out her left hand, studying the pale etching of his name on her ring finger. "So you're proposing a sequel."

"Not just a sequel—a sequel that's better than the original."

"Is that even possible?"

"It's rare, but it happens. *Evil Dead 2* was far superior to the original."

"*Evil Dead 2*?" She burst out laughing. "You're using a movie called *Evil Dead 2* as the model for our marriage?"

"The whole thing was genius! The hero had a chain saw for an arm!"

"That's the most romantic thing I've ever heard."

"Hey, I'm up for the challenge if you are."

"If you're in, I'm in," she assured him. "Always. Here's to a perfect Hollywood ending."

"To us." *Clink.* "Big kiss, fade out, roll credits."

Beth Kendrick grew up in New England, but now lives in sunny Arizona, where she dreams of white Christmases and colorful fall foliage. She hasn't watched a horror movie in years, as doing so requires her to sleep with the closet light on. (Yes, really.) She is the author of *The Lucky Dog Matchmaking Service* and *The Bake-Off*, along with six other novels.

CONNECT ONLINE

www.bethkendrick.com
facebook.com/bethkendrickbooks
twitter.com/bkendrickbooks

Center Point Large Print
600 Brooks Road / PO Box 1
Thorndike ME 04986-0001 USA

(207) 568-3717

US & Canada:
1 800 929-9108
www.centerpointlargeprint.com